For three special women, the perfect gift is one that keeps on giving...

It's loving and being loved in return. It's opening home and heart to a lonely child, giving her someone to call 'Mummy' and 'Daddy'—and giving each other someone to call 'husband' and 'wife.' The perfect gift is…

Motherhood.

Join Gemma, Nora and Christina as they, each with the help of a lonely child in need of a home and the love of a very special man, receive this most precious of gifts.

KATHLEEN EAGLE

is a transplant from New England to Minnesota, where she and her husband, Clyde, make their home with two of their three children. She's considered writing to be her 'best talent' since she was about nine years old, and English and history were her 'best subjects.' After fourteen years of teaching students about writing, she saw her own first novel in print in 1984. Since then, she's published many more novels with Silhouette® Books that have become favourites for readers worldwide. She also writes mainstream novels and has received awards from Romance Writers of America, *Romantic Times* and *Affaire de Coeur*.

EMILIE RICHARDS

Award-winning author Emilie Richards believes that opposites attract, and her marriage is vivid proof. 'When we met,' the author says, 'the only thing my husband and I could agree on was that we were very much in love. Fortunately, we haven't changed our minds about that in all the years we've been together.' The couple has lived in eight states—as well as a brief, beloved sojourn in Australia—and now resides in Ohio.

Though her first book was written in snatches with an infant on her lap, Emilie now writes full-time. She loves writing about complex characters who make significant, positive changes in their lives. And she's a sucker for happy endings.

JOAN ELLIOTT PICKART

is the author of over seventy novels. When she isn't writing, she enjoys watching football, knitting, reading, gardening and attending craft shows at the town square. Joan has three all-grown-up daughters and a fantastic little grandson. In September of 1995, Joan travelled to China to adopt her fourth daughter, Autumn. Joan and Autumn have settled into their cozy cottage in a charming small town in the high pine country of Arizona, USA.

Kathleen Eagle
Emilie Richards
Joan Elliott Pickart

A Mother's Gift

SILHOUETTE®

DID YOU PURCHASE THIS BOOK WITHOUT A COVER?
If you did, you should be aware it is **stolen property** as it was
reported *unsold and destroyed* by a retailer. Neither the author nor the
publisher has received any payment for this book.

*All the characters in this book have no existence outside the imagination
of the author, and have no relation whatsoever to anyone bearing the
same name or names. They are not even distantly inspired by any
individual known or unknown to the author, and all the incidents are
pure invention.*

*All Rights Reserved including the right of reproduction in whole or in
part in any form. This edition is published by arrangement with
Harlequin Enterprises II B.V. The text of this publication or any part
thereof may not be reproduced or transmitted in any form or by any
means, electronic or mechanical, including photocopying, recording,
storage in an information retrieval system, or otherwise, without the
written permission of the publisher.*

*This book is sold subject to the condition that it shall not, by way of trade
or otherwise, be lent, resold, hired out or otherwise circulated without the
prior consent of the publisher in any form of binding or cover other than
that in which it is published and without a similar condition including
this condition being imposed on the subsequent purchaser.*

*Silhouette and Colophon are registered trademarks of
Harlequin Books S.A., used under licence.*

*First published in Great Britain 2000
Silhouette Books, Eton House, 18-24 Paradise Road,
Richmond, Surrey TW9 1SR*

A MOTHER'S GIFT © Harlequin Books S.A. 1998

The publisher acknowledges the copyright holders
of the individual work as follows:

WAITING FOR MUM © Kathleen Eagle 1998
NOBODY'S CHILD © Emilie Richards McGee 1998
MOTHER'S DAY BABY © Joan Elliott Pickart 1998

ISBN 0 373 48358 9

76-0004

*Printed and bound in Spain
by Litografia Rosés S.A., Barcelona*

CONTENTS

Dearest Reader,

I was delighted when my editor invited me to write a story for this particular story collection, because I already had the gem of a story about adoption in mind. It came from a regular feature in the Sunday newspaper—you'll know what I'm talking about when you get into the story—*two* regular features, really; one about children, the other about pets. All youngsters need loving homes.

I once told my mother that I was not going to add to the population when I grew up. There was no shortage of children in the world, I declared, but there was a critical shortage of parents. I was going to adopt. My mother said that was a fine plan. She knew well that I was never at a loss for a plan. I've since given birth to three children, and my husband and I believe that was a fine plan, too. Either way, children are a blessing, but they are also a responsibility. When I 'spake as a child,' blithely saying what I would and would not do when I was old enough to choose, I took my own parents' commitment for granted. Now I understand my mother's knowing smile. Having the baby is just the beginning, hardly what being a parent is all about.

I appreciate those who have the courage to make the choice that I once boasted that I would make. I embarked on parenthood the easy way, but you have chosen to adopt children or to foster children, you have thought long and hard, searched your souls, waited, kept watch, reached out, gone the extra mile. Congratulations, Mum! Way to go, Dad! I'll pass on the cigar, but let this story serve as a hearty handshake.

All my very best,

Kathleen Eagle

WAITING FOR MUM

Kathleen Eagle

The author wishes to acknowledge the helpful folks at Petco in Minnetonka and All About Pets in Golden Valley, especially the wise and wonderful Miss Elizabeth, for insight into the pet supply business.

My thanks, also, to Connie Brockway, kind-hearted foster mother to four-legged creatures great and small, for telling me all about the terrific 'Pet Haven' foster care programme in Minneapolis.

Dedicated to two of my favourite animal lovers, Leslie Wainger and Elizabeth Eagle.

Prologue

Mrs. Bowles was coming today, and Laurel had run out of good hiding places. She couldn't squeeze behind the toys under the stairs anymore because Barbara's Body Magic machine was back there now. The Bottoms Upper had taken over the hall closet, and Ski Slim had been towed up to the attic, where it was either too hot or too cold for hiding. Today it was just too stuffy.

Barbara had told her to find something nice to wear and put her hair up in a ponytail. She liked it better loose, but Barbara said it looked neater in a ponytail. "You want to look your best for Mrs. Bowles. She's going to put your picture in the newspaper."

Laurel didn't want her picture to be in the newspaper, but she didn't want to make Barbara feel bad, either. She was feeling bad enough about moving. Barbara had lived in Minnesota all her life, and she didn't want to move now. She kept telling Laurel how sorry she was. But the house was up for sale, and Terry was supposed to start his new job in California pretty soon. He wanted to have everything "wrapped up" by Christmas, which didn't give Mrs. Bowles much time to find a place for Laurel.

Laurel liked living with the Kopeckis. She liked the twins, even though they were only three and couldn't do much. She liked having her own room for a change, and she liked her school pretty well. She also liked it that the only person at school who knew she was a foster kid was her fourth-grade teacher, but if Mrs. Bowles put her picture in the paper for being one of the "Waiting Children," then everyone would know that Laurel didn't have any parents.

Her mother was only a dim memory, and she'd never had a father. She'd been with her grandma for a while, but she'd died, too. She'd had three foster homes. Mrs. Bowles said it was hard to find the right "fit" sometimes, but she was eligible for adoption, and soon the "fit" would be found. She just needed a little "exposure," as one of the Waiting Children they put in the paper every week. There were tons of Waiting Children—there was a wait just to get your picture in the paper—so Laurel knew she was supposed to feel lucky to be next. She didn't.

"Laurel?"

Barbara was calling from the top of the stairs. The only escape was the walk-out basement door. Laurel held her hand over her head and rubbed her thumb over the tips of her fingers. *Sprinkle sprinkle.* It was an old habit from when she was just a little kid. Fairy dust. She used to pretend that it would give her special powers, make her disappear or make her appear to be something else, but now she only did it for luck. Sometimes it worked, sometimes not.

This time it worked. She dashed across the backyard without anybody calling her back. She slipped through the space where the slat was missing in the wooden fence and skipped through the Fosters' yard. It was a long way to the strip mall if she followed the streets, but if she cut through people's yards she could get there a lot more quickly without passing Mrs. Bowles on the street. Mr. Perkins had told her twice not to run through his side yard, because it made his dog go crazy, but she could run fast— maybe even beat the rain that was just beginning to fall—and the fairy dust was working. So far she was invisible.

The store was just opening for Saturday business. The official greeter offered a cheery ''Welcome to Pet Palace'' and asked Laurel if she had any questions. She said no, she was just going to look at some things.

''I might get a dog pretty soon, and I want to make a list of the things I want to get and how much they'll cost.'' She picked up a card from the comment-card table. ''Can I use this pencil? I'll put it back.''

''Sure. What kind of dog are you thinking about?''

''Is it Pet Adoption Day today?'' She glanced at the empty kennel that was sitting in front of the leash display, where, on previous Saturdays, she'd visited with dogs and cats who needed homes. ''I might get a dog from the pet adoption lady if she has the kind I want. I want one that's not too big, not too small, kinda friendly and doesn't bark at kids just for nothing.''

"Have you asked your parents?"

"I'm still in the planning stage." She held up the paper and pencil. "That's why I'm here. I'm making a plan."

"And you're here by yourself?"

"I just came ahead to get started on this. Figuring out what we need." She knew she could stay in the store only as long as she had a purpose. They always noticed when kids came in and hung around without their parents. More than once she'd been told to "run along now."

"So, you're here with somebody?" the greeter lady asked.

Laurel smiled her best good-kid smile. "I'm just waiting for my mom."

Chapter One

Tom Tallman was cordial to all of his customers, even the ones who weren't housebroken. He welcomed the piddling Lab pups and the crabby old Yorkies with equal courtesy. The sign on the Pet Palace door welcomed all critters, great and small, "as long as their humans behave themselves." He sometimes thought about adding, "and do their business in cash," but then he would have been tempted to add another line about critters doing their business outside, and Corporate might not be amused. Without critter business, there was no Pet Palace business.

Business had been good lately, especially on Pet Adoption Day, which was every other Saturday. Tom's fishing day. Unfortunately, he was between fishing seasons. Camille Peterson, his assistant manager, had covered Saturdays all summer so she could have them off when her kids were in school. Now it was Tom's turn. As good as adoption day was for business, it just wasn't Tom's thing. That was what he'd told Camille when he'd tried to get her to take one more Saturday.

"Not your *thing?*" she'd said with a laugh. "Pets are your business. It says so right on the door."

"Yeah, but adoption isn't. Those cages take up too

much space, and they draw swarms of kids, and some of those animals are so…''

He shook his head rather than come up with a word like *ugly* or *wretched* and have Camille jump all over him for being a hardcase. At this point in his life, there was no reasonable, intelligent explanation for the funny feeling he got in the pit of his stomach as he peered through swags of rain and past whapping windshield wipers at the huge Pet Adoption Day sign out front.

Explainable or not, he certainly wasn't going to mention any funny feelings to Camille. Instead, he had offered her overtime pay and tickets to the zoo on Sunday for her whole family.

She'd admitted that she was tempted, but she didn't want to set a precedent. ''Saturdays are mine now,'' she'd said.

So, here he was, and he was late. Tom was never late for work, but today, Pet Adoption Day, he was late. The store was already open—he would have to remember to thank Beth Evans, the stock supervisor, for that—and there were already a dozen cars in the parking lot. He could always count on Beth to get the show on the road. He parked behind the store and slipped in through the back door. Not that he was hiding anything. He was, after all, the manager, and he was in charge. He spent most of his waking hours at the store, so he wasn't going to apologize, didn't have anything to apologize for.

"Sorry I'm late, Beth." He shed his slicker, scattering raindrops on the cement floor of the stockroom. "Traffic, rain, road construction. Take your pick."

Beth suggested another alternative. "Pet Adoption Day."

"I didn't offer that one." He tossed his slicker over a coat hook. "You had the boys help drag all the stuff in for it and get it set up? The cages and stuff?"

"Kennels, Tom. We sell them. Why is it that when you're selling them, you have no trouble with the word *kennels?*"

"Slip of the tongue." He glanced at the computer screen on Beth's desk. The cursor was blinking over the price list for Poochie Pal toys. "The adoption program is great for business, but it feels so disorderly. Like you've got everything organized, and in comes this stack of cages."

"Kennels," Beth corrected as she reached for the ringing phone. "Of course he's here. We were just going over the fish inventory, and I'm telling him how short you are." She laughed as she flashed Tom her you-owe-me-one look. "Short means short. You of all people should know that. Yeah, he's on his way." She shooed him from her domain as she hung up the phone. "Marsha says she needs a manager at register two."

On his way from the back of the store to the front,

he noticed some signs that would need changing today and a shelf of canned food that needed to be fronted and filled. He made a mental note to call Beth when he got up to the registers. He rounded a corner with a reasonably occupied mind and nearly trampled a little girl.

She looked up, surprised, as though he'd interrupted some little-girl reverie over puppy carriers. Her babyish face was pale except for the rosy blush in her cheeks. She reminded him of a china baby doll he'd seen in a magazine ad, but the look in her big brown eyes was remarkably grown-up and sedate.

It was she who greeted him first.

"Is there anything I can help you with?" Tom asked her.

"What's the price of that dog bed up there, please?"

He quoted her the twenty-five-dollar sticker price on the plaid bed on the top shelf, which was well above her reach.

She wrote the numbers down next to a little picture she'd drawn on the back of a comment card. "Do you think it would be big enough for a dog about the size of the one in the 'Spotlight' cage?"

There, he thought. Other people thought of them as cages, too. "I haven't seen the dogs we have here today. What kind is it?"

"A mixed breed. He sort of looks like Tramp from *Lady and the Tramp*. How big do you think Tramp is? It's kind of hard to tell in a cartoon, because it isn't real, so you think of the dogs like they're people.'' She gestured, smiling like some other cartoon pixie, trying to distract him from his duties. "Come on. I'll show you.''

"I'll check him out later.'' He glanced around the end cap, fully expecting to find more of her kind lurking near the peanut bin. "Are you doing a project for school or something?''

"No. This is what I'll need when I get my dog.'' She fanned several comment cards out like a hand she'd just been dealt. More drawings, more prices, more pixie wishes. "See? I've picked a collar, leash, food dish, water dish, bed. I only picked two toys. I think that's enough to start, don't you?''

"I think so. Those are good choices, too. Are you here with Mom and Dad?''

"I'm waiting for my mom.''

"Did she drop you off?''

"Not exactly, but she'll probably meet me here soon. What time is it?''

He checked his watch. "It's eleven-thirty. Your mom knows where you are, then.''

"I live really close to here. I come here on Saturdays a lot. I never see you. Do you work here?''

Tom told the little girl that he was the manager, and that Saturday was usually his day off, and that if her mother wasn't with her and didn't know where she was, he was concerned about her being in the store all morning, but if she needed to call home…

From her post at the adoption display, Nora Cassidy couldn't help hearing the whole exchange. Her ears had a way of homing in on Tom Tallman's voice like an owl picking up on mouse talk. She couldn't help it. He obviously avoided her like the plague—he hardly ever came into the store on adoption days—but she found him irresistible. Abandoned-puppy irresistible. Big blue eyes, always looking so concerned about the placement of every product and every sign. When something was amiss, he always looked sad about it. Not displeased, but genuinely disappointed, as though his stock boys had let him down.

Abandoned-puppy blues. Nora never turned her back on that kind of forlorn.

Or that kind of handsome. Tom Tallman was the kind of a guy who turned heads when he walked in the door. He had what Nora's mother would call "a commanding presence." You saw, you stared, you thought, *wow,* and you waited for him to speak to you first—at least, she did. If you had to speak to him right away, you looked for some sign of permission, an unspoken invitation, which he quietly gave to one or two people at a time. He was not a crowd player.

Some of the people who worked at the store thought he was antisocial, a little stuck on himself, maybe. Nora was not one of those people. She knew a loner when she saw one, and her instincts told her that this loner was also lonely. He'd been managing this store for at least a year, and he was utterly efficient, but he certainly hadn't gone out of his way to make any friends.

She would have been happy to go out of her way sooner, but everybody knew that if it was Tom's day off, it must be Pet Adoption Day. Nora's Second Chance Ark day. Nora wasn't used to being avoided. Unnoticed, yes. Unlike Mr. Tallman, Nora was someone people routinely overlooked unless she spoke up and made her presence known. Which she did. Routinely.

She peeked around the Complete Canine Cuisine end cap display and ogled a bit, since his back was turned. There was nothing plain about black slacks and a white shirt on Tom Tallman. She wondered whether he was a swimmer. Bicycler, maybe. Runner. Maybe he...

The little girl was looking up at him anxiously. She was a regular visitor, a pet-dreamer, but obviously her parents were not. She asked plenty of questions about the animals, but she never asked about taking one home. Nora had asked the child's name once, and she remembered because it conjured such a pretty image. Laurel.

"No, she isn't worried," the child was saying. "I

mean, she knows how much I like to come here. I
mean...you don't want me hanging around, huh?''

Tom glanced away uncomfortably and sighed.
''We're not exactly a place to hang out. You're welcome to—''

''I have a job for Laurel to do,'' Nora said. The
man and the girl turned at the same time. She ad-
dressed the child. ''If you're interested, and if it's
okay with your mom.''

''A job?''

''I desperately need a dog walker today, and I'm
willing to pay—''

''Oh, you don't have to pay me. I'll do it. I love
to walk dogs.'' Laurel pocketed her wish cards and
made a beeline for the kennels. ''Which one do you
want me to start with? I'm a really good dog walker.
I can walk two at a time if you want me to.''

''One at a time, starting with Dumpy.'' Nora
opened the kennel door and blew a kiss to the gray,
shorthaired mutt. The dog hopped through the opening and sat immediately at her feet. ''This is
Dumpy.''

Tom eyed the proceeding from the length of an
aisle, as though he suspected some rare contagion
might infest Nora's Ark. ''Saddled with a handle like
that, he's going to have a tough time finding a
home.''

''Oh, he's my favorite. He was abandoned at a
dump. Isn't that terrible? And just look how cute he

is." Nora attached a leash to the D-ring on the dog's collar, then ruffled his floppy-tipped ears. "Yes, Dumpy, you're my guy, aren't you? Yes." A black-and-white dachshund-cocker cross whined from another kennel. "Now, don't get huffy, Pickle, you're my favorite, too."

Tom chuckled. "Pickle?"

Nora looked up. He'd edged closer, like a curious child. "She's always getting herself into one. The other day, during afternoon recess, she quite literally got her butt in a sling when she tried to swipe an old inner tube and got hung up on a garden stake."

"Afternoon recess?" He laughed as he gestured at the sign. "Is this what you do for a living?"

Nora laughed. "This is what I do for a *life*. The dividends can't be deposited in the bank. But the program is self-sustaining. I get city funding, and the Humane Society gets involved." She handed Laurel the leather loop at the end of Dumpy's leash. "Now, don't let him pull on you. Tell him to heel, and use his name first. Say, 'Dumpy, heel.'" The dog attended to Nora like an obedient soldier. "Yes, he knows. He's a good boy." She rewarded him with a pat on the head. "I also do some training, and that actually does pay pretty well," she told Tom.

They watched the automatic doors fly open as Laurel sauntered out, a well-behaved dog in tow. The rain had subsided, but it was still a puddle-gray day.

"She's been here all morning," Tom said. "Some

people try to use us as a day-care facility, or a zoo or something. 'Go in and look at the fish while I go shopping.' I hate to kick the kids out, but we can't baby-sit them, either.''

''She was shopping, though. Making her wish list.'' She offered an apologetic smile on the girl's behalf. ''Not causing any trouble for anyone.''

''You never know.'' He wagged his head. ''Seems like a nice kid, but where are her parents? You don't want to end up calling the cops for a kid that age, you know? She tries to walk out with something, or she's here all day and nobody shows up for her.'' He gave Nora that seriously bluer-than-blue-eyed look. ''Believe it or not, I don't much like being the bad guy.''

''I believe it. What kinds of pets do you have?''

He glanced toward the Small Companion sign at the far end of the door.

''You personally,'' she said quickly, trying to imagine him with a cat in his lap. ''At home, I mean.''

''I have an aquarium.''

''No dogs or cats?'' He shook his head. ''How about children?''

''I'm not married.'' His gaze drifted above her head. ''Anymore. Uh, ma'am…''

Nora turned to see what was going on behind her back to take his attention from their exchange of essential facts. A woman was watching her Siamese cat make himself at home in the self-serve, fill-your-own-pail kitty litter bin. To him, life was a beach. He'd already reached the cover-up stage.

"This is wonderful," the heavyset woman enthused. "Such a pet-friendly store. It's so nice of you to provide a litter box for your guests. And such a nice big one."

"It isn't really…" Tom signaled a passing teenager wearing the store's blue-and-red polo shirt. "Richard. Service ninety-one."

The hint was lost on the satisfied customer as she gathered up her cat. "I've been shopping at The Happy Pet, but this store is much friendlier. You've thought of everything."

"Where?" Richard asked his boss, as he scanned the floor. Ninety-one would be a puddle. Ninety-two would be a pile.

Tom jerked a thumb at the kitty litter bin. Nora had to suck her cheeks in to keep from bursting out laughing.

It took a moment to sink in, but when it did, Richard did an incredulous double take. "No kidding?"

Tom gave a plastic, I-kid-you-not smile.

"Can we…?"

"Just shovel and smile."

"Oh, what a beautiful kitty." The woman brought her contented Siamese over to a cage containing a large white cat. "Look, Harrison. Wouldn't he make a lovely playmate?'' Harrison hissed. The woman turned to Nora. ''Would they get along?''

''Neutered male? I'll bet you're the king of the house, aren't you, Harrison?'' With one finger Nora stroked the Siamese under his jaw until he tipped his head to the side, closed his eyes and purred. ''Dickens should probably go to a one-cat family. They probably wouldn't be playmates. At best, they'd probably ignore each other. You might want to introduce a kitten into Harrison's domain.''

''He's so pretty.'' The woman smiled at Tom. ''Thank you for the pit stop.''

Tom shook his head, but only slightly, as he watched the woman stroll down the aisle with about fifty dollars' worth of cat supplies in her shopping cart.

''Maybe it's not a bad idea,'' Nora said. ''Kitty pit stop.''

''The health department would love that.'' He pulled a foil pouch from his pocket and wagged it at Nora as he spoke. ''You need a few pointers on salesmanship. She was ready to take that cat.''

Nora couldn't quite tell what he was waving at her until he tore open the pouch, shook a brown nugget into his palm and offered Dickens a treat through the kennel bars. *Better be tuna flavored,* Nora thought. Dickens sniffed, then nibbled.

''I'm not selling them,'' Nora said. ''I'm placing them in good homes. Dickens needs a home with an

empty kitty throne. Do you happen to know of one?''
Dickens lifted a paw to say he'd have another bite.
Surprisingly, Tom obliged. ''Yours, maybe?''

He pocketed the pouch, turned and teased her with
half a smile. ''There's only one throne at my place,
and I have a tendency to leave the seat up.''

''Dickens would understand. He has his male habits, too. And there's no better fish-watching companion than a cat.''

''I only have a few fish left. Big, ugly, mean ones
that have survived my neglect. If I flushed them
down the toilet, they'd be a threat to the gators in
the sewer.''

''Ah, they're back already,'' Nora said with a welcoming lilt, effectively dismissing his bogus callous-
ness. Laurel was grinning ear to ear. ''Dumpy's had
a good time, hasn't he?''

''I don't think you're going to sell that one, either.'' Tom spared the panting mutt a pat on the
head. ''I see characteristics of at least a dozen breeds.
Who'd put greyhound legs on a dachshund body?''

''As I said, I'm not selling, I'm *placing*. If no one
takes him today, I really need a temporary foster
home for Dumpy. He's been penned up too much.''
She willed Tom to look up, and when he did, she
gave him her brand of salesmanship. Guilt. ''All he
needs is one good foster parent. Just temporarily.''

''I'll ask around.''

Hmm. Not quite the response she'd hoped for. "Okay, Laurel, it's Pickle's turn."

"If her mom comes looking for her…"

"She probably won't." Laurel handed Dumpy's leash to Tom and took Pickle from Nora. "But I'll be watching for the car, just in case."

"If I see her…what does she look like?" Tom was pulling another pouch from the other pocket. Left for cats, right for dogs, Nora observed.

"Just regular. Kind of medium hair and nice eyes, pretty clothes. We'll be right back."

"She'd make a great witness," Tom muttered as Laurel skipped out the door again. He tossed Dumpy a beef treat. Nora smiled when Dumpy made an effortless catch.

"You get the feeling we're being…" A passing stock boy distracted Tom. Or brought him back, perhaps. "Richard, tell Beth to make a sign for the litter bin that says, uh…"

"No cats?" Richard teased.

Beth's smiling face popped up from behind the stack of empty pails. "No dumping?"

"Where did you come from?"

"Dispatch," Beth said. "I got another call from the front. They don't need a manager at register two anymore. I forged your signature. As for the sign, how about if we come up with a new universal symbol?"

"There you go." Tom cocked a finger at Beth. "There's a limit to our friendliness."

"I hear The Happy Pet just put in an indoor fire hydrant."

"Damn. The pet supply wars are heating up. The next directive from Corporate will have me turning Grooming into a doggie spa."

"What do you think, Dumpy? Could you go for a massage?" Nora was still smiling, Cheshire cat style. "He'd be satisfied with a little scratching behind the ears."

Tom took the hint, reluctantly.

"You're not a cat man. Admit it. You're a dog lover at heart. Do you live in a place that won't take dogs?"

"Yeah," he said with a laugh. "It's my own place, and I made the rule. No dogs allowed. Bent it a couple of times in the past, but not for a while now." He handed Nora the leash. "I'll get out of your way so you can get to work on finding homes for these guys."

He headed for the cash registers, just beyond the maze of impulse racks—treats and grooming aids, toys and sweaters. Nora didn't realize she was watching until he disappeared. She could have sworn she'd heard a bubble burst.

"What a nice cat."

Nora turned to the woman who was admiring Dickens. "We just got a kitten, who seems a little

lonely," the woman said. "Would they get along, do
you think?"

"They just might," Nora mused, stepping up her
*place*manship. She explained that an older cat often
accepted a younger charge as long as everyone understood who was boss, and she proposed her trial-
placement alternative for Dickens. The woman decided to go home and get her kitten, but Nora had
her doubts about seeing her again. She'd end up with
another kitten.

When Laurel came back, Nora watched her play
with Pickle. "What I need right now is more foster
homes."

"*Foster* homes?" Laurel made it sound like a foreign word.

"Temporary homes for the animals, until I can
find permanent homes."

This was her ace in the hole, the feature of her
shelter that really placed it a cut above the others.
She worked hard at finding volunteers, at educating
them and encouraging them to get their friends involved. Most of them were women who cared about
animals and made a place for them in their lives.

"I have a few foster parents on call, but I need
more," she told her new assistant. "It's so much
better for them to have a family. I have to keep them
in runs and kennels, and I can only give so much
individual attention. I'm only one person."

"You don't have any kids?"

"I have all these kids." Nora looked lovingly on her charges. Dumpy and Pickle tuned in, as though their names had been called. Dickens was busy raising a leg, like the regal courtier, positioning it for a washing. "It isn't the same, I know, but I'm not married. If I ever get married, then I'll definitely have human kids. At least, I hope I will. Right now, these lovely critters are my kids."

Laurel scratched Pickle's silky head. "You really put them in foster homes?"

"I do, and it works out well. They get to be with a family, and we're able to get to know them better. Understand what they need." Nora watched the child for a moment. She knew a girl in need of a dog when she saw one. "Do you think your parents might…?"

Laurel shook her head sadly. "We won't be here after Christmas, probably."

"Moving?" Laurel nodded. "Where?"

The girl shrugged, as though the answer were as illusory as the question. "Can I be your regular dog walker?"

"If it's all right with your parents."

"It is. We live close by." Laurel stood up and took a quick survey to see who was around. "I think that man likes Dumpy, don't you? I think he needs a dog, and you can just tell he really wants one, but it's kinda like his mom won't let him have it, so he holds back."

"Mr. Tallman is his name. Tom. And he did say 'no dogs allowed' was his own rule."

"Yeah, but the way he said it, you could just tell it wasn't final."

"Spoken like a true kid." She was watching a young woman read the sign that explained the program. The woman nodded, offered Nora a passing smile, then squatted next to Pickle and extended a hand for a get-acquainted sniff.

"That's Pickle," Nora said. "Are you interested in a dog?"

"Pickle walks like a lady," Laurel said cheerfully. "I'm the regular dog walker, and I just walked her. She didn't pull on the leash at all. She's a perfect size for a kid my age." And then, what had become the question of the hour, "Do you have any kids?"

Tom was trying to help Krissie, the new cashier, count down her drawer while he kept an eye on Ron, the stock boy he'd assigned to swab the aisles. Ron had a party to go to, and he had twice proclaimed his halfhearted efforts to be finished. One more "Can I go now?" and Tom was going to tell him to hit the road.

If everybody would just take care of his own job, then Tom could help the animal shelter lady load up the last of the unwanted cats and dogs. He could, of course, assign someone else to give her a hand—normally he would do just that—but he found himself itching to help Nora pack up her ark himself. One of those itches that would not fade away of its own accord, and it felt strange. How long had it been?

Since Kathryn. Now, that really made it feel strange. No resemblance whatsoever. This pert, freckle-faced little redhead was a far cry from the wife he'd lost four years ago, the woman he missed every waking hour of his sterile day. He'd stopped dreaming about her, though. He'd stopped dreaming completely.

But the itch was real, and the only way to scratch it was to let himself get in close to those pathetic, unwanted animals and lend a helping hand to this chirpy little redbird named Nora. She had her hair clipped up on the back of her head, and there was a piece flopping over the clip that reminded him of a bird's tail. When she didn't have anyone else to talk to, she chattered with the animals in that same friendly tone, with that same elfin smile. He'd met a pixie and an elf today, and he had to admit, they were both pretty cute.

Cute? Since when had he been attracted to *cute?* The handful of women he'd gone out with since Kathryn's death had been tall and svelte and quietly sophisticated. Much like Kathryn.

Nothing like Kathryn. There was no other Kathryn. *Remember that, Tallman.*

The springy red tail caught his attention again.

"Let me help you." He took the cat carrier from her. She looked surprised, as though he'd stepped out of a spaceship. Hadn't he been perfectly friendly to her earlier? "I've always wanted to see how you keep the tigers away from the wolves on an ark."

She laughed. "It's nothing less than a miracle."

"What? Peace on the ark, or my help?"

"Both, maybe, along with the fact that we placed two cats and two dogs today. That's not too bad."

"How many more do you have?"

"Too many. I need foster homes." She eyed him, sizing him up for something as she handed him a second cat carrier. "Do you feel charitable today? Do you happen to have a fenced yard or just a—"

"You're barking up the wrong tree, Noah."

"Nora," she corrected. "And I can offer you one who won't bark or bother your trees."

He shook his head. "I'm gone all day."

"I'll give you a pair. They'll keep each other company until you get home."

"A pair of those?" With a nod he indicated the dogs sitting at the ends of the two leashes in her hand. Pickle and Dumpy. "Those are the homeliest animals I've ever seen. I don't think even Noah had a pair like that."

"Of course he did. Where else did they come from?" She led the way toward the back door, chattering while he followed with the pink and blue cat carriers. "You and Dumpy would become good friends," she promised. "After a couple of days, you wouldn't want to give him up. I have a knack for matching people up with animals."

"You do, do you? What would I have in common with a sorry-looking critter like that?"

"He's beautiful." They'd stopped at the back door, she with her two dogs on their leashes, he with his hands full of her boxes.

She looked down at the gray mutt, then back at Tom, linking the two of them somehow with a look, a wish, a romanticist's vision. "He's one of a kind," she claimed. "If you were looking at puppies you might not see that, but Dumpy's old enough to be a real somebody. That's what people don't understand about older dogs. They all want puppies, and puppies are just like eggs in a carton. But you take Dumpy, here, he's a very special soufflé. He's all ready for you."

He caught himself smiling and thought about trying to curb it, but he let it go; he couldn't really help himself. Her wistful expression was sweet.

"You're like a kid in a Norman Rockwell painting. The one with the Free Kittens sign on her red wagon. She kinda looks sad, like the last thing she wants to do is give those kittens away."

She frowned a little, as though she were flipping through some mental catalog. "Is that a Norman Rockwell painting?"

"It should be."

She looked at the dogs. "They need homes."

"They need *good* homes. He's better off with you than with me. Anyway, I'm doing my share for the animal kingdom. I'm the palace guard. I stock all their favorite toys and treats." He nodded toward the front of the store. "Did you check the donation bin?"

Her smile said that she had. "I'll come back and collect our donations tomorrow. Maybe people will be feeling more charitable on Sunday."

Damn, he thought. How could his customers resist this most worthy of causes?

After she left, he hauled a dozen bags of premium dog and cat food up to the front of the store and loaded them into the donation bin. Then he told Beth to ring them up while he wrote out a check.

"And if you tell anyone about this, I'll fire you on the spot."

Chapter Two

They called her Mean Jean. Tom's boss, District Manager Jean Farmer, wasn't really mean, but she was certainly demanding. It wasn't unusual for her to set up one of her brainstorming meetings at Tom's store on a Sunday evening. During the summer, he hadn't minded so much. He could depend on Beth and Camille to get the store all shipshape while he had a relaxing fishing weekend, at least through Sunday morning. He would come back refreshed and ready to deal with Mean Jean, while Beth and Camille scooted home to spend Sunday afternoons with their families. He'd been able to head off some of Jean's wackier promotional gimmicks that way.

Now that the schedule was changed, there was no weekend getaway for Tom, no resting up before the meeting and thinking up good reasons why he couldn't judge a coloring contest and didn't think stupid pet tricks would go over well with his customers.

Stupid employee tricks?

Well rested, he'd had a ready answer for that one. Something about a dignified environment. Friendly, yes, but dignified. They didn't need to do cartwheels down the squirrel-feeder aisle.

But now he was coming off a twenty-hour week-end with the soulful eyes of orphaned animals burning holes in his brain, and he was in no shape to face Mean Jean's selling-machine mentality. He didn't doubt that she had some bizarre "event with a capital *E*" to spring on him.

"Singles Night At Pet Palace."

"Single pets?" Tom asked, affecting nonchalance while shifting his brain into skeptical overdrive.

"*People.* Pets don't spend money. People spend money." Jean was one of those high-energy skinny people who paced while she plotted, wagging her finger over every point. "Single people and their pets. From eight to eleven, the store will be open to singles and their pets."

Mean Jean's tone broached minimal debate. Tom watched her wander toward the pop machine end of the break room, her three-inch heels grinding on the cement floor. She was a striking African-American woman. She always dressed like a district manager, and since she was Pet Palace's only female district manager in the Twin Cities area, she got to determine the dress code. It was chic and powerful.

"We'll do ten, fifteen percent off, serve cookies, cat and dog biscuits, play suitable middle-class burbs fun-night music, like 'Hound Dog' and 'Stray Cat Strut,' some icebreaker games, like…" Menacingly manicured finger raised, she twirled to face him. "Spin the flea spray bottle?"

"Was that the punch line?"

"There is no punch line. I'm completely serious, and I think it's a brilliant concept. Pet owners tend to be wholesome, loving, responsible people. That's exactly what you'd be looking for in a date, right?" She folded her arms and gave him that get-with-it look. "If you ever dated, that's what you'd be looking for, Tallman."

"People don't come to this store looking for dates. They come for dog food."

"Now that's where you're wrong, Tallman, and if you went out once in a while, you'd realize that." She swept her jacket back and sat on the break table—not fully, just one skinny hip and part of a thigh—which was no big deal, since she weighed nothing.

He glanced at Marsha, the head cashier, whose face signaled a jelly doughnut alert. He shrugged. Too late now.

Mean Jean went on. "Singles are always on the lookout for new ways to meet people in a safe, wholesome environment. They bring their pets, it adds a sense of security, gives them something in common, something to talk about."

"Wouldn't it be better to try this in one of the rural stores?" Tom smiled. "Like Fargo, say, in January. I hear people get pretty desperate there in January."

"I could always send you to Fargo in January,

Tallman, just to get the ball rolling. Of all my store managers, there's no one better suited to launch this idea for us because you *are* the man.'' She looked to Marsha for support. ''Right? It's obvious.''

''*The man?* This is not a man thing, Jean. Singles night at Pet Palace is just not a man's kind of thing.''

''Oh, Tallman, you'd be surprised. Men like to think of women as pets, anyway.''

''Do we want to encourage that kind of thinking?''

''We want to encourage people to make Pet Palace a place they think of fondly and long to visit frequently. A fun place. Maybe even a romantic place.''

He groaned. ''We sell dog food and kitty litter.''

''Speaking of which, I noticed that sign in the litter bin. That is not an inviting sign.''

''You're damn right it isn't. We can't have—''

She stopped him with the point of an acrylic nail as she perked her ear toward the front of the store like a whippet detecting rabbit munchings. Somebody was rapping on the glass door.

Tom took it as his cue to claim a break.

''Tell them you're closed,'' Jean called after him.

He smiled when he saw Nora standing there in a pool of sodium vapor light. She waved, said or mouthed something unintelligible, and it struck him that she would have been a welcome sight even if Mean Jean's heels hadn't been clicking on his tail.

''It's Nora. The Ark lady,'' he announced over his

shoulder as he pulled a wad of store keys from his pocket.

"Noah the Ark lady?"

Jean was already forgotten background noise. Tom was busy unlocking the door.

"I'm sorry. I forgot you close earlier on Sunday," Nora said. Her face was autumn-chill pink—very pretty with her freckles and cinnamon-colored hair— and Tom wondered how long she'd been standing outside. "I came for the food donations. I probably should have just come back tomorrow, but Mother Hubbard's cupboard is pretty bare. If there isn't much of a dole, I might need to…" She glanced at the bin. "Wow, you had some generous shoppers today."

"I'll load it up for you."

But Jean had other fish to fry. "Let's get Nora's opinion of the singles-night idea." And she proceeded to explain her scheme, while Tom tried to sneak a discreet peek at the back of Jean's skirt. "Are you married, Nora?" she was saying. Nora shook her head. "Don't you think it would be a wonderful way to evaluate a prospect?"

"Prospect?" Tom interjected. No sign of doughnut jelly. It probably wouldn't dare stick to her.

Jean ignored him. "The way they treat children and animals is a primary indicator, don't you agree, Nora? I just think animal lovers look for opportunities to include their pets in their social activities, and this could become a regular thing. It stands to reason that there are a lot of single people out there with pets, doesn't it?''

Nonplussed, as any normal woman would be, Nora glanced at Tom, looking for some clue.

He shook his head. There would be no getting out of this one. ''I have a feeling you'll be short on guys, Jean.''

''That's where you come in. You're a single man. You know other single men. For this first time, anyway, we'll need to recruit.''

''My tropical fish aren't real portable.''

''A Pet Palace manager without a cat or dog? How did that happen?'' Jean scanned the rafters. ''He needs a dog. Nora, Tallman needs a dog.''

''Tallman doesn't need a dog,'' Tom said emphatically. ''Tallman practically lives at Pet Palace and has no time for a dog.''

''We can promote Singles Night on Adoption Day,'' Jean rhapsodized, taking Nora by the arm. ''Talk up the foster parent program. Take in a foster pet and bring it to Singles Night. You scratch my belly, I'll scratch yours. Perfect!''

Nora's glance bounced between Tom's thoroughly disgusted countenance and Jean's euphoric one. ''I do need more foster homes. I don't want to twist any arms, but sometimes the temporary placements work out better than people anticipate.''

''We could make every Saturday a Pet Adoption

Day, and we could offer more information about the need for foster homes, if that would help.''

Tom watched the plan mushroom before his eyes, like a nuclear explosion in the pet supply war. As he carried the bags of pet food out to Nora's van he resigned himself to overseeing more gimmicks. The two women were still chattering about in-store flyers and a bulletin board feature. Pictures of lost pets gracing the bulletin board were one thing. People were looking for those animals, wanted them back, *wanted them.* Pictures of Nora's orphans were something else. He would be looking at abandoned creatures every damned day of the week.

And then on Saturdays they would be coming in with Nora. Maybe he didn't mind that so much. Maybe they could get together for coffee. Nothing serious. Just coffee. Maybe.

''Don't worry,'' Nora whispered to him after she'd escaped Mean Jean's clutches by following him out the door. ''I won't push.''

''Push?'' He glanced up quickly. The light from the security lamp glistened merrily in her eyes. He couldn't tell whether she'd read his mind, or simply found his situation amusing.

''Dumpy. I wont dump him on you. He has to go to someone who can appreciate his exceptional qualities.''

''It would only be for one night.'' He loaded the last bag of dog food into the back of her van. He was thinking that if he had to be stuck with a pet, he didn't want it to be some stranger. "Nobody's going to show up for this. It'll be the first and last Pet Palace Singles Night."

"Be that as it may, Dumpy doesn't go in for one-night stands anymore. He's a sensitive dog. What you need is a showy animal, one who's too self-assured to worry about being accepted or rejected by mere humans. A poodle, maybe?"

"I don't like fussy dogs."

"I know! What you need is a cat."

He groaned as he shut the van door. "What I need is a small break. These events of Jean's are driving me crazy. A sale on dog food brings people in, right? But that's too simple. Instead, we decide to double as a dating service. Triple as an adoption agency."

"I won't push that, either. Every other week is fine."

The sorry-to-bother-you look in her eyes stabbed him with guilt. "You only unloaded four animals yesterday. You never told me how many you're housing. Does it get crowded?"

"It varies." She turned the key in the van door lock. "I have a small hobby farm that I've fixed up for sheltering small animals. Unfortunately, the demand increases as winter approaches."

"Winter's a bad time all around."

"You wouldn't mind if I let Laurel help me out on Saturdays, would you?" She looked up at him and quickly refreshed his memory. "The little girl who was here yesterday. Apparently her family will be moving soon, so she can't have any pets."

"If you've got something for her to do, and if it's okay with her parents."

"She asked if she could be my regular dog walker."

"I don't much like it when I have to run kids out of the store." He smiled. "Believe it or not."

"I believe it." She stood there looking at him for a moment, her misty breath mixing with his in the cold night air. "I've never had a child," she said quietly. I've imagined the joy of having one, but the pain of losing one is probably beyond what I can imagine."

So she'd heard.

He nodded once, and that was all. He spoke of it to no one. It was not something he wanted to think about, let alone talk about. He'd lost them both in the same accident, and for a while he could neither think nor talk. He was lucky to put one foot in front of the other and get through the day. His wife and his son were the only real family he'd ever had. A truck sliding through a stop sign on an icy road had crumpled their little car like an aluminum can, crushing them both. He'd been a zombie for the first year, a lunatic for the second. He was fine now, human again. But he never talked about delicate things, like love or pain or loss. Not with anyone.

Maybe she read all that in his eyes or in his reticence. She nodded, too, just once, and then she
glanced away. "I'll check with Laurel's mom, just
to be sure it's all right."

"Will this food last you a while?"

"This really helps." She looked at him again, this
time with a shy little smile. "Would you be interested in seeing Nora's Second Chance Ark sometime?"

"I'm sure it's a fine shelter, but I'm not an in-
spector." He shrugged. "Birds and fish are one
thing, but I don't like seeing cats and dogs in cages."

"Neither do I." She opened the door and climbed
into the driver's seat.

He claimed the door handle before she could shut
it. "Mean Jean hasn't left yet, which means she
hasn't had her final word." He lifted the bottom of
her long wool coat, which was trailing over the
threshold, and draped it back over her lap. "Let's get
together for coffee sometime."

"I'd like that."

Laurel had agreed to let Mrs. Bowles take her pic-
ture in return for permission to spend Saturdays at
Pet Palace. Nora insisted on getting on the phone
with Barbara, but Laurel carefully avoided calling
Barbara by name until she put Nora on the phone.
"Her name is Barbara," Laurel whispered. "She

wants to know am I sure I'm really helping and not getting in the way."

Nora assured Barbara that she appreciated Laurel's help, and that she was good with the animals.

"She'd love to have a dog or a cat, I know, but we just can't," Barbara explained at the other end of the line. "Allergies, you know, plus the situation is temporary."

"That's what Laurel said. I'll enjoy her help as long as she's still here."

"It'll all work out for the best. It'll be hard when the time comes, but I just know things will work out. Laurel's the kind of kid that adapts. She'll be fine."

"Change is always hard, but Laurel's so friendly, she'll make new friends in no time." Nora offered Laurel an encouraging smile. Laurel returned a tight, stiff-upper-lip response.

Moving was hard on kids, Nora thought. When she was growing up she'd moved several times with her own family, which was why it had been so nice to put down roots when she'd inherited her grandparents' farm.

"Thanks for giving her something else to think about," Barbara said. "With any luck, maybe she can continue with this kind of thing after we move."

"This will be good experience for her. If she wants to stay until we close up shop, I'll see that she gets home safely." She hung up, turned to Laurel

with a smile and smoothed back the wisps of hair
that had escaped the girl's blond ponytail. "All set."

"She didn't say anything like...?"

"Like what?"

"Like about me not being here after Christmas, or
like..."

"She said that maybe you could do this sort of
thing wherever it is you're moving. There are animal
shelters all over the place, and they all need volunteers to spend time with the pets. Zoos use volunteers, too, so even though you can't have animals at
home because of the allergies in your family, there's
no reason why you can't have animals in your life,
since you obviously don't have the problem. Is it
your mother?"

"What?"

"The allergies."

"Oh." Laurel shrugged. "Everybody but me, I
guess."

"Lucky you. Where are you moving?"

"Um. I'm not sure." She was suddenly halfway
out the office door. "Should I take Dumpy out
first?"

"He'd love that."

Tom sauntered over to the collection of kennels
during a lull. Nora was on a roll, having placed two
animals within half an hour. Tom wasn't rolling. His
jaunty step was clearly a cover-up. He surveyed the

pickings, but the look of resignation in his eyes said it all.

"Okay, here's the deal. It's either Singles Night or some kind of masquerade thing at Halloween, so I think I'm going for Singles Night. Let Ed Lundey over at the Brooklyn Park store dress up like a purple dinosaur." His gaze landed on Dumpy. "I guess I need a pet of some kind to set the right example."

"What kind would you like, Mr. Tallman?" Laurel asked. "We have cats."

"I'm not a cat person. Cats ignore me."

"Cats ignore everyone," Nora assured him. "I'm sure Socks ignores the president."

"Yeah, well, the president doesn't peddle cat chow."

Laurel took the hint from Nora's glance. "Dumpy won't ignore you." She opened the kennel door and let the dog out. He sniffed at Tom's trouser leg. "Look, he wants to be friends."

"I don't want to be friends. Just acquaintances." But he lowered one knee to the floor and greeted Dumpy with a face-to-face ear scratching. "You are the homeliest... What color would you say he is? This isn't even a color. It's every color of dog all run together. It's..."

"Dumpy color," Laurel supplied. "He could be a new coloring crayon."

Tom chuckled. "This is going to be just for one night, Dumpy."

"There's a minimum requirement," Nora informed him. "One week, unless we place him sooner. After a week you have the option to return or extend."

"I have a lake cabin. I always go up there whenever I have a day off."

"Dumpy would love that."

Tom looked up at her. "You said you wouldn't push."

"You said you needed a companion for Singles Night. Dumpy's willing to do that for you, I think. Aren't you, Dumpy?" The dogs perfunctory panting could have passed for a smile. How could the man resist? "Dogs are amazing. They give so much and ask so little in return."

"I don't know if I can do a whole week, but a day at the lake…" Tom stood up slowly. "Would you like to come, too?"

"I would," Nora said carefully. Her heart was suddenly pounding a mile a minute. "If I can get my usual sitter to look after my charges. She's a teenager, and you know how you have to work around their schedules."

"See, that's the problem with having pets. They tie you down."

"That's not the only problem. They're also expensive. There's premium food, toys, beds, invisible fences. Look, flavored bottled water." She pointed to the product on a nearby shelf and glanced at him.

He smiled sheepishly and shrugged. "Whatever sells."

"It's not a problem for me, Tom. Just give me time to make the arrangements."

Chapter Three

Tom had diligently laid the groundwork for the store event they were now calling "Pets And The Single Owner Night," or PATS ON (the head). Nora's idea, mostly, although Tom had gleefully added the acronym to the sign.

"PATS ON the butt?" one of the stock boys had suggested, so Tom had quickly penned the parentheses before some graffiti artist got to it first.

Then came the flyers and an offer from the Humane Society to help Nora cosponsor the event. Mean Jean's buddy from one of the local radio stations offered to bring in a disk jockey to do a live broadcast, and the photographer who usually did their "pets with Santa" gig offered to be on hand for PATS portraits. "It'll be like a prom night," she said, and she pledged part of the proceeds to the foster pet program.

Laurel took charge of the bulletin board. Nora supplied snapshots of pets needing homes, and Laurel used colored markers to print their names. Nora added a little description of their needs and personalities—a job that Laurel declined because she said her spelling wasn't that good. But she did contribute lots of little animal sketches, which she said she'd learned to do from a book. "See? You just use circles," she said, and she demonstrated for Nora, turning out a wonderful sketch of Pickle, followed by one of Dickens and another of Mitzie. "I don't think we should put Dumpy up here," she said. "I think he should stay with Mr. Tallman."

"We can't make Tom keep him," Nora said dutifully, although she had some of the same thoughts—along with a host of others, all about Tom.

"He wants to, though. I know he does."

"I think he does, too, but it has to be his own choice, and not one made out of pity or guilt. He has to make room in his life for another life. It's not just something you buy and put on the shelf. So he has to see if he's ready."

"He's just about ready. You can just tell." Laurel was hunched over the table again, working on another sketch. "This one's gonna be for Mr. Tallman."

"We'll need to get the dogs ready for the party next Saturday. If you want to, you can help me pretty them up a little, and then maybe you'd like to stay and be my assistant. I'll call your mom and see if it's okay."

"It'll be okay. I know it will." Laurel looked up at the nearly finished bulletin board. Her sketches were neatly arranged with the Polaroid pictures of the animals. "Do you think they're embarrassed about being up there for people to kind of pick over?''

''Who, the animals?'' Nora was pleased with the way the bulletin board looked. It featured animals that wouldn't be in the store for the party. The pictures had been taken at home. ''Why don't we take some of the ones we have here today? You can pose with them.''

''I don't like to be in pictures too much,'' Laurel said.

''How about a picture of you and Mitzie and Pickle?'' Nora grabbed the camera, but Laurel shook her head and backed away. ''Not for the bulletin board,'' Nora said. ''For you to keep.''

Laurel's face lit up. That was different.

The party wasn't supposed to start until after the store closed on Saturday, but Tom started feeling queasy well before the appointed hour. Part of him hoped that when they closed the doors, there would be no one left but employees. Another part of him wondered who among the store customers might be there for the party. He'd sworn he wasn't going to think of this as *his* party—he hadn't thrown a party in over four years—but he knew he was about to take the whole thing personally. If people came, he would have to live with the success of a damned singles party. If they didn't, he would have to live with the whole town's rejection of Tom Tallman.

He clung to Dumpy like a security blanket. It was as though having the dog gave him a reason to be in his own store. If the party worked, they were cool. If it didn't, hell, Dumpy didn't care. Why should Tom? He started greeting people with an invitation to "stick around for the party." To his astonishment, many of them said that was what they'd come for. The disk jockey started his patter fifteen minutes before Tom closed on a store full of singles and their pets.

"How about a tune from Three Dog Night? It's all about a bullfrog named…what's a good name for a bullfrog?"

The response threatened to shake bags of food loose in the upper tiers of the store's shelving. "Jeremiah!"

Tom wasn't the best mingler, but Dumpy made it easier for him to play the host among guests who were not of his choosing. And, after all, a customer was a customer. Like the would-be comedienne who appeared to be petless for the evening, but had a name tag shaped like a cat. The order of the evening was to greet the animal first.

"What an interesting dog. What kind is he?"

"He's, uh…" Tom wasn't too keen on the way the woman was examining Dumpy's ears, as though she thought she'd find a label under the floppy tip. "He's my kind of dog. One of a kind."

"What's your name, sweetie?" She glanced up at Tom's name tag, then back at the dog.

"Dumpy." Tom figured he could take his pick of who was the sweetie.

"Dumpy? You should be Humpy, then. Humpy and Dumpy." She laughed as she finger-combed her short, dark hair. "But you're not, you're Tom. So you're Tommy and Dumpy. How sweet." She gestured toward the front of the store with a cup of red punch. "Speaking of dumpy, are the items dumped in that box by the door for sale? Some of the bags are torn. It must be the bargain bin?"

"That's the *donations* bin. Did someone remove the sign?"

She craned her neck. "Oh, I see. Silly me. I guess I didn't read the fine print."

It wasn't exactly fine print. "The food goes to needy animals. You're welcome to pitch in."

"I certainly will," she promised, still looking around. "*Is* there a bargain bin, Tommy?"

"Just Tom, no..."

"No *me?* No *me* on Tom's tail?" She laughed again. "Oh, dear, that was bad, wasn't it? A very bad tail joke."

Tom glanced at Dumpy, who was looking dolefully up at him. They were obviously thinking exactly the same thought. Tom pointed to the clearance table. "Anything on clearance is an extra fifteen percent off tonight. You ought to check it out."

"Doggone it, I think I will."

He smiled, nodded and resisted the urge to duck into the office and lock the door. He asked the disk jockey to announce that any donations to the food bin would go to Nora's Second Chance Ark. Then he went looking for a friendly face. Where was Nora? Or Laurel?

"I'm not much of a party animal," he told Dumpy as he searched the kennel aisle. Dumpy whined. "It shows, huh?"

An orange tabby pranced across the end of the aisle. The floppy tips of Dumpy's ears quivered as he perked them and whined again.

"Forget the feline, Dumpy. I need a friend here. Where's Nora?"

Dumpy knew the name. He raised his head, wagged his stubby tail and looked around, all set to play bloodhound.

"Let's try the cookie bar. Want a cookie?"

Dumpy definitely did.

Nora was nearby, talking to a prospective cat adopter. The yellow Lab on the end of the woman's leash was checking Dickens out, nose-to-nose. The dog was more enthusiastic than the cat, but at least Dickens wasn't hissing. "I think they like each other, don't you?"

"That's as friendly as Dickens ever gets with a dog."

"He's so beautiful. I've always wanted a cat."

The small, smartly dressed woman edged closer to Nora's side, raising her voice a notch above the strains of "Muskrat Love," which the deejay had dedicated to all the rats in the room. "How does that foster placement deal work again?" the woman asked.

After the woman moved on, Tom took her place. "Are you having any success?"

"I think I've placed a dog, a rabbit and two cats already. Plus…" She fished several business cards out of the side pocket of her flowing skirt. "A possible corporate sponsor, one symphony concert, two dinners and one movie."

Tom scowled. "What?"

"Well, one of the dinners goes with the symphony, so that's really only—"

"There aren't that many guys here."

She held up three fingers. "The sponsorship offer came from a woman."

"And the offers of food and entertainment came from…" He was scanning the milling crowd in the aquatics section for likely suspects.

"There are quite a few men here, Tom. I'd say you have a rousing success on your hands."

"Damn. She'll want to make this a regular thing. You have no idea how much I…" He looked at Nora again. She had her hair fixed up in a little bun, its deep russet color accented by a spray of tiny white flowers. Soft stray wisps of hair framed her sweet, girlish face. In her winter white dress—it was the first time he'd seen her in a dress—she might have been, good Lord, a blushing bride, and all he could think of was that you were supposed to be able to kiss the bride. That, and the fact that he was seeing her gorgeous ankles and shapely calves for the first time.

Again he checked the crowd for mooning admirers. "Three, huh?"

"Surprised?"

"Not at all." He drew Dumpy closer. "Where's Laurel?"

"She went to look for the snake. Did you know there's somebody here with a snake?"

He shook his head, only half-aware of what he was saying no to, because he was noticing so many things he hadn't noticed before. Tiny ears, shaped like a little bird's egg. Had they always been covered before?

"We're still on for the lake, aren't we?"

"Well, let's see," she said, taking out her cards again. "Did you give me your card?"

Card, hell. He leaned closer to one of those tiny ears. "Let's go now."

"We can't go now. This is your party."

"It's not just me." He squatted next to Dumpy, hooked his arm around the dog's neck and struck a humble petitioner's pose. "It's both of us asking.

Humpy and Dumpy. Please rescue us from this madness.''

The laughter first bubbled in her throat, then burst forth in vibrant ripples.

He grinned. "Irresistible, huh?''

"Absolutely.''

He stood, his gaze claiming hers as he took the cards from her hand and tore them in half.

"Oh, but the—''

"I owe you two dinners, a concert and a movie.''

"And a corporate sponsor.''

"I'm not a corporation. How about a private sponsor?''

She smiled. "One foster dad in the hand is worth a dozen corporate sponsors in the bush.''

"You already hooked me as a foster dad. How good are you at hooking fish?''

"The season's over, isn't it?''

"*Netting* fish, then.'' He pulled a list from his pocket. "The next stupid party game is Pairs Fish-Netting. I need a partner.''

"What in the world is Pairs Fish-Netting?''

"I have no idea, but it's right after Pin the Tail on the Hamster.'' She laughed, and he hastened to add, "Mean Jean the party machine must have stayed up nights thinking these up.''

Two days later Tom took Nora to his cabin on Lost Lake. It was only a two-hour drive from Minneapolis, but it felt like a different world. The cabin was nestled deep in the woods at the end of a long gravel road. A screened porch overlooked the placid blue water, which mirrored the trees' red and yellow party clothes, their final celebration before stripping down for a long winter's nap. They'd stopped at a store on the way for the makings of a picnic supper—fruit, cold meat, bread and cheese—which they shared on a glider on the porch while they listened to a pair of loons herald dusk's early falling.

"How long have you had this place? It's so beautiful and quiet and..." Her gaze settled upon a swing made of thick rope, which hung from a huge oak. The sling seat hung low to the ground, and Nora imagined short legs and rubber-toed tennis shoes dangling above the glide path, a small voice pleading, *Higher, Daddy!*

The glider creaked as Tom shifted beneath the afghan that covered both their laps. There was a confession in the look she gave him—*I wonder about them*—and untold sadness in the look he returned. *I miss them still.*

"We were married for seven years before we had Mark," he said at last. "Kathryn had miscarried twice. She called Mark our miracle baby. He was five when the accident happened." He snapped his fingers. "Just like that, they were both gone. It's been four years. I haven't had anyone else up here. You're the first guest in four years."

She nodded. The call of the loon echoed across the lake. No answer this time. Such a lonely sound. "I don't know what to say. That's a long time, a lot of hurting. Why do you do it alone?"

"You know another way? If someone cut off your right arm, who would feel it besides you?"

"Those who love you. Your family, your friends."

"That semi wiped out my whole family. As for friends…" There was an invitation in his eyes.

She was hoping he would say it, put it into words. Assumptions were dangerous to the heart, especially the heart of a woman who was not the kind to turn men's heads. In a room full of women, Nora knew she was likely to go completely unnoticed. Men like Tom went for the tall, sleek, resplendent sort of woman, not the short, cute one.

"Man's best friend." She smiled wistfully at Dumpy, who was stretched out at their feet as if he already owned the place. "Like most clichés, it's based on truth. They've done studies, you know. Dogs sense human emotions. They know when to give you some space and when you need comfort. They even know when you're approaching before they can physically sense you." She turned to Tom, who obliged her with a incredulous look. "No kidding. They've set up video cameras and found that dogs will anticipate their human companion's homecoming before the car is within view or hearing distance. Some cats will do it, too."

"They get to know a person's schedule?"

"Nope. They've tested with random arrivals. The animals still go to the door before they could possibly see or hear the car."

"Who's doing this testing?" He surprised her by lifting a finger to trace the outer edge of her ear. "Pet industry people?"

"Independent, unemotional researchers." She closed her eyes, trying to tamp her emotions down, keep them contained within the fluttery basket of hubbub her stomach had suddenly become. She took a deep breath, let it out slowly, then smiled into Tom's baffling blue eyes. "When do you want me to take Dumpy back?"

"You were right about him being an easy keeper. I guess I'm in no hurry to give him up."

"That's not quite the answer we require, but it's getting there."

"When do you want me to kiss you?"

She swallowed hard. He smiled softly. She cast about for something clever to say, but all she could come up with was shy prudence. "That's not something you want to rush into, either."

"That's not the answer we require, but it's better than *never*." He leaned closer, so slowly that she thought she might shatter by the time his lips touched hers. Her eyes drifted closed just before she felt his gentle kiss, sweetly and softly undulating like the water lapping the lakeshore. When he took his lips

from hers, she wanted to haul him back, but she resisted. She ran the tip of her tongue over her lower
lip, coveting every last bit of the taste of him. She
opened her eyes slowly.

He was smiling. "When do you want me to kiss
you again?"

"Would *now* be considered rushing?"

He set their plates aside and took her in his arms.
"Now would be a good time for you to anticipate
my approach and meet me at your door."

His next kiss promised more from him, demanded
more from her. Parted lips, hunger traded for hunger,
tongue seeking tongue. His hair felt silky between
her fingers, his shoulders strong and powerful beneath her slender arms. She could feel the pounding
of his pulse—at least, she thought it was his; maybe
it was hers. Or maybe it was theirs, surging together
to make one driving heartbeat.

He praised her ears, sucked one lobe and tickled
just below it with his tongue. He praised her freckles
and her small breasts—he said small *sweet* breasts—
but he didn't venture beneath her clothing. He merely
held her and kissed her and finally whispered something about the bedroom being close by.

"No," she said, but she clung to him, buried her
face against his neck and could not think of letting
go. "That's not something I want to rush into, but I
do… I do…"

She wanted him. He wouldn't tell her that she

would be the first since Kathryn. It would sound hokey, like some stock seduction line rather than proof that he wasn't trying to rush her. Instead, he said he was sorry.

"Please don't be," she whispered, kissing his neck in a way that could well send him skyrocketing through the porch roof. "Let's not do anything we'd be sorry for. I like you much too much for that." She looked up at him. "Besides, I don't want you to get me confused with the memories that must surround you in that room."

He nodded. "I understand."

She held on tight. She was so small, so enchanting, sparkling with something he'd begun to think of as elfin magic. She looked into his eyes so eagerly, so like a child who desperately wanted a roller-coaster ride but didn't quite dare climb aboard.

And he was *so* ready to be ridden.

She licked her lower lip. "We're not sorry about the kissing, are we?"

He laughed uneasily. "I don't know about you, but I'm not." One more tongue-flicking over that lip and he'd show her how un-sorry he was.

"It's kind of a good way to test the waters, isn't it?"

"That depends." He tucked a strand of hair behind her ear. Damn, she had the cutest little ears. "On whether this test is being conducted by independent, unemotional researchers."

"I don't know about you, but I'm not."

"Touché." He drew back, but he kept his arm around her. He wasn't going far. "You're right. I guess I've been independent and unemotional for quite a while. It was the only way I could survive." With two fingertips, he traced the small point of her chin. "I like you, too, Nora. Much too much. If I start jumping all over you the minute you walk in the door, all you have to say is *Down, boy*. I'll behave."

"I know the difference between a dog and a man. I know how to love both, although…" She smiled. A little sadly, he thought, although the evening shadows offered her considerable shelter for her feelings. "I have a lot of experience caring for dogs, but men are another story. Dogs seem to return my affection much more readily."

"Ah." He couldn't imagine any whole and healthy man deflecting her affection, but if such an animal existed, he wanted to hear about it, wanted to get his number. "Once bitten, twice shy?"

"I've never been bitten by a dog." She shrugged. "I've never actually been bitten by a man, but I've had one or two nibbles that strengthened my resolve to stick with dogs. They're faithful."

"Men aren't?"

"I'm sure some are. It's just that…" She put her hand to her own chest, fingers splayed over her sweater. "It's just that if I don't hang on to something here I'm going to fall much too hard."

"What are you hanging on to?"

"My clothes."

In near darkness they looked at each other, then smiled at each other, each acknowledging the other's needs. "How about some old-fashioned stargazing?"

"It's a little cold," she allowed.

"Which only means we'll both want to hang on to our clothes. Would you feel safe with me in a hammock? I just got it this summer." He stood up, took the woven backyard bed off its storage hooks and held it aloft by its wooden slats. "Completely empty hammock. No memories whatsoever, but it's great for stargazing. Grab that." He pointed to a bundle sitting on a willow twig chair.

"Sleeping bag?"

"It's not a sleeping bag." She picked it up, looking for clues as to what else it might be. He quickly cut her off before she could argue. "It's a bundling bag. Strictly for bundling. Not sleeping."

"And the difference is…"

"When you're bundling, you hang on to your clothes."

"I see." She tucked her bundle under her arm and opened the screen door while he grabbed one more thing. "And what's that for?"

"Dumpy." The dog was up and out the door at the mention of his name. The lake had been puppy love at first sight for Dumpy. Tom tossed the cedar-filled burlap cushion over one shoulder. "The ground's kinda cold. This is the indoor-outdoor model."

"You bought him a bed?"

"No big deal. Hell, I get an employee discount."

She laughed as she trailed him down the well-worn path to the dock. He plopped Dumpy's cushion in the grass, then pushed the hammock stand onto the dock and strung the hammock up. Nora dutifully added the sleeping bag to the arrangement, kicked off her shoes and crawled in. Dumpy curled up on his cushion.

"This is the tricky part," Tom told her. The hammock was as wide as the dock, but he managed to make his entry without tipping her over or losing his balance. It felt good to achieve the feat before her very eyes, then stretch out next to her, take her in his arms and hold her warm body close to his while autumn air nipped at their noses and the stars dazzled them overhead. The water lapped at the old wooden pilings beneath them, and it felt as though they were drifting in a canoe.

They whispered to each other of the wonders of the night, the names of the stars, the bittersweetness of the season and the beauty each saw in the other's face. They kissed and touched tentatively, and giggled about how risky it would be to let passion take over in a hammock suspended over a lake.

"In Minnesota."

He unbuttoned her blouse.

"In October."

He unhooked her bra.

"At night."

He covered her small breast with his big hand and played with her nipple until she gasped with the exquisite pleasure of it.

"Are my hands cold?"

She shook her head.

"Is this all right?"

She groaned. "Better than all right. But please don't..."

"I promise not to bite or push or rush or any of those things. I need to touch you, but I need to go slow, too." He kissed her, slowly and deeply. "Go slow, get to know you." He kissed her again, deeply, touched her more slowly.

"Are your hands cold, Nora?"

"I don't think so."

"I need you to touch me." He found her hand, drew it between them, beneath his sweater, his shirt, pressed it to his bare belly and shuddered from head to toe.

"Cold?" she whispered.

"No, not at all." Her hand stirred over him, and he closed his eyes and let the feel of it stir him. "It feels sweet and warm and completely new."

* * *

Nora was still riding high from her visit to Lost Lake. As far as she was concerned, that which was lost had been found. Tom had called her every night since, and she'd practically had to nail her shoes to the floor to resist running to Pet Palace for a sack of pigs' ears or a bundle of alfalfa. She couldn't afford pigs' ears, and she had plenty of alfalfa. They'd met for breakfast on Saturday before the store opened, and he told her he'd gotten the concert tickets he'd promised. Now she was riding even higher.

Business had been brisk that morning. Laurel had single-handedly placed two calico cats and a mixed-breed puppy. Nora was a little distracted, but she couldn't stop singing Laurel's praises after the paperwork was all signed and the pets delivered into the arms of new owners.

"Laurel, this looks just like you." Marsha stuck her head out the office door. She'd been counting down her register drawer, and she was waving a newspaper clipping. "On the back of this coupon in the Sunday paper. It's your picture, isn't it? What did you do? Did you win a contest or something?"

"Let's see."

Nora was on her way to check it out, but Laurel grabbed her arm. "It's nothing, just some silly—"

"Here's a bigger clipping." Marsha brandished a whole stack of them now, some neatly clipped, others torn from the paper in a big scrap. "Well, sure it's you, it's…"

"It can't be nothing." Nora was already taking a peek over Marsha's shoulder.

It was a nice picture of Laurel, although Nora had seen much bigger smiles on the child, and brighter eyes. She was sitting in a Boston rocker in front of a fireplace, holding a book on her knees. Nora started to tell her how nice she looked. Then she read the caption, and her heart dropped into her stomach.

"Waiting For Adoption. Would You Be Laurel's Mom and Dad?"

Chapter Four

Laurel's face got so hot she could feel the red glow. Her stomach pushed up into her throat. She wanted to shrink up and disappear right before all the staring eyes. *Pouf,* like magic. She couldn't, of course, so she eyed the door, thinking a quick dash might be an okay second choice, if Mr. Tallman would just get out of the way with that big cat tree he was helping a customer take out to her car.

"Laurel?" Nora laid a hand on her shoulder. It didn't feel like a real hand, more like a big doll's hand. "We didn't know."

Laurel shrugged the hand away. "It's no big deal. My foster parents are moving, so they just did that. I didn't want them to. I can just go to another foster home." She glanced up at the bulletin board. Some of the pictures had been taken down--the animals they'd placed in new homes—but Nora had more to put up. "They said probably nobody I know would see that in the paper. Like kids from school and stuff."

"They probably won't."

"I know one kid who has to cut out all the coupons for her mom. I never thought it would be on the back of a coupon."

"If she sees it, what does it matter? If she's your friend…" There was that hand on her shoulder again, heavy with pity. "We're your friends."

Laurel shrugged again. "I'm gonna take Corky out now."

She wasn't sure where she was going, but she needed to be by herself. As soon as she had the leash in her hand, she started for the door. But Mr. Tallman was still messing with that cat tree, so she headed for the back of the store. "I'll use the back door," she muttered. She had to go to the bathroom anyway.

Tom had noticed the long face and the attempts to console. "What's up with Laurel?" he asked as he added a shopping cart to the file of them just inside the door.

Nora showed him the clipping. "I wonder what kind of 'special needs' they're talking about, besides stability," she was saying as he looked at the face in the picture and she read the rest of the accompanying article.

He knew exactly what the child had been thinking when they'd snapped this picture. He knew just how she'd felt. She was a tiny pawn in a huge chess game, and all she could see was row after row of squares, all the same except for the alternating colors. It wouldn't matter much whether they put her on a white one or a black one. She still wouldn't be able to see the edge of the board.

"'Lived with relatives before being placed in foster care,'" Nora was reading over his shoulder. "And we know they're moving. I just assumed Barbara was her mother." She looked up at him, plaintively, as though he'd just pushed the boat away and she was still standing on the dock. "We've spent a lot of time together, and she hasn't mentioned anything about being in a foster home."

He looked at her, looked through her, knew full well she had no idea. "Why would she?"

"I don't know. I guess because we're friends. I thought she would be moving."

"She will be."

"Oh, gosh. Poor kid."

"Don't let her hear you say that." He had hold of Nora's arm now, feeling foolishly defensive, oddly exposed. "Don't let her see it in your eyes. Okay? Don't change the way you look at her."

"Of course not. This doesn't change anything, except that I wish…" She shook her head sadly. "She said she didn't want them to put her picture in the paper. I'm sure this kind of exposure helps them find homes for kids, but you kind of hate to see her advertised this way."

"It definitely spoiled the illusion she had going for herself," he allowed quietly, and he had to admit, at least to himself, that the girl's ruse was a good one. Probably put a lot of her worries on hold, at least on Saturdays. "We all thought she was just a regular kid, and so as long as she was here, that's what she was.''

''Regular?'' Nora watched him hand the coupon back to Marsha, who'd been waiting patiently to finish counting down so she could punch out. ''I think she's a pretty special kid.''

''Do you?'' He waited until Marsha had disappeared into the office before casually suggesting, ''Give her a home, then.''

''Oh. Gosh.'' She looked at him, wide-eyed, clearly thinking *who, me?* ''That's a big step.''

''Bigger than taking in homeless animals?''

''Much bigger. Besides, I'm not married. I can't adopt a child.'' The *who, me?* melted, but instead of the dismissal he might have expected, he saw something else. The entertainment of possibilities. ''Can I?''

''I don't know what the rules are, but that thing from the paper says she'd like an adoptive family with pets. You sure qualify there.'' He shrugged, trying hard to stay cool. ''You'd probably qualify for foster care.''

''But if they can find a permanent home for her, good adoptive parents, a real family, that would be better, wouldn't it? I'd just be another temporary stopover for her, which isn't what a child needs. She needs—''

''Maybe I don't want to be adopted.''

They turned to find Laurel standing next to the

kitty litter bin, clutching the mixed-breed shepherd's leash in both hands. She'd been crying, but the tears were gone now. She'd replaced them with quiet rage.

She glared at Tom. "You're trying to get Nora to take me, just like another puppy nobody wants. Maybe I don't want to just be handed over to somebody. If I could get a job, I could take care of myself."

"I believe you could." He meant it. He wasn't patronizing her. He could tell she was building her shell, layer by layer, just by the way she was standing there with her little shoulders so square, hardly trembling at all. He wanted to go over and stand with her, but he didn't dare. His own shell had too many weak places in it.

He shoved his hands into his pockets and resorted to the all-knowing adult attitude. "It seems as though we're always trying to make matches. Singles nights and adoption days. Newspaper shots. Trying to match everybody up, and that includes children who need new parents. Everybody means well, Laurel, but sometimes we fumble around a lot."

"Meaning well just isn't enough sometimes," Laurel informed him.

"I know."

"I wish you hadn't seen that stupid article. I wish you'd just throw all those stupid things away and forget about it."

"We can't throw them away or we'll be in serious

trouble with Mean Jean." He took a step toward her, and she immediately stepped back. The message was clear. It was no good making lame excuses for the ways of the adult world.

"We know what we know, Laurel, so you don't have to try to hide it anymore." Across the ten-foot gulf of space, he looked her directly in the eye. She was his equal. "That's pretty good, isn't it? You can just tell us how it's going, you know, right up front. Barbara's been pretty nice, huh? She lets you come in on Saturdays, no problem."

Laurel shrugged. "Yeah. I like her a lot better than the last one I had. She wouldn't let me do anything."

"See, so sometimes matches work out pretty well, like with Barbara."

"I'm not very good in some of my school subjects."

"Which ones?" He nodded toward the bulletin board. "You're very good in art. I know that."

"So what? That's just the fun stuff. I'm not good at the important stuff, like reading and spelling."

"Maybe we can help." Nora was permitted to move close to her now, squat next to the dog, take the child's hand.

Tom felt a little left out as he stood there watching, witnessing, aching for the child, for the dog, for himself.

"Laurel, you've helped me a lot," Nora said. "What you do here on Saturdays is important. These animals have special needs, and you have a way with them. Don't think I haven't noticed." She scratched Corky's head. "Friends help friends."

"I still wish you never saw that picture. It's like, when you put the pictures up on the bulletin board, and some of the animals get picked, but some don't. I don't like them to see that their picture is still there and the others have been taken down." Laurel's lips trembled. Tears welled in her eyes. "Maybe it doesn't bother them, but it bothers me."

"I know just what you mean, sweetheart." Nora took the child in her arms. "It bothers me, too."

Over Nora's shoulder, Laurel squeezed her whole face up, like a purple prune, and Tom recognized it for an outward sign of what her insides were doing. She struggled hard with those tears, and in a moment she beat them back. Anyone else might have been surprised to see how quickly the child brought her emotions under control, but Tom wasn't. He knew exactly how such mastery was earned and honed.

Unnatural reserve ruled the rest of the day. Business took over. Customers unwittingly obliged by filling in the gaps between the diplomatic words and the unspoken ones. Offers were made. Most were politely rejected. A short break? A can of pop? A ride home?

Barbara usually had to stick her head in the door when she picked Laurel up, but this time Laurel was watching for the car. Nora chided herself for feeling just a little relieved. Nothing had changed, but everybody was acting as though it had. Nobody had done anything wrong, but it felt as though somebody had.

"Why do you do this?" Tom asked her as he loaded a kennel into the little two-wheel trailer she sometimes pulled behind her van. "You can't possibly find homes for all the animals that people abandon. Eventually some of them get put down."

"They do, yes."

"How do you deal with that? I mean, I could probably tell myself—" He slammed the tailgate shut, fastened the latch and turned to her with an expansive gesture. "Hey, you win some, you lose some. But somehow I can't imagine you saying that."

"I find homes for most of them." He gave her a doubtful look, which she resented. "No, really, I do," she insisted. Finding homes for abandoned animals was, as she'd once told him, more than a cause, more than a charity. It was her life. "I put pictures in the paper and on bulletin boards. I bring them to the store and put them in front of people's faces. I want people to realize that having a litter of puppies or kittens is more than just a way to teach the kids where babies come from. It's more animals needing more homes."

He already regretted his bit of nay-saying. She could see that in his eyes. They were standing near

the parking lot security light, which cast his handsome face in garish light, exposing the sadness he
tried unsuccessfully to mask.

"No, I can't place them all," she said, gently now.
"There are times when there's no room at the inn
and no choice but to put one down. At times like that
I have to think about the homes we've found, the
pets we've placed."

"Nobody wants the older ones." The cars whiz-
zing behind him on the Interstate were a counterpoint
to his dull, flat words. "They want babies and tod-
dlers." With a shrug, he apologized for straying into
territory neither of them wanted to tangle with. He
shook his head. "Puppies and kittens," he amended.

But she knew what he meant. "I'm going to call
the number in that ad," she assured him.

"I had no right to—"

"No, it's okay, Tom. You didn't know she was
there." She touched his arm. "You made a sensible
suggestion, and I'm going to follow up on it." She'd
been thinking about it all afternoon. She'd said nothing to Laurel, of course. "I'm going to call the Adoption Network. I'll find out what their guidelines are.
But with that picture in the paper, some nice family
is bound to ask for her. Maybe lots of nice families."

"Strangers," he said. "People checking her out to
see if she's bright enough, cute enough, good
enough. You're not a stranger. You accepted her, included her in all this just as naturally as..." He

sighed, stared at the storefront, shook his head and sighed again. "All I could think about was that she was hanging around too much."

"That concern comes with your job, Tom."

"My job." Again he shook his head. Then he looked at her, as though he were seeing her differently now. The doubt was gone, at least for the moment, and he was willing to believe. He put one arm around her, hand on her shoulder as though they were about to come up with some sort of plan together. He checked his watch. "Is it too late to make that call?"

"It's Saturday, and it's after five." She reassured him with a smile. "I'll call first thing Monday morning."

"Let me know what you find out, okay?"

He returned her call on Monday morning, as soon as he got her message. "What's the scoop from the adoption folks?"

"They've had some response to the ad," she told him. "Serious interest, they said, which I think meant they didn't consider my inquiry to be serious, because I told them I was single and asked whether I might qualify as a foster parent. The woman said they hoped to arrange an adoption with a…" Her voice trailed off a little, and he imagined her reining it back in and trying to pump it up with a little cheer. "You know, a good family. That's best, isn't it?"

"Sure, I guess. That's best." Any disappointment she was in for now was his fault. He'd made an impulsive suggestion, planted a seed in her brain like some callow adolescent sowing...

"When are you going to invite me over for dinner?"

"Dinner?" She made it sound like an unfamiliar concept. "You...want me to cook for you?"

"You don't do that sort of thing?"

"I can cook," she claimed tentatively. Then, with assurance, "Of course I can cook. When can you come?"

"Whenever you want me. When would that be?"

"That would be..." She kept him hanging, smiling, thinking *Say it, Nora, say all the time.* "Any time you're free."

Close enough. He looked at his watch. "I'm free in two hours. Would I be more welcome if I brought dinner with me?"

"You would be completely welcome under any circumstances. Two hours is good. Plenty of time for me to—"

"I'm inviting myself for Chinese takeout, which I'm taking over. How's that?"

She laughed. "You're *taking over,* huh?"

"Taking over to your place. Taking takeout out to the farm. Over to the farm. How do I get to the farm?"

Nora imagined him sitting on his desk the way he

sometimes did when he was willing to take a few extra minutes with a phone call. She gave him detailed directions, because it was a little complicated and she didn't want him to get lost. She didn't want to lose him. Now that he'd finally taken notice of her, she didn't want him to lose his way. These were the thoughts she carried in her head as she straightened up the living room of the small farmhouse, gathering the scattered newspapers into a stack for recycling, running around with a dust cloth, a dust mop, a vacuum cleaner and a cobweb catcher. Visitors often came to Nora's Ark, but seldom to her house.

She didn't want to lose Laurel, either. She had no claim on the child, and she couldn't offer her the perfect two-parent situation, but she could offer a home with pets. Animals galore. A shelter like Nora's Ark wasn't a project just any child could deal with. Animals that might be gone tomorrow still demanded love and care today. But Laurel took it all in stride. She'd cheerfully parted with some of her favorite critters, animals she longed to have as her own pets. But she understood the nature of Nora's Second Chance Ark. They liked each other—Laurel and the animals, Laurel and Nora—and they would undoubtedly do well together under the same roof, even if it was only three hundred cubits by fifty cubits.

But the Adoption Network wasn't looking for a

Second Chance Ark. They were looking for a Mom-Dad-kids home, which was a sound plan. A very sensible plan. Nora had made the call. She'd gotten some information, and she'd decided to do what she could, to offer what she had. She'd been thinking about all that, too, and she remembered Laurel's response to Tom's suggestion. Maybe she didn't want to be adopted. It all seemed so one-sided—the doing the offering, the fostering, the adopting. It was all being done to the child, as though Laurel had no feelings, no say, nothing to offer herself. Lopsided, Nora thought. How did these things get to be so lopsided?

Some two dozen dogs announced Tom's arrival. Nora threw her jacket on and ran outside to greet him. She wanted to show him around before it got dark.

"I only took one wrong turn, and I corrected for that quickly," he told her as he held the car door open for Dumpy. "C'mon out, fella. You remember this place?"

"Hi, Dumpy. How's my sweetie?" She had to greet the dog with an upraised knee. "Down," she reminded him firmly, and when he obeyed, she gave him an affectionate reward. "I had him cured of that, Mr. Tallman."

"Uh-oh."

"There's no reason to let him jump on people."

"He didn't tell me he knew any better."

"Well, he does." She spread her admonishing look between the two of them. "So you're bringing him back to me with bad habits?"

"He's just visiting. We've decided to keep each other, me and Dumpy, bad habits and all."

"I knew you would," she said happily as she led the way toward the large, white, free-span facility that bore the Nora's Second Chance Ark sign. "But, remember, you don't have to tolerate bad behavior."

"Is she talking to me or you?" Tom asked the dog.

Dumpy whined.

They'd reached a row of kennels with attached chain-link runs on the south side of "the ark." Barking and whining dogs in all shapes and colors greeted their former neighbor. Butts wiggled, tails wagged, paws clambered on the gates.

"See, Dumpy? Somebody's already moved into your old digs," Nora said, explaining the presence of a scruffy, scrawny yellow Lab, who was obviously much in need of Nora's care. "Most of the bigger dogs get these outdoor accommodations, unless it's winter and they've been house dogs. Then I keep them inside. I take in paying boarders when there's room, usually in the summer. This is the time of year we start getting more abandoned animals. Fall and winter." She pointed to three acres of fenced field. "That's the play yard."

"Do they all go out at the same time?"

"Some dogs play together just fine, but we do have our occasional troublemaker. Some have been abused, others are just terribly antisocial. It's hard to change that in an adult animal. But they all need exercise."

She opened the door to the ark and ushered her visitors in. "That's why the volunteers are so important. They help with so many things, but mostly they help me give the animals a second chance to learn how to be sociable, to learn how to be around people. It's not a problem in all cases. Most of the animals—guys like Dumpy—are really easy to love. But some of them have been treated badly somewhere along the line, and you have to be very careful where you place them."

"Like maybe not around small children," Tom assumed. He was eyeing the setup now, from partly concrete floor to open-rafter ceiling.

"Exactly. Well? What do you think of my ark?"

The animals were housed in wire cages, kennels, hutches, small pens, whatever worked best. Rabbits, guinea pigs, the occasional goat or potbellied pig all found shelter in the ark. One corner was an enclosed cat area with climbing trees and a door to an outdoor enclosure. And there were plenty of dogs.

"How do you take care of all this?"

"How do you take care of Pet Palace?" The look he gave her said there was no comparison. "You have a schedule," she reminded him. "You run a tight ship."

"Yeah, but this is…"

"This is where I spent most of my summers when I was growing up. The minute school got out, I was ready for Grandpa's place. My mother was born and raised as a farm girl, and I was always a farm girl at heart." She stopped to greet a collie who'd just whelped eight squirming pups. She already had homes lined up for three males and a female.

"This is kind of like farming, only I don't market the animals the same way, obviously," she explained as she led Tom between the rows of pens. There was plenty of barking and yipping, but she was used to talking over it all. She took people through the ark almost every day. "I inherited the place from my grandfather. I sold some of the land, got a very good price for it, which I invested, and that enables me to do this."

"You're still only one person."

"I have a paid assistant, who comes in part-time, and I have a host of wonderful volunteers. But you see why the foster care program is important. I have to get them out of this environment and into homes as quickly as possible so that they continue to be suitable companions for people."

"You take in horses, too?"

They'd reached the box stall at the end of the ark. Nora smiled as her big bay beauty came over to say hello. "This is Chauncy. He's mine. I almost sold him last winter to make room for more orphans, but I just couldn't do it. Too selfish, I guess. But he does help bring in volunteers. I've got two horse lovers who help me out a lot in return for the privilege of riding whenever they like. It works out well for us, doesn't it, Chauncy?"

"Selfish isn't a word that springs to mind, Nora." She turned, found him watching, smiling. He joined her in rubbing the horse's neck. "You're not selfish."

An awkward silence passed. She suddenly felt a little embarrassed, and he seemed overwhelmed by it all. It was probably not the best idea in the world for a woman who was seriously interested in a man to show him her barn full of stray animals. Probably something like the mother of a dozen young kids looking for a husband.

"Are you hungry?" Tom asked finally. "I hope you have a microwave. The sweet and sour has become the sticky and cold."

She figured she might as well lay all her liabilities on the table. "Microwave reheating is all I know how to do anymore."

He liked the house. It reminded him of his lake cabin, which was rustic but homey. Nora's house was country-style homey. From the light shining through the leaded-glass eyebrow over the front door to the thick, hand-braided rag rug on the other side, the house itself gave a man and his dog a welcome feeling. Once Grandpa's home, now Nora's home, it felt more like a family place than his own house, empty but for the memory of family. He hung his jacket on the coat tree, while a small, foxy-looking mutt greeted Dumpy in the foyer.

"This is Vixen," Nora said as she squatted to pet the dog. "She's mine, too. I have to be very strict with myself about my own adoptions."

He let the house draw him in. It had nine-foot, coved ceilings, hardwood floors and, from the look of the layout, lots of small, cozy rooms on two floors. He chided himself for expecting it to smell like wet dogs and cat litter boxes. It didn't. Not that there weren't a couple of cats peering regally down at him from carpeted perches on an eight-foot cat tree.

"I'll bet you do."

"Which brings me to Laurel." Nora tossed her own quilted jacket on the coat tree and turned to him. "I've made some calls. I can get on the list for foster care and get inspected, investigated and certified, but meanwhile, they're looking for an adoptive home for Laurel."

He nodded. She'd laid it on him like a report he'd assigned her to do. He'd been out of line with his suggestion, and he'd felt guilty about it ever since he'd made it. He had no right to try to guilt this woman into taking charge of a child. But the woman was Nora, and the child was Laurel, and every time he thought about either one of them—or, worse, about the two of them together—he had the craziest thoughts. The wildest visions of the three of them, maybe. Together.

He smiled. "What do you say we nuke the fried rice?"

She took the brown bag and led the way through the blue-and-white dining room. He noticed that she had already set the table with what must have been Grandma's good dishes and put on a stack of romantic CDs. He noted that the kitchen was "neat as a pin." She laughed and assured him that the oven was especially clean.

They ate by candlelight. She scolded him for slipping Dumpy a bit of beef from his plate. He laid a fire in the fireplace, and they piled pillows in front of it, sipped a little wine, cracked open their fortune cookies and teased each other about what they said. She was, according to her fortune, "a connoisseur of fine food."

"You've been a frog long enough," he read aloud from his strip of paper. "You're about to turn into a handsome prince."

"Let me see that." She reached for the paper, but he held it out of reach.

"You doubt me, princess? I've got a palace."

She looked into his eyes so long and hard that he almost wished he hadn't asked. He should have just reached for her, pulled her close, put his cold lips on hers. But it wouldn't work that way. He was the one who'd forgotten the way, and she had the magic. He had such crazy visions lately, but she had to believe and touch him and show him the way.

"I'm afraid to kiss you," she said at last.

"Why?"

"If you get any handsomer, I'll never get my other dinner, or my movie, not to mention my—"

"Take a chance."

She put her arms around his neck, closed her eyes and covered his lips with a warm, loving, life-giving kiss. Damn, he thought, he was a fairy tale come true. There was a prince in him after all, a man with crazy visions of filling his life with love once again. He took his elfin princess in his arms and returned her kiss in full measure.

Her cats, aloof on their perches, supervised this full-measure kissing with detached interest. Dumpy finally whimpered a little, just to remind them that he'd come for a visit, too.

"Sorry, fella. It's too late for you," Tom said. Nora smiled at him. "But not for me. Sweet heaven, it's not too late for me."

Chapter Five

On Saturday, Laurel didn't show up for adoption day.

Nora wanted very much to look on the possibility of a bright side to the girl's absence. "Maybe they've found her a new home already."

She said it as an upper, but it felt like a downer. She knew it was selfish of her, but since Tom had suggested that she offer the child a home, the idea had lingered in her mind, getting better and better. She'd started thinking of the bedroom on the east side with the dormer window as Laurel's room. She had checked into the school situation and decided that with a little driving each day, it would be possible to spare Laurel a transfer. She kept having the same niggling thoughts over and over: *Maybe they won't find anyone else. Maybe they'll let her come live with me.* Pretty selfish thoughts.

"They couldn't have finalized anything," Tom told her as he absently stroked one of two pairs of bunny ears that were up for adoption. "Not so quickly."

"Maybe they're introducing her to a new family today. Or maybe she's sick." She touched Tom's arm. "She might be sick. She's never missed an adoption day. Maybe she's—"

He looked up from his stroking. "Maybe you should call."

"I don't have any right to interfere with..."

He challenged her with a look.

"You're right. I'll call."

When Nora identified herself, Barbara lowered her voice. "Laurel says she isn't feeling well today, but it doesn't appear to be anything serious. A few sniffles."

"What about...?" She picked up a pencil off Tom's desk and scratched a few marks on his memo pad. "Has anyone come forward to adopt her?"

"There's a family doing some preliminary paperwork, and there have been others who've shown interest."

"Oh." She drew a circle. *Preliminary.* It was just preliminary. "Well, that's...that's reason to be hopeful, isn't it?"

"Oh, yes. But I've been doing foster care for a while, and I know how often these things fall through for the older kids. Lots of potential snags."

"How does Laurel feel about it?"

"I don't know. She's been pretty quiet."

"Maybe I could stop over and see her. I'm tied up with the animals today, but if you wouldn't mind, maybe I could stop in after school sometime?"

"I'm sure she'd like that." There was a little indistinct whispering on Barbara's end of the line. Then, ''When she's feeling better, I know she would.''

''Is she up to coming to the phone?''

''Um…'' More whispering. Pause. ''I guess not.''

''Oh.'' Understandable. ''Please tell her I…we miss her.''

''I will.''

She was still sketching when she hung up the phone. Big circles, little ovals, overlapping here and there, just the way Laurel had demonstrated. But Laurel's were much better.

Tom's shoes appeared in the office doorway. By the way his knee was bent, she could tell that he was leaning against the frame, and from the silence, she knew that he was waiting for a report.

''She didn't want to talk to me,'' she said without looking up from her pitiful sketch. ''They've done some preliminary paperwork on a family interested in adopting her. A very nice family.'' She filled in part of an eye. ''I mean, I'm sure they're very nice.''

''If that doesn't work out, they might still place her with you.''

''That's right. They might.'' She plunged the pencil into the black cup and heaved herself out of his chair. ''They have to do what's best for Laurel.''

''Exactly. Are we on for the lake this week?''

''Tuesday, right?'' He nodded. ''It wouldn't be right for me to tell her that I offered to take her,

would it? I want her to know that I'd be pleased to
have her, but I don't want to interfere with…''

''Is she sick?''

''I don't think so. And she's not a baby, Tom. She
knows exactly what's going on. She must feel so
uncertain and vulnerable and…'' She moved closer
to him. ''So scared.''

He nodded again, looking into her eyes as though
he had something to say, but he wasn't sure what
words to use. He turned away without finding them.

The sketch on his memo pad had him mesmerized.
Nora's version of Laurel's circles, ripples in his lake
plans, soft cords around his heart. He knew what it
meant to be homeless. You could have a place to
stay and still be homeless. He'd been homeless before he'd met Kathryn. He'd been homeless since her
death. He had a place to stay, but it had taken a
scruffy mouse-colored dog to make it feel like home
again. In Nora's kitchen he was home again. In her
yard, on his porch, even in the store, he was home
again. At that moment, sitting there in his own skin,
he realized that he'd found home again.

They weren't cords; they were circles. Ripples in
his reclusive plans, but, damn, if they didn't make
him feel as if he'd finally broken through the surface
and found a breath of air.

''I'm going to lunch,'' he told Nora as he shrugged
into his jacket. She couldn't have gone with him even

if he asked her, which he wanted to do but couldn't if he was going to do what he had in mind, which was probably harebrained, but, hell—he reached into the bunny box to stroke those powder-soft ears—he was in the pet business. "I see you had a rabbit customer this morning. You're down to one. Can I bring you anything?"

She looked at him curiously. He usually didn't take a lunch break.

"Gotta go home for lunch now that I have a dog to worry about. Fish were a lot easier."

"But they don't lick your face when you're..."

"Happy." He smiled and reached out to touch her cheek. More powdery softness. "Dumpy likes to get his licks in when I'm happy, as if to say, 'This is it, Tallman. Laugh a little. Smell the roses.'"

"And have you been doing that?"

"You know I have."

"Do my eyes deceive me?" Beth had sneaked up on him from behind the Know Your Pet book spinner, and she was grinning like a bargain hunter on double coupon day. "Or is there some hanky-panky going on under the Palace stairs?"

"Taking a lunch break." Tom tossed Beth the keys to his office and the rest of the kingdom. "Nora doesn't work for me, so it's not hanky-panky."

"Then it's safe to assume that my eyes are *not* deceiving me."

"I'm safe in assuming that your eyes are not receiving the shipment from Fowl and Fin that should be pulling up to your dock any minute.'' She was bouncing the keys, giving him that caught-you-red-handed look. ''You aren't safe assuming anything, so don't start spreading any—''

Beth was already sauntering down the Tabby Tuna aisle singing, ''Tommy's got a girlfriend.''

''Where's the respect?'' He grinned at Nora. ''I don't mind if you don't. I was thinking about carving our initials out there on the lamppost. What do you think?''

''It's a metal pole.''

''I like a challenge.'' He nodded toward a couple approaching one of the dogs with their hearts on their sleeves. ''You've got customers. I'll be back in an hour.''

His plan was to take Dumpy for a walk in Laurel's neighborhood, which was only a few blocks from his own. He'd briefly met Barbara Kopecki, the plump woman who answered the door, when she'd come to the store for Laurel. She seemed like a nice woman. He knew that most foster parents were nice people who were interested in helping kids. Without them, where would kids like Laurel be?

Bottom line, where would he have been?

''Stopped by to see if Laurel's feeling any better.''

''Laurel?'' Barbara called over her shoulder. ''I'm glad you came, but, um, the dog…''

"We're just out walking."

"My twins are allergic, so I can't..." Again over the shoulder, "Laurel, there's someone here to see you."

He could hear cartoon voices on TV, the chattering of a small child, the whirring of some mechanical toy. He smiled wistfully, remembering the sound of his own child's favorite windup train. Reminders still hurt, but not as sharply these days, he realized, especially when Laurel appeared at the door.

"How are you feeling?"

"I'm feeling okay." She pushed the storm door open wider when she saw her old buddy. "Hi, Dumpy."

"Got a cold?"

"A little one." She looked up from her nose-to-nose greeting with the dog. "You're not taking him back, are you?"

"No way. He's my dog now. Would you like to come..." Tom glanced up at Barbara, who had stepped back to hold the door. She nodded. "And take a walk with us? It's nice out."

"I'll get my jacket." Laurel turned to her foster mother. "Is it okay?"

"It's okay if you feel okay."

Laurel disappeared and returned with her jacket in two shakes of Dumpy's tail. Barbara shoved a stocking cap in her hands, and they were on their way. "I

had a sore throat this morning," Laurel explained as
she pulled the blue cap down over her ears.

"Better now?" he asked, and she nodded. "Here,
I usually have…" Tom handed her Dumpy's leash,
then pulled a piece of cellophane-wrapped candy
from his jacket. "Yep, lemon drops. I got into the
habit of keeping a few in my pocket for my little
boy. My wife got after me about it, said he might
choke on them. I'd say, heck, he could choke on a
piece of chicken." He gave her a tight smile. "We
were careful. We were always so careful."

"I'm sorry he died."

"Me, too." He held out his hand for the candy
wrapper, which he pocketed. "I'm sorry you were
embarrassed to have us see that article in the paper."

"It doesn't matter."

"It matters that it bothered you. It mattered to us
that you didn't come in today because of it."

"I don't know what they're gonna do with me,"
she said after some silence. "I know Barbara feels
bad. They didn't mean to adopt me, but they would
have let me stay with them if it wasn't for them
moving, and Terry's job having to change because
where he worked got bought out, and stuff like that."

"I'm sure the Kopeckis are going to miss you."
He offered her another lemon drop. "Who's your
caseworker?"

"Her name is Mrs. Bowles."

"Mine was Mrs. Kidd." Laurel looked up at him,

wide-eyed. He smiled, nodded. She was still staring at him as she tucked the candy in her pocket. "I remember asking her if the Kidds had any kids, and she said her job was to be the shepherdess for other people's kids. You mean the strays, I asked, and she said—" He pitched his voice up an octave. "'Heavens, no, Tom. My kids will not be allowed to stray.'"

"You were a *foster kid?*"

"I was."

"How come?"

"My mother couldn't take care of me, I guess."

She nodded. She understood perfectly. "Mine died."

"Mine, too, eventually."

A car passed. The driver rolled the window down and tossed a cigarette butt onto the street, and the strains of some polka music emerged, as well. Tom had learned to polka at his wedding, but the vision that popped into his head was of him teaching Laurel to polka, maybe twirling her around the dance floor at her wedding. What joyous circles those would be.

They turned a corner together. He listened to the rhythm of their combined footsteps—Dumpy's four feet padding on the sidewalk, Laurel's two steps for every one of Tom's. Natural music.

"I thought about running away," she said abruptly, "but I'm kinda scared."

"I tried it." He clucked his tongue. "Bad idea."

"What happened?"

"I didn't have anyplace to go. Ended up getting picked up by the police, which was lucky, I guess. I was thirteen, old enough for serious trouble, but still young enough to steer clear of it. Mrs. Kidd helped me steer clear."

"How did she do that?"

"She found another family to take me in. They treated me very well."

"Did you get adopted?"

"No, I didn't." He looked at her, smiled a little. Her nose was getting red. Reminded him of Nora's bunny. "It worked out okay. I made a few friends, stayed in school, went to college, got a good job."

"Why can't I decide where I get to live? Why can't I pick?" She wasn't whining for a new toy. She just wanted answers. "Because I'm just a kid?"

"To be honest, Laurel, that's part of it. It's not fair, that's for sure, but it's the way things are." They'd reached the end of the block. They stopped. Dumpy stood at the end of the leash, panting, patiently waiting on the whims of his humans. Tom offered Laurel his hand.

She looked at it for a moment, extended at an angle, palm down. No demand, no supplication, just a wordless offer from a man who had once been a father to a child who had never had one. She glanced across the street. There was no traffic. She was a big girl. She'd been crossing the street by herself for some time now.

She looked up at him as she took his hand. He smiled, thanked her with a simple nod, and they crossed the street together.

"What I wanted to tell you is that there's no shame in being a foster kid. I know it feels like there is sometimes, but you've got to try to fight that feeling off."

"It's hard to."

"I know." He gave her hand a quick squeeze. "Hardly anybody knows I was a foster kid. I never tell anyone. Even now, I don't want anyone feeling sorry for me. You know what I mean?"

"Yeah."

"Before I got to know you and Nora, I didn't like being in the store on Pet Adoption Day," he confessed. "I didn't like seeing the animals in their cages waiting for somebody to take pity on them and give them a home. I really hated that."

"Yeah, but they do get homes. I like it when the little kids get to hold them for the first time, and you know they've been wanting a pet for a long time, and now they've finally got one."

"I like that part, too. But you know what? I almost missed seeing that part. We have to let people see them. We can't hide them away. If we do that, they'll never find homes."

"Dumpy, heel."

The dog slowed his pace.

"You're a natural," Tom said with a smile. "I

went out to Nora's place last night—Nora's Ark. Have you been there?'' Laurel shook her head. ''Then we've gotta take you out there soon. You know, there used to be a city pound where they'd take all the stray animals, and it was a bad scene. Nora's way is much better.''

''Nora knows a lot about taking care of pets.''

''But we have to help her put up their pictures and publish them and show guys like Dumpy off, so that even hard-hearted guys like me get to see them, finally decide to give it a chance and find out...'' He laughed when the dog looked up, pleased just to hear Tom speak his name. ''That's right, Dumpy, you showed me. We get along pretty good. Dumpy and me, we were made for each other.''

''It's embarrassing to have your picture up.''

''I know.'' Again he squeezed her hand. ''Ah, honey, I know. But the embarrassment will pass. Believe me, you put up with it for a little while, and it'll pass. Something good will happen, and you'll forget what you had to put up with to get it.''

''Are you sure?''

He wanted to be sure. ''Would you like to go back to the store with me? Nora could really use your help.''

''I guess I could.'' She reversed their direction by walking around him, using him as an axis. ''We're not going to stop being friends, are we?''

''No way.''

"I hope my new family won't live too far away, because if they don't, I can still come to the store sometime."

"If you don't, we'll go looking for you."

They walked back to the Kopecki house, spoke to Barbara, then took Dumpy back to his new, very own backyard. On the way to Pet Palace, Laurel forgot about any sore throat she might have had. She would soon be back on the job, and suddenly she'd found new purpose.

"You really like Nora, don't you?"

It wasn't the red light at the intersection that made Tom smile.

"Do you love her?"

"You don't beat around the bush, do you?" He chuckled. "I really, really like Nora. A lot."

"Just say it." Laurel was fairly popping out of her seat belt. "You love her."

"If I'm in love with her—and I say *if*—don't you think she should be the first one I say it to?"

"Yeah. Probably. Green light."

He glanced up, accelerated and gave Laurel another smile, which was all the cue she needed.

"When are you gonna tell her? Today?" With the twitch of an eyebrow he tried to warn her against rushing him, but she was having none of it. "You can't keep it a secret. You'll bust wide open."

"I will, huh?"

"Or else you'll, like, be keeping it a secret, and

keeping it a secret, and pretty soon time passes, and your hair turns gray, and your teeth start falling out...." He was laughing by now, watching her animate her fantasy with her hands. "Pretty soon you've got a cane, little glasses on the end of your nose. And she's been waiting all this time, because she loves you, too."

"You sure?"

"Yeah, but she doesn't know if you love her, because you're keeping it so *secret.* Finally you hear she's getting married to some other old guy, so you call a cab, because you're too old to drive, and you go to the church, and you can see through the window that she's almost all the way down the aisle."

"But it's taking her a while."

"Well, yeah, she's old, too. Plus, she had to get all the dogs and cats ready for the wedding."

"They're lined up in the pews."

"Little bow ties, little hats." Her eyes sparkled as her hands created the shapes beneath her chin, over her head. "So you're running as fast as you can, which is awfully, *ter*ribly slow, trying to make it up the steps to the church, and she looks back through the door..."

"I think I've seen this movie."

"And you mouth the words." Her little mouth silently formed them for him, while he pronounced them aloud. "I...love...you...Nora."

She nodded, clapping her hand over her heart.

"Just as you have a heart attack and drop over on the church steps."

"The end."

"It could be," she told him with an instructive finger. "Or she could grab the preacher by the hand, hop on a Great Dane, ride down the aisle and out the door, and get to you just in time."

"In time for what?" They were pulling in to the Pet Palace parking lot. "I'm too old for a honeymoon."

"Yeah, but you're never too old to say the words. The preacher could say the whole thing really fast— I do, I do, husband and wife, kiss the bride..."

"So I at least get a kiss."

The question checked her chatter as she drew a slow smile. "Have you kissed her yet?"

"That's none of your business."

"You have, haven't you? I can see that little sparkle in your eyes." The car was parked now, but neither of them opened a door. They eyed each other, the vestiges of merriment easing them back to reality. "You should just tell her," Laurel said. "What are you afraid of?"

"A lot of things." He knew he wasn't going to get off that easily. "What am I *most* afraid of?" She nodded. "Getting too attached." She nodded again. "You, too?"

"Me, too." She drew a kid-quick frown. "But isn't kissing, like, *attached?*"

"Not permanently." His mind fixed his lips on Nora's, and he smiled. "Just for a little while."

"It looks kind of slobbery sometimes, like you'd be getting somebody else's spit in your mouth."

He laughed.

"Does it taste like somebody else's spit? I mean, can you tell the difference between yours and hers?"

"Hers tastes better," he told her when he could get the words out, laughing the way he was.

"Nora's?"

"Yeah. Nora's."

Laurel beamed.

"Hey!" He reached over and tickled her under the chin. "You little weasel."

"So just tell her. 'Nora, I like your spit better than mine.'"

His sides were about to split. "Oh, that is beautiful."

"Or you could tell her you love her."

"That might sound a little better."

"It's just another way of putting it. I mean, if you're gonna slobber all over somebody and let them slobber all over you…"

"I see your point. And if I wait too long, we're liable to be drooling all over each other anyway."

"Yu-u-ck." She unsnapped her seat belt. "Do you have to go around tasting a bunch of spit before you find the right one?"

"No, not…not really. You really don't." She was

grinning at him, all sugar and spice. In five short years this little girl was going to be a knockout.

Tom noticed party-boy Ron loading dog food into the back of a van.

They drove vans now, these wild teenage boys, he thought.

"In fact, Laurel, if you ever start thinking along those lines, I want you to bring the boy around to me, and we'll conduct some lab tests, a little test-tube flavor analysis. You wouldn't need to have any icky boy's lips attached to yours at all."

"Good." Her smile assured Tom that his wisdom was undeniable. When he got out of the car, he felt taller.

On their way into the store she told him, "Grown-ups are lucky. If they want to get attached to somebody, they can just ask them. If they don't, they don't have to."

He knew then, after four bleak years, that he wanted to be attached again.

And he knew, when Nora greeted them like not one, but two, missing and dearly missed connections, that he was ready to ask her.

"You said you'd be back in an hour," she reminded him after she'd welcomed them back to the Palace.

"Laurel and I had some things to talk about."

"Like what?" Her smile invited an answer from both of them.

Laurel's hair sprang to attention when she peeled off her stocking cap. "All I know is, the only kind of love I want is just love at first sight. No slobbering."

"Really," Nora said, looking at her curiously.

"Nora, you want to come into my office a minute?" Tom winked at Laurel. "I've got something I want to tell you before I get too old."

"Too old?"

He took her by the hand and headed for the office. Ron tried to head him off with a request to leave early, and Beth trailed him with an urgent message from Mean Jean. "Give me five," he told them both before shutting everyone out but Nora.

Ron looked at Beth. Beth shrugged. A moment of silence passed.

"You like my *what?*" Nora howled behind the office door.

Beth looked at Ron.

"Is he harassing her?" Ron whispered.

"She doesn't work for him. I don't think it would be considered—"

Ron shushed her. More silence.

"I told him it sounded better the other way," Laurel said as she moved in to join the watch. Ron and Beth looked to her for more clues, but she just giggled. "Guess she likes his, too." Then she thought about it and made a clownish grimace. "Ick."

"When did you decide this?" Nora asked him as their lips parted after a doubt-defying kiss.

"That I love you? The first time I laid eyes on you." Her doubts resurfaced. "Okay, *decide* is the operative word here. I loved you the first time I laid eyes on you, but I was afraid to call it that until today. So…how does *my* spit taste to *you?*"

"Let me try it again." Arms around his neck, she drew herself up, up, for a deep, delightful, open-mouthed kiss. "Oh, yes." She sighed. "Oh, yes, you are *most* delicious, Tom Tallman."

"My spit," he clarified.

"Your spit, your sweat, your tangy skin."

"What do you say we get married?"

"Married?"

"You know…" He rocked her in his arms, tipping his head from side to side. "I do, I do, husband and wife, hurry up and kiss the bride before you have a heart attack."

"Are you nervous?"

"Damn right I'm nervous." But he kissed her again anyway. "What I'm most afraid of is that you'll say no."

"Really?"

He mouthed the words *I love you.*

She mouthed them back to him.

He attached his mouth to hers, tasted her again, again and again, and he thought, *yes.* Hers was infinitely better.

Epilogue

Something good *had* happened, just as Tom had promised.

It worked out even better than the way Laurel had dreamed up, and all because of a great picture that had made the front page of the newspaper, along with some pretty schmaltzy footage on the ten-o'clock news. Thanksgiving was fat-newspaper, slow-news day, Tom had said, and a wedding at Nora's Second Chance Ark, attended by more animals than people, was great feel-good material. The wedding had attracted so much attention that eleven dogs—one for each of Laurel's years—and seven cats had found new homes.

"Be sure to mention your first date at Pet Palace," Mean Jean had prompted from the groom's side of the ark. "We're planning a PATS ON Christmas party." The cameraman had zeroed in on her, and she had displayed a white-gloved handful of Kitty Kibbles and one of cracked corn. "Instead of rice," she'd explained. "Compliments of Pet Palace."

Nora had protested a little bit on rushing the wedding—she never liked being rushed—but Tom had thought it was a good idea to get married if they expected to get a kid. The kid they were expecting to get was Laurel, and they had to fill out a lot of papers and pass "mustard" with Mrs. Bowles. Laurel wasn't sure what mustard had to do with anything, but she was willing to pass her caseworker everything in the refrigerator if it would help get her name changed to Laurel Tallman. Nora had really liked the idea of becoming Nora Tallman. She said she'd been a short woman long enough.

Naturally somebody had to move, and it had to be Tom, but he said that not too many guys around the lake could claim they got to go home to an ark. After moving Tom and moving Laurel, they'd even spent part of Christmas vacation helping the Kopeckis pack up for their move to California. Barbara finally unloaded a bunch of exercise equipment in her moving sale.

"Will you girls shake a tail feather up there?" Tom called. "The ark sitter's here. We've got places to go, things to do. Final adoption papers waiting to be signed."

Laurel could just see him standing at the foot of the stairs with his coat on. He was going to have to get used to not rushing. Girls didn't like to be rushed. That was what Nora said.

Tom and Nora. They'd said she could call them anything she felt comfortable with, and she was comfortable with Daddy and Mom. She just had to get used to thinking the words. She'd waited so long, she was almost afraid to believe, so whenever the doubts bothered her, she raised her hand and rubbed her fingers together just above her head, *sprinkle sprinkle.*

"Want some fairy dust, Vixen?" She sprinkle-sprinkled over the little red dog, who was enjoying her sunny window seat. "It works pretty good. Just make a wish."

Nora peeked in and smiled. "Go down and tell him to give me five."

Nora was still brushing her hair. She'd spent so much time fussing over Laurel's hair, she'd almost forgotten about her own. But of course, Nora's always looked pretty.

Nora's? *Mom's.*

Sure enough, he was down there pacing, and Dumpy was sitting on the rag rug, watching him, waiting to see if he would get to go, too. She remembered the first time Tom had almost run her over in the Pet Palace aisle. He'd scared her. Maybe she'd scared him a little bit, too. But this time the sight of her at the top of the stairs put a twinkle in his eye.

"You ready to become a Tallman?"

She felt like a princess, descending the stairs in the green velvet dress they'd bought at Christmastime. "Is there an oath I have to take?"

"It goes something like, 'I do, I do, daughter and parents, kisses all around and don't slobber.'"

Straightfaced, she tipped her head from side to

side as she repeated the words, as though memorizing her lines.

"You got it." He reached for her hand. "Now let's—"

"Daddy!" Laurel grinned. It sounded just fine, as if she'd been saying it for eleven years. "Be patient, now, Daddy. We're waiting for Mom."

*   *   *   *   *

Dear Reader,

When I was asked to be in this collection, I couldn't say no. All of use have issues that are particularly dear to our hearts, and one of mine is adoption. I absolutely believe that each and every child deserves a home where he or she is loved and valued, and adoption is just one of the ways we, as a society, can make that happen.

My husband and I are adoptive parents. Our daughter came to us from Calcutta many years ago, a six-year-old fascinated by the extravagance of our American home and by the flickering picture on our television set, which carried the image of Mother Teresa, who she had last seen in an orphanage so far away.

But when I think about adoption, I also think about the other families I met on our own adoption journey. The friends who had their hospitalisation benefits cancelled when they tried to adopt a child with severe medical problems. (They went ahead with the adoption anyway.) The friends who took children with fatal illnesses, with mental handicaps, with severe emotional problems. None of them were saints or martyrs. They were simply people who believed they could make a positive difference in the life of a child. And they did.

I'm delighted to be a part of this collection of stories. I'm thankful to be the mother of four children who bring joy into my heart every day. And I'm particularly happy that my own experience with adoption brought me into contact with so many wonderful people who change the world one child at a time in beautiful and extraordinary ways.

Warmest wishes

Emilie Richards

NOBODY'S CHILD

Emilie Richards

Chapter One

"Nobody's here, damn it. Something tipped them off!"

Farrell Riley gave his partner, Cal, a curt nod as he tried not to breathe in more air than he needed to sustain life. The house smelled the way it looked, fetid and filthy. Months of garbage had been carelessly shoved to the borders of most of the rooms to make walkways, and even now, with a dozen of Hazleton's finest plowing through the house, a rat feasted contentedly not more than ten feet from his shoe.

"They must have gotten out just seconds before we surrounded the house," Cal said. He sounded the way Farrell felt. Disgusted, tired. Pissed. The house on Keller had been watched for days, the raid carefully planned. The small city of Hazleton, Ohio, had its share of drug problems, but not enough that losing to dealers was a ho-hum experience. Nearby, the slamming of doors and angry shouts testified to the frustrations of his brothers in blue.

"It doesn't look like they need us anymore." Farrell gave a halfhearted kick at the rat, which had moved closer, like a friendly puppy expecting a treat. Farrell and Cal had been called in as backup, but clearly, the unit in charge could handle the remains of the unsuccessful raid on their own.

"I'll get the word." Cal holstered his gun and left Farrell and the rat alone in what passed for a bedroom.

While he waited, Farrell did another visual survey, although by now he knew exactly what he would see. A bare mattress spilled its guts in a corner, and a frayed sleeping bag lay crumpled at its foot. A chest of drawers, with only two of its three drawers intact, was covered with bottles and vials. The kitchen was a makeshift drug lab, but this room had been used for storage as well as sleeping. Boxes of chemicals were stacked in the corner opposite the mattress, and Cal's cursory search of the closet had revealed more of the same.

Farrell shoved a hand through his unruly dark hair and wondered, as he always did, about the choices people made. Some undetermined number of people had made a conscious decision to live, eat and sleep in this hellhole. They had chosen to make and sell illegal, mind-and-soul-destroying drugs. And what had they gotten in return for this pathetic example of the Puritan work ethic? Filth and rats and, at the moment, cops crawling all over their humble home.

Farrell was an orderly man. Everything he owned had its own special place and could be found in a matter of seconds. Clutter made him uneasy, and this house would have made him crazy if he'd been forced to stay overnight. Now, with no way to bring order out of chaos, he did the only thing he could think of. He closed the closet door with an angry shove and turned to go in search of Cal.

"No!"

For a moment Farrell stood very still and wondered if his imagination was running away with him. He thought he'd heard a child's cry. But no one else was in the room.

The bedroom was silent again, except for the noise of cops rummaging through the adjacent hallway. Farrell did another quick exam, but the closet was the only possible source of the sound. He turned the doorknob and pulled the door toward him until it was wide open; then he shone his flashlight inside.

And he saw what Cal, who had examined the closet first, had not.

"Oh, sweetheart..." Farrell squatted on the floor so that he could peer between two tall stacks of boxes. Two very blue eyes peered back at him, tear-filled eyes over a streaming nose and a mouth that trembled inconsolably.

The little girl—at least, he thought by the length of the hair the child was female—tried to wiggle farther away from him. But she was literally boxed in, with no place to go.

"I didn't know you were here. You must be scared to death," he said as softly as his baritone could manage.

She didn't even blink. She stared at him as if she were waiting for him to raise his fist, as if that was what she expected.

Some emotion as dark as the closet shuddered through him. "It must be lonely in there." He sat back a little to show her he had no intention of hurting her. "I'd be scared, if I were you."

Her lip wobbled, and her nose ran. But she still didn't blink.

"And I think I'd be hungry," he continued. "Are you hungry?"

She didn't nod, but something changed behind her eyes, as if she were reassessing him.

Farrell wished that he had something to give her, some offering that would convince her he could be trusted. Cal had a package of cupcakes in their patrol car, but Farrell knew he couldn't leave her long enough to go for them. "If you come with me, I have a surprise." He smiled at her, something he didn't do often. His cheeks and lips felt rusty from disuse.

She didn't move. She watched him, her blue eyes taking in everything from the unflinching gray of his eyes to the tips of his highly polished shoes.

He didn't know which of them would have given in first if it hadn't been for the rat. With the bravado of a domestic pet, it came closer to investigate this new turn of events. The child's eyes flicked in its direction; then, with a small cry, she launched herself at Farrell.

He hardly had time to catch her. She was sobbing in his arms, babbling incoherently, with her arms wrapped in a death hold around his neck. He got to his feet and shooed the rat with his foot. Then, with the too-thin body plastered against his, he went to report what he'd found.

The child was filthy and almost naked. Despite the cool spring evening and the unheated house, she had been dressed in nothing more than thin cotton underpants when she had jumped into Farrell's arms. The house had yielded no clothes for her to wear, but Cal had produced a Police Athletic League sweatshirt from the squad car trunk, and Farrell had slipped that over her head to keep her warm. The sweatshirt fell well past her feet.

Right now she was sitting on his lap, a position she absolutely refused to relinquish, and nibbling on a cupcake. He had expected her to wolf it down, but her response was sadder. She nibbled, as if she had to make this unexpected treat last for hours. She nibbled as if she was uncertain another meal would ever turn up.

Farrell leaned against the back seat with his legs over the side while he and Cal waited for Child Welfare to come and claim her. Red-haired Cal, who at twenty-four was admirably broad shouldered but fast gaining a pot belly, rested his back against the car. "How old do you think she is?"

Farrell shrugged. "I don't know anything about kids."

"I'm guessing about two. I have nieces and nephews."

Cal's wife was expecting their first child, so Farrell knew his partner took an interest in all things family. "I bet none of them look like this one, do they?"

"Sometimes…" Cal cleared his throat. "Sometimes I wish we could make the laws, not enforce 'em."

"That's why we vote." But Farrell's voice conveyed his own anger at a system that didn't always protect children.

"Yeah. Well, I didn't vote for any law that lets parents hurt their own kids."

Farrell shot him a warning glance. The child was young, but there was no telling how much she understood. "She'll be taken care of tonight. That's something."

"Yeah. Something."

A beefy officer who was still wearing a protective vest came over to join them. Sergeant Archie Weatherstone had been on the Hazleton police force for twenty years, and he had seen everything, including plenty of abortive drug raids. But now even Archie shook his head at the sight of the little girl. "Got some bad news."

"You ever got any other kind?" Cal said.

Archie's voice had a permanent rasp from too

many cigarettes. "Child Welfare's emergency team is otherwise occupied. They can't come for another hour, at least."

"So what do we do? Take her to the station?" Farrell looked down at the child in his lap. She was still trembling, and he couldn't imagine putting the little girl through more hours of terror. "I don't like this."

"Don't worry. They gave me an address. They have emergency foster homes set up for situations like this one. You can take her to this one yourself. That's where she'll spend the night, anyway. Then, as soon as the team's free, they'll go there and do the intake exam."

"A home?"

"Yeah. The woman in charge is expecting you."

"A home with a bed? Food?"

"No bars on the windows. No maniac juvenile offenders. A home."

Farrell nodded, and the knot in his stomach unclenched a little. "Yeah. Okay."

"Think you can pry her loose long enough to hook her into a seat belt?"

Farrell made a stab at trying to extricate the little girl from his lap. She went rigid as a barn beam, and her lip began to tremble again.

"It's the law," Archie reminded him.

"How far's this house?"

"Galeon." The section of Hazleton Archie named

was fifteen minutes away from Keller Avenue, a residential area on the way up, but still best known for its old houses in need of renovation.

Farrell wrapped his arms around the little girl. "Galeon, huh? We can take the back roads."

"I won't arrest you. Do what you want." Archie gave him the address and walked away.

"I'll drive slow and careful," Cal said. "You know, you look pretty good with a kid on your lap."

Farrell covered the little girl's feet with the hem of the sweatshirt. "Take a picture. It's the last time you'll see it."

"Nah, Sheila and I are making you a godfather. Remember?"

Farrell slid off the seat, still gently holding the child, who was spilling cupcake crumbs on his perfectly pressed pants. "Let's go."

Gemma Hancock checked all her preparations for the third time. A child. She was getting a child. She couldn't really smile. Any child who came to her in the middle of the night was a child who had undergone trauma. She grieved for all neglected children. In a perfect world a foster home would never be needed. But although her fondest wish was that her own services would someday become obsolete, she was glad that tonight she had a home and love and good sense to offer a child in crisis.

A child. A little girl.

The telephone rang and she almost yanked it off the kitchen wall. "Hello?"

She listened as Marge Tremaine, the caseworker who had first called to ask if she could take the abandoned child, explained that things weren't going well with the emergency team. Marge sounded rattled, an unusual condition for a woman with multiple years in a job that most people left after a short stint.

Gemma saw headlights as a car pulled in to her driveway. "I'll evaluate the situation. If I need to have someone come and take a look at her tonight, I'll let you know."

Marge was grateful and perfunctory, in a hurry to get back to her crisis. She promised that if all was well, she would see the child first thing in the morning. Gemma hung up just as the doorbell rang.

She straightened her sweater as she headed for the front of the house, and wished she'd had time to brush her hair.

The police officer standing on the other side of the door was tall and lean. She had a brief impression of hair the color of bittersweet chocolate and a face as stern as the Old Testament Jehovah.

"Gemma Hancock?"

She smiled, but she had already lowered her gaze to the tiny bundle in his arms. "Right." The little girl had been sleeping, but now, as if she felt a stranger staring at her, her eyelids parted.

Gemma's heart thudded against her breastbone.

"Hi, there," she said softly. "You look comfortable."

The little girl began to cry silently, gigantic tears that slid down dirt-streaked cheeks. Gemma's smile didn't waver, although her heart beat double time in sympathy. "Well, of course you're feeling sad."

"She hasn't said a word," the police officer said. "Not since I found her. No, that's not quite true," he added, as if telling the story exactly the way it had happened was important to him. "She said something, but I couldn't understand her."

Gemma nodded. She looked back up at the man with the child in his arms. He was taller than she was by six inches, at least, and his sober expression reminded her of old "Dragnet" reruns. But this man was the looker that Jack Webb had never been. He was, in fact, as ruggedly masculine and appealing as any man she had ever seen.

"She seems to like where she is," Gemma said. "But you're going to have to turn her over to me eventually."

"Is anyone else here? In case you have a problem?"

She knew exactly what he was asking. At first glance she didn't necessarily inspire confidence. She was small-boned and deceptively fragile in appearance. She had wide pale green eyes that always made her seem a little lost, and fine shoulder-length blond hair that looked as if it should be tied up in ribbons.

"I'll be fine," she assured him. "I'm trained for this."

He hesitated for a moment, then held out his arms. The little girl began to shriek. Gemma had taken in his skeptical expression as he'd tentatively offered the child. Now he snatched her back as if Gemma was planning to roast her for supper.

"No!" The little girl clung to him, refusing to let Gemma take her.

"Well, she knows one word," Gemma said.

"She doesn't like you."

Gemma couldn't be angry at him. He probably had children of his own. He was probably an exceptional father. "Officer…?"

"Riley." He balanced the little girl against his chest.

"Does she have a name, too?"

"Not one we know."

"It's not that she doesn't like me," she explained patiently. "It's just that she's comfortable with you. She feels safe."

"I don't know anything about kids."

She suspected he knew a lot more than he thought he did. "Were you the one to find her?"

He gave a gruff nod.

"I'll bet she sees you as her rescuer." She brushed the little girl's lank brown hair off her filthy forehead. The child flinched.

"What are you going to do?"

"The question is, what are *you* going to do? If you have to leave immediately, I'll have to take her and that will be that. But if you have a few minutes to help calm her, that would be better." *For both of you,* she added silently.

"I guess I can stay."

She tried not to smile. She knew that, deep down inside, he had absolutely no intention of relinquishing the child until he was sure she was okay.

A second cop came up the walkway to stand behind Officer Riley. He grinned at Gemma appreciatively. "You a foster kid or a foster mom?"

Since there had been nothing provocative about the comment, she gave a friendly nod. "We're going to take the transfer slowly. Could you use a cup of coffee?"

The man clapped his hand on Officer Riley's shoulder. "I've got to run back to the station before we sign off."

Officer Riley looked pained. "Go ahead. Just stop and pick me up when you're finished."

The other man nodded and took off again.

"Come on in." Gemma stepped aside. "I have a rocker in the living room. Let's try that."

"Is anyone else home? Will we wake up your husband? Kids?"

"No, I live alone." She didn't add that this child was her first placement. He was edgy enough about leaving the little girl.

She watched him do a covert examination of the house as he followed her into the living room. She had moved into the house one year after her husband's death. She still had more work to do on the old shingled colonial, but she was proud of what she had accomplished so far.

The week she moved in, she had stripped 1970s orange shag carpeting, and sanded and varnished the oak floors underneath. She had removed four layers of wallpaper and painted all the walls with indestructible paint made especially for children's rooms. She had decorated with attic finds and garage sale specials, but the overall effect was warm and homey. Better yet, there was nothing here that was more important than a child who might accidentally damage it. It was a house designed for children, and even though she had lived in it for only a year, it was home.

She settled Officer Riley and his bundle in an old wicker rocker that had once graced someone's front porch. She had painted it white and sewed a colorful red-and-blue-checked cushion for the seat. Now it sat beside her front window, where she could watch the world go by as she rocked a progression of children to sleep.

She was more than ready for that experience.

Officer Riley looked incongruous against the lacy wicker. She wished that she hadn't randomly tied red and blue ribbons through the canes. It was too hard not to smile at the sight of a large-boned, six-foot cop in a sober black uniform framed by two dozen perky little bows.

"I made her a snack," Gemma said.

"I already fed her a cupcake."

"Oh. And it stayed down?"

He looked uncomfortable, as if that was something he hadn't considered. "Yeah."

"That's a bonus." She left and returned with a plate of crackers, cheese and grapes, and a glass of milk. She set them on a table beside him, then went to the sofa for an afghan, which she carefully tucked over the child on his lap.

She realized Officer Riley's face was just inches from hers. He seemed to realize it, too, although he didn't shift in the seat. "She wasn't dressed when we found her. My partner loaned her this sweatshirt."

He had eyes of such a dark gray they were nearly black, hooded, guarded eyes that told her as much about the man as a six-page biography. She straightened. "I'll be sure he gets it back. I have clothes of all sizes here. I'll find her something comfortable to wear after she's had a bath."

"You're going to give her a bath tonight?"

"We'll see how she does. I'm going to take my cues from her."

He seemed to relax a little. "Good." He directed his attention to the child on his lap. "Are you still hungry? The nice lady's made you something to eat.''

"She can call me Gemma." Gemma reached for the plate and squatted beside the chair, holding out a cracker to the child. The little girl considered it, then lifted it from Gemma's fingers.

"She eats slowly, like she's not sure where her next meal is coming from."

"She'll have plenty to eat here. But probably nothing as good as a cupcake from her personal hero, Officer Riley."

She got to her feet and started to move away, and she was surprised when he touched her hand. She did not believe in electricity between men and women. She had never experienced it, despite having a satisfactory sexual relationship with her husband in the years before their marriage began to disintegrate. But she felt the oddest sensation when Officer Riley touched her. A stirring inside her. A restless fluttering of her senses.

After Jimmy's death, she had sworn off men, and she hadn't yet regretted that decision. But now she wondered how easy it was going to be to keep that vow.

"My name's Farrell," he said.

"Farrell Riley. Born to be a cop?"

His lips twisted into a wry, humorless smile. "Not even close."

She wanted to probe, but not as much as she

wanted to move away. She already knew that this man, with his steel gray eyes and his roughly chiseled features, was complicated right down to his soul. She didn't need a man, and she didn't need complications.

She just needed the child sitting on his lap, and the other children who would pass through her life.

"I'll leave you two alone." She took a step backward, then another, before she squared her shoulders. "I'll be in to check on you in a few minutes."

"We'll be here."

She went back into her kitchen, with its sunny yellow walls and red tile floor. But when she got there, she leaned against a counter and wondered why Farrell Riley had made her feel things she had given up believing in a long time ago.

Chapter Two

Farrell always had his morning coffee at the kitchen table where he read the headlines, the sports section and the comics. He wasn't a slave to routine, but the simple morning ritual gave him pleasure. He liked good Colombian coffee, the way sunlight freckled the walls and floor of the old duplex, the sounds of his neighbor's children playing in the backyard. He liked waking up slowly in his own apartment, with no one to answer to except the landlord.

This morning the paper still lay on the front porch, and the coffee remained in the can. He shrugged into a sweater and slid his feet into loafers, grabbing his car keys off the hallway table on his way out the front door.

Farrell had been sure it wasn't a good idea to give Gemma Hancock his telephone number. He still didn't know what had possessed him. Last night he had rocked the little girl to sleep and tucked her into a warm, clean bed in a cheery pink room, and he should have been done with her then. The child was in good hands. He couldn't have asked for a kinder, more conscientious foster mother. Almost anyone else would have pried her from his arms and scrubbed her within an inch of her life. Gemma had been more concerned about the child's spirit.

Gemma Hancock.

He started the engine and backed carefully out of his driveway. Gemma Hancock had been a real surprise. At first glance she had reminded him of dandelion fluff: one good puff and she would scatter in a thousand different directions. She was delicate in appearance, one of those women some men wanted to spend their lives protecting from reality.

She wasn't fragile or scatterbrained, of course. She was filled with good sense and goodwill, and she seemed to know acres about kids. What she didn't know was that Farrell Riley didn't get involved. He had left his phone number on a whim, that was all. She wouldn't have called him if she had figured that out. But she *had* called him.

The phone had been ringing as he stepped out of the shower. He had dripped water on his bedroom carpet as he answered it.

"Officer Riley?"

He had recognized her immediately. She had a soft, sweet voice that would soothe any child in crisis. "Mrs. Hancock?"

"Gemma. Right. Our little one is inconsolable this morning. I don't know if it will help or hurt things more, but if you'd like to stop by sometime in the next couple of hours, I think she'd be awfully happy to see you."

Our little one.

He almost hung up the phone at that point. Did he really want to know what happened to this child? Did he really want to go back to the house with the cheerful cream-colored walls, the polished woodwork, the kitchen with its red tile floor, its slate blue cabinets, its cheerful yellow wallpaper?

He hesitated long enough to make her contrite. "Oh, I'm sorry," she said. "You probably have a family of your own that keeps you busy. It's just that—"

He wasn't sure why he answered that. "No, I don't. I'll come over in a little while. Just as soon as I'm dressed."

There was a short pause, then an audible intake of breath. "You're sure you don't mind?"

"I'm sure."

"Then we'll look forward to seeing you."

Now, as he pulled up in front of the old shingled colonial with its wide porch and Easter bunny wreath on the front door, he wondered again exactly what he was getting into. He didn't know anything about kids or women so maternal they were willing to nurture somebody else's children.

But even as he told himself this made no sense, he knew why he had come.

He had come because he couldn't make himself stay away.

At the front door, he heard the little girl's wailing

before he could raise his hand to knock. A moment later Gemma answered with the screaming toddler resting on her hip.

Gemma had a beautiful smile, a Madonna, earth mother, the-world-works-exactly-the-way-it's-supposed-to smile, and she used it now. "She doesn't like baths."

"I suspect she's had very few."

At the sound of his voice, the little girl raised her head from Gemma's shoulder and stared at him.

Something clenched inside him as her tears forgot to fall. "Hi, sweetheart."

She pitched her little body toward him, and he took her from Gemma's arms. "Do you mind?"

"Except for ten minutes in the bathtub, she's spent the last four hours welded to that very hip. No, I don't mind."

"Has she been screaming since she woke up?"

"No. We made friends over breakfast. But in her eyes, the bath was not a plus."

He examined the child. Her newly washed brown hair was clipped back from her face with pink poodle barrettes, exposing a skin so pale, she looked as if she'd never seen the sun. And even though her face was clean, there were still dark circles beneath her eyes, circles that didn't belong on a child's face. "You washed away a month of dirt."

A shadow crossed Gemma's face. "I almost wish I hadn't."

He cocked his head. He didn't understand.

"She's got some nasty bruises," Gemma said.

The fury that had simmered since he had found the child in the closet threatened to erupt. He swallowed. The child rested her head against his chest and sniffed and shuddered.

"I have an appointment with the pediatrician this afternoon for a good checkup." Gemma stepped aside so he could enter the house.

He followed her to the kitchen. The house smelled like cinnamon and yeast, and as they neared the kitchen, the smell of coffee joined the others with mouthwatering intensity. His stomach rumbled.

Gemma stopped at a restaurant-sized stove and motioned him to a seat at the table. "We were up early, so I baked fresh cinnamon rolls. Our little friend helped me. She can shake a cinnamon can like nobody's business."

Our little friend. Farrell settled the child against his chest. She had burrowed her fingers into the yarn of his sweater with fierce possessiveness. Obviously the sweater would go before she did.

"How do you like your coffee?" Gemma asked.

Farrell looked up. Gemma, in a leaf green dress the color of her eyes, was standing in front of him with a plate heaped with fragrant rolls.

For a moment he could think only about how he liked his women. Not warm, soft-spoken and infinitely feminine, like this one. He liked his women remote, casual and ready to move on at a moment's notice. He didn't encourage relationships. He dated, and sometimes he dated long enough to have sex. But he carefully chose women who didn't want more, women who for their own reasons wanted no ties and no heartaches.

This woman was one big heartache waiting to happen.

"Maybe you'd rather have juice. Or tea?" She wrinkled her forehead. "No, you're definitely not the tea type. A cop who drinks tea?" She laughed.

"I like my coffee black."

"Easy to please."

He watched her search for the perfect mug, then pour coffee right up to the rim. He did not want to notice the way she moved, as if she was slow dancing to music that no one else could hear.

She didn't hover. She set the mug far enough from him that the child couldn't grab it; then she settled herself across the round oak table, which was set with place mats shaped like brightly colored pieces of fruit. His coffee sat on an apple, hers on an orange. A half-eaten bowl of cereal with a child-sized spoon beside it rested on a banana.

"I hope we discover her name." Gemma sipped her coffee with unconscious grace.

"Has she said anything today?"

Gemma looked at the little girl. "No, but she understands what we say to her, don't you, honey? I've told her that's what I'll call her, because her hair is the color of honey.''

''Does she know what honey is?''

''She does now. I showed her, and she dipped her fingers in the jar. That kept her busy for a little while.''

''How did she sleep last night?''

''Sporadically.''

''I'll make it my business to follow up on this.''

Gemma didn't ask him to elaborate. Both of them knew he was talking about finding the little girl's parents. ''Well...'' She smiled. ''So, Officer Riley...'' She appeared to make a decision. ''Farrell. Does this happen to you often?''

''Does what happen to me?''

''Do you find yourself in strange kitchens providing support and counseling?''

''Is that what I'm doing?''

''Well, I appreciate your coming, and so does she.''

''How do you handle everything when you have a whole bunch of needy kids at the same time?''

''I don't know. This is my first placement.''

For a moment he didn't comprehend. ''Your first...?''

Her eyes twinkled. ''Yes. I just finished the training last week. That shows you how desperate the county is for good homes.''

''Then you've never—''

She stopped him with a wide grin. "Don't worry. I've been training all my life to do this. I have a degree in child development, and I taught preschool for three years before—" She halted abruptly.

He never probed. He did now. "Before?"

The grin disappeared. "Before my husband died."

"Oh."

She sat back, taking her coffee with her. "I taught middle-class children who went straight from their mornings with me to music classes and gymnastics. They saw their pediatricians and dentists every six months, wore designer clothing with matching hair ribbons or baseball caps, and read *me* stories. I wanted to do something more personal and challenging. So here I am."

"If you wanted challenging, you picked the right job."

"I know."

The cinnamon roll melted in his mouth. He tore off a hunk and held it out in front of him. The little girl took it and repeated the behavior he remembered from last night. She nibbled.

"She'll gain weight quickly," Gemma said. "She has a good appetite."

Farrell wondered what he was doing sitting in the coziest kitchen he'd ever seen with a girlchild in pink-footed pajamas on his lap and a woman with a smile as warm as summer sitting across the table. A woman who defined the word.

"So do you," Gemma added.

For a moment he didn't know what she meant; then he looked down and realized both cinnamon rolls were gone and his coffee cup was empty. He didn't know when he'd had anything as good as the rolls. He couldn't help himself. He grinned.

Gemma smiled, too, then took his dishes to the sink and refilled his coffee cup. "I really shouldn't have asked you to come. You have the kind of job you probably want to forget about in your off hours. I wouldn't have called except that, well…"

"It's okay. You were just thinking of her."

She brushed his arm as she leaned over to set the cup in front of him again. He inhaled the scent of steaming coffee and something new, something sweet and feminine that emanated from her and reminded him of lilacs. He remembered that he'd felt this same surge of unadulterated longing when he had touched her hand last night, and now, like then, he stiffened in denial. "I have to get out of here in a few minutes."

"I'm sure you do."

He found himself picking up the coffee cup, though he'd already had his fill. "Will she stay here long, do you know? Or will they move her as soon as a place in another home opens up?"

"No, she'll stay right here."

So the child would stay with Gemma, who had probably taken better care of her in the past twelve hours than anyone else ever had in her whole sad lifetime. The child would stay until the parents were found, and possibly, a reunion was attempted. Or the child would stay until the parents' rights were terminated—a process that might take years—and she was placed for adoption.

Farrell knew that even though this solution was faulty, the child was more than lucky to have landed with Gemma for the time being. "She'll be happy here as soon as she settles in."

"Would you like to see the backyard?" Gemma looked startled at her own question, as if it had just popped out. "It's probably silly, but I'm proud of what I've done with it."

"You're a gardener?"

"Not much of one. No, bring your coffee and come see. Let's find out if our friend will come with us if you're not carrying her."

Our friend. He set the child down, and although she whimpered, she was not nearly as upset as he'd feared she might be. He stood and stretched, then extended his hand. She slipped her tiny one inside and padded beside him toward the door on the other side of the kitchen.

Gemma led them out to a small deck. "I bought the house because of the yard. It's a double lot. Apparently the previous owners never went outside, so it had grown into a jungle. I had to hire professionals to prune everything down to size. But see what you think.''

Farrell realized he was in a child's paradise. He stood beside Gemma with the little girl clinging to his hand and looked over the storybook creation. A weeping willow tree sat in front of a tall wooden fence, with a tire swing hanging from one massive branch. Beside it was climbing equipment consisting of timbers, posts and thick rope net stretching over what appeared to be the hull of a ship.

Closer to the deck was a wooden playhouse, complete with tiny window boxes under windows just tall enough for a child to see out. Curving even closer— right up to the steps, in fact—was a free-form sandbox large enough for four or five children to play in without endangering each other.

A picnic table sat off to one side, with a barbecue not more than a few yards away. Forsythia in full bloom bordered one fence, and an apple tree stood in front of the other. Brick pathways ran from one piece of play equipment to another, and flower beds just waiting for summer annuals circled the playhouse and deck.

''One of my brothers-in-law built the playhouse and the deck.'' Her voice dropped a notch. ''The other one put together the climbing ship. They're good guys right down to the bone.''

He suspected they adored this ethereal sister-in-law with her serene expression and her soft blond hair curving to her shoulders. He doubted she'd even had to ask for their help.

She gazed up at him. "I just wanted you to see it. So you'd know…"

"So I'd know she's in good hands?"

"Exactly."

"I didn't doubt it."

"You did last night."

His voice sounded like steel against steel. "Look, it doesn't matter what I think." He tried to soften his words. "I'm just the cop who brought her here. But for the record, I'm glad this is where she landed."

She hesitated just long enough that he knew she was scrambling for an answer. He hadn't meant to sound so harsh. But he was suffocating on the intimacy of standing beside this woman with a small child clinging trustingly to his hand. Both of them thought he was more than he was. Both of them thought he was somebody who gave a damn.

And right now, he was afraid they might be right.

"Well, I know you have to be getting back." Gemma rested her hand on the little girl's arm. Farrell looked down and saw the child weave her fingers through Gemma's.

The child was going to be fine. She didn't need him anymore.

The relief he should have felt didn't materialize. "I'd better get going."

"Thanks again for coming. It did the trick."

He squatted to say goodbye to the child. "Hey, sweetheart, I have to go now. Be a good girl, okay?"

She wrinkled her forehead, as if she were going to cry. Before the tears could fail he stood and faced Gemma. "I hope the doctor's visit goes well."

"Would you like to know what he says?"

He was out of this now. Done. If he had a place in this case, it was to find the scum who had abandoned this child. But what could he say? That no, he wasn't interested in how the little girl was? He was many things, but never a liar.

"I'd like to know." He met Gemma's eyes and saw questions she was too polite to ask. "Will you call me?"

"I'd be happy to. But not this early in the morning, I promise."

"Call me any time you want." He turned away before he could take back the words. But, of course, he'd already said them and wouldn't retract them, anyway. Worse, much worse, he'd meant every one of them.

Chapter Three

The report room of the Hazleton police station was a wasteland of battered metal desks and ringing telephones. Farrell sat at one of them, tackling what seemed like a bottomless stack of paperwork. Usually he tolerated filling out forms in triplicate better than most of his colleagues did. He understood the need for record keeping, but today it seemed like a huge waste of time. He didn't want to write up his part in finding the little girl in the closet. He wanted to search for her parents.

"You got a minute?"

Farrell looked up to find Archie standing in front of him with an open folder. "You have something?"

"I sent Brady and Scanlon out to question the neighbors last night after you left. Most of them didn't want to talk."

Farrell wasn't surprised. People protected themselves and their families in the only ways they could. "Did you discover anything about the little girl?"

"An old lady who lives next door claims that the kid's name is Mary. She said the kid's mother used to come and go at the drug house a lot, and one day a couple of months ago she caught the old lady out on her back porch and demanded that she baby-sit.

The poor woman was afraid to say no, and the kid ended up staying at her house for most of a week until the mother finally came back to get her.''

"And she didn't tell anybody?'' Farrell shook his head.

"She was scared. I don't think she would have talked to us last night, either, but she's moving to Detroit in a few days to live with her son. I guess she thinks she'll be safe.''

"What does she remember about the mother?''

"She never got a name, but she gave a pretty good description.'' Archie looked down at his folder. "Long dark hair. Short. Overweight. She said the woman was missing a tooth or two in front. The description matches one a neighbor across the street gave us. They both guessed her age at somewhere around twenty-two or twenty-three. Most of the time she was seen with a man, and they were pretty sure he lived at the house.''

"Anything else?''

Archie closed the folder. "Nothing. They could be in California by now. Who knows? We'll run what we came up with last night, but we're probably never going to catch up with them. They'll find another house somewhere, set up business…'' He shrugged.

Farrell knew the answer to the next question already. "So what about little Mary?''

"She'll be better off with the state than with a mother who abandons her whenever it's convenient.

After a while—a long while, probably—some judge will admit she's been deserted and terminate the parents' rights. Then, if she's not too badly damaged by what she's been through, they'll place her somewhere more or less permanent. But at least nobody will drop her off with strangers for days at a time.''

"Some consolation."

Archie dropped the folder on Farrell's desk. "She's a cute little thing. It's too bad we probably won't find the mother. She might agree to give up the kid. It's happened before."

Farrell didn't tell Archie that if he had his way, it was going to happen again. He did his job, and he did it well. He didn't take on personal missions, and he didn't become obsessed with crimes he couldn't solve.

Not usually.

Archie leaned over so his face was closer to Farrell's. "Heard the foster mother at that home you took her to was something else."

Farrell looked up and saw the speculative expression in Archie's eyes. He knew where Archie had gotten his information. "Cal never knows when to shut up."

"He tells me you stayed with the kid until she fell asleep."

"She was sobbing her heart out."

"This foster mom, she live by herself?"

Farrell heard the interest in his superior's voice. "Does it make a difference?"

"Could. It sure could. She might need some home security. A regular patrol, you know?" Archie winked.

Farrell arched a brow, but Archie just laughed. He was still laughing as he strolled away.

"She'll need vitamins. Lots of good things to eat. I want to do some blood work before you leave." Anna Choi, a pediatrician who worked with Child Welfare's clients, looked down at her chart. "I think she's not quite two. I want you to make an appointment for developmental testing. We have a psychologist in this building who understands cases like this and knows what we're looking for."

Gemma balanced her new charge on her knee. "Can she settle in a little first? I don't think anything we'd learn right now would be completely accurate."

"Oh, he'll take everything she's been through into consideration. But we need some results now, so we'll have a baseline for comparison."

Anna stepped into the hallway and signaled for her nurse. "Will you take our patient down the hall and get her a toy from the basket?"

The nurse, an older woman with a friendly smile and superior child management skills, coaxed the little girl off Gemma's lap and out of the room. Dr. Choi turned to Gemma. "I didn't want to discuss this in front of her. We don't know how much she understands.''

Gemma nodded.

"She's got some serious bruises."

"I know."

"They're consistent with what I've seen in other cases like this one. Somebody got angry and took it out on her. That's why I got some pictures. We may have to use them if the mother returns and wants her daughter back.'' Dr. Choi sighed and blew a strand of hair off her forehead. ''Believe me, I've seen much worse. She's almost healed, and I didn't see anything to indicate broken bones, either recent or prior. But I'm going to order some X rays, just to be sure we know what we're dealing with."

"Whatever you need."

"This might be hard for you to believe, but this kid might be one of the lucky ones."

Gemma made a sound of disbelief.

"I know," the doctor said. "She's been slapped around, not so badly that she'll have any lasting physical effects, but badly enough that we can use the evidence in court. She's survived and come this far. If we can intervene and keep her from going back to a bad situation, then she has a chance to grow up more or less normally. Not all kids get that chance."

"I want to protect her." Gemma's voice cracked with emotion.

"Don't get too involved," Dr. Choi warned. "All you can do right now is take this one step at a time."

"Just as long as the next step is making sure she doesn't go back into an abusive situation."

Dr. Choi folded her arms and leaned against her examining table. "You know we can't always prevent that, don't you?"

Gemma did know, and she'd thought she was prepared. But even after one night with the little girl, she felt fiercely maternal.

"Take good care of her while you have her," Dr. Choi said. "Right now, that's the one thing you can do for sure."

By the time Gemma made arrangements for X rays and shepherded the little girl through the process, both of them were starving. Gemma knew a deli that cut peanut butter and jelly sandwiches into stars and moons for their pint-size customers, and it was only after they were sitting at a window table looking over a busy street that she realized the police station was directly across the street.

Two stars, a moon and one turkey sandwich later, Gemma found herself choosing a giant slice of cheesecake to go. "You don't have a bow, do you?" she asked the proprietor.

He didn't, but he cut loops of string and fastened a carnation from one of the tables in the center of the plastic foam container. With the cheesecake tucked under one arm and the child tucked under the other, Gemma crossed the street.

Inside the station, she approached the woman in uniform sitting behind the reception window. "Hi, is Officer Riley in?"

Gemma hadn't had time to think about what she was doing. But by the time the question left her lips, regret was already taking the place of impulsive goodwill. What had convinced her to bring Farrell the cheesecake? For that matter, what had possessed her to choose a restaurant directly across from the police station? She had wanted to say thank-you, but there were less personal ways to do it. She set the bag on the counter between them. "I can just leave this with you if he isn't."

The woman didn't lift her head. "I'll check. Take a seat."

Chastened, Gemma nearly told the woman to forget it, but her charge began to rub her eyes, as if either a nap or tears were imminent. Gemma took the bag and moved to the side of the room, murmuring soothingly, "Hey, it's okay. We'll be going home in a few minutes."

Home. It wasn't the little girl's home, of course. She might stay with Gemma for years. She might stay only days. At any time, the woman who had abandoned her might decide she wanted her daughter after all, and the courts might agree to give her a second chance. Then Gemma would be required to

hand her over. She swayed to console the child, closing her eyes for a moment. When she opened them
again, Farrell was standing in front of her.

"Oh…" She forgot everything she'd planned to
say. She had only come to thank him again and to
repeat what the pediatrician had said. But for moments she just stared up at him and wondered what
it was about this man that made her feel safe and
under seige at the very same time.

She already knew he was a man who didn't waste
words. He didn't waste any now. "I have some
news."

She nodded, as if that was the entire reason she
had sought him out. "Do you?"

He bent his head to speak to the child. "Hi, sweetheart. I hear your name is Mary."

The little girl, who was no longer nameless, held
up her arms so that Farrell would take her.

"Mary?" Gemma rolled the word on her tongue
as she handed the child to him. "That's easy
enough." She felt an unwanted connection to the
woman who had given this child both life and a traditional name. "I don't suppose you have a last name
to go with it?"

Farrell smiled down at Mary, who wrapped her
arms around his neck. He didn't look at Gemma.
"I'm afraid not. That's all we know for now."

Gemma admired the strong sweep of his jaw. His
dark hair was cut short, but it was thick and wavy

enough to defy the closest supervision. She wondered if the man was the same way, if under the guarded exterior there was something inside him that couldn't quite be tamed.

She reached into the paper bag and pulled out the container. "We came to say thank you. We brought you something."

He turned his attention to her. She already knew that he hated emotion. He had probably been raised by a stern father who had taught him well. But now the expression in his gray eyes was not as remote as she had expected. It was, in fact, warm, maybe even probing. "You didn't have to do that."

"I know. And it's a silly present, really. I mean, you probably eat across the street all the time. It's their cheesecake. But it looked so good…" She realized she was babbling. He was smiling at her. A smile that made something inside her catch and hold. "If you don't take it, I'll eat it myself." She smiled back.

"It's a nice change from doughnuts."

She laughed, and his smile broadened in response. "We were in the neighborhood. I took…Mary to the doctor."

"What did he say?"

"*She* said Mary looks fine. She needs some extra weight and vitamins. Her throat's a little red, but Dr. Choi thought she's probably just coming down with a mild cold."

"That should be fun for you."

"Oh, we'll do fine."

"What will you do if you ever need help with her? Do you have…anyone who can lend a hand?"

She heard the hesitation over "anyone." With something akin to pleasure, she wondered if he was asking whether there was a man in her life. But before the pleasure could build, another possibility struck her. Perhaps he just wanted to know if she was going to continue to bother *him*. The thought horrified her.

She hastened to reassure him. "Oh, I have plenty of family nearby. In an emergency I can always call on them. We'll be fine. And I promise I won't bother you again. I still feel bad that I had to call you at home this morning."

"I don't."

For a moment his answer didn't register. Then she realized that he wasn't just being polite. He meant it. The pleasure began to build again. "You're very kind."

"Not words I hear often."

"I don't know why. Maybe nobody else looks under the surface." She realized how presumptuous that sounded. "Look, I didn't mean that. Everything I say to you seems to come out funny."

"Everything you say comes out wonderful." He looked down at Mary again, as if he had revealed

too much. "I have to get back to work. Shall I trade
you a little girl for that cheesecake?"

She held out the bag. "Mocha chocolate chip.
Please ignore the carnation. It's probably wilted by
now."

He took the bag and leaned over, sliding Mary into
her arms. They were tangled together for a moment,
shoulders against shoulders, arms looped, as they
made the transfer. Mary whimpered, but she settled
against Gemma as Farrell edged away from them.

For just the briefest moment Gemma had felt his
weight bearing down on her and his hip pressed
against hers. Her heart was speeding faster; she could
feel color suffusing her cheeks.

And that was when she knew what a dangerous
game she was playing. She had not come to say a
final thank-you. She had not even come to reassure
him about Mary's health. She had come to see him
once more, to watch the way his steel gray eyes softened to pewter when he looked at the little girl, and
the way they sometimes softened when he looked at
her. She had come to see his smile, that rare but
infinitely rewarding smile that was already becoming
an addiction. She was playing a dangerous game,
playing with fire, in fact, because despite the fact that
Farrell was fighting it, too, there was an attraction
igniting between them that neither of them would be
able to ignore if they were thrown together again.

"Well, we've definitely kept you long enough."

She used Farrell's trick; she gazed down at Mary to avoid looking in his eyes. "And Mary's fading fast, aren't you, sweetheart? It's naptime."

Farrell leaned over and ruffled the back of Mary's wispy hair. "Take care of her."

"Oh, I will."

"I'll let you know if I hear anything worth reporting."

She wondered if he would. Or would he just pass on his information to his sources at Child Welfare and count on them to get the news to her? She turned away. There was no point in speculation. She had asked more of this man in the past hours than she had asked of her husband in all the blighted years of their marriage. She couldn't ask for more.

"Thanks again." She looked over her shoulder and smiled a casual goodbye. "Hope you enjoy the cheesecake. It deserves a superior cup of coffee to wash it down."

"Believe me, nothing at this station compares with yours."

"My pot's always on." She wanted to yank her tongue out. "If you're ever in the neighborhood."

"I'll remember that."

She didn't trust herself to say another thing. She headed for the door, and, with Mary on her hip, she left the station without a backward glance.

Chapter Four

"Relax, Gemma. The doctor says Mary's ears are fine. Her temperature's just a little elevated. She's breathing, even if she doesn't sound too great. She has a cold." Gemma's oldest sister, Patty, settled back in the wicker rocker with Mary on her lap. Anyone who glanced at them would have taken them for mother and daughter. Patty's hair was the same light brown as the little girl's, her eyes the same vivid blue.

Gemma must not have looked convinced, because Patty added, "Honestly. You can stop worrying."

Gemma knew Patty was right. During Mary's exam, Dr. Choi had warned her that the little girl might be coming down with a cold. And now, three days later, the cold had been confirmed during a second appointment. Gemma knew better than to worry. She had wiped a thousand little noses in her days as a preschool teacher. But in those days she'd sent the children back home after school for their mothers to take care of.

"I'll take her if you're tired," Gemma offered.

Patty waved Gemma to the love seat against the nearest wall. "I'm not tired. Sit and take a break. I'm used to this."

Patty had married young, and nine months later she had presented her graduate-student husband, John, with twin boys. Two years later the second set had come along. All the boys were rambunctious, and Gemma doubted that Patty had ever spent more than five minutes with one of them in her lap before he squirmed away to see what mischief the others had gotten into.

"This poor baby hasn't had a good night's sleep since she arrived." Gemma settled herself on the love seat, where she could observe her sister and Mary. Patty pretended to be thoroughly sick of her own children, but she never missed the chance to mother someone else's.

Patty smoothed Mary's hair back from her forehead. "I'm guessing this will be the worst day, then she'll start to feel better. How are you doing? Want me to send John over tonight to help you walk the floor? I'd come, but the last time I spent the night away from home, the dishwasher sprang a leak, Mark got the chicken pox, and Dillon fell and knocked out a tooth. John was beside himself."

"Baloney. John can handle the boys with a hand tied behind his back. You just hate being away from them for too long, and you want a good night's sleep."

Patty rolled her eyes, but she didn't deny it. Patty adored John, too. "You'll be all right? You look tired. Seriously, one of us can help if you need it."

For some reason Gemma pictured another man, not John, walking the floor with Mary that night. John was blond, and this man was not. John talked about everything. This man chose his words carefully and seemed most comfortable with silence.

Gemma shook her head. "No, I'll be fine. I had a lifetime of uninterrupted nights to rest up."

"You were always there when I needed you. Remember when the babies were cutting teeth?"

Gemma remembered, and she remembered how part of her had envied Patty during those months, both for her beautiful babies and the warmhearted husband who loved her.

"You handled everything without a fuss," she said. "And so did John."

"A little birdie tells me that the cop who brought Mary here is a total hunk and as single as John is married."

For a moment Gemma wasn't sure she'd heard her sister right. Since childhood, Patty had been good at suddenly changing the subject to throw her off guard. "A little birdie?"

Patty turned up one hand in defeat. "Okay. One of my neighbors is married to your cop's partner."

"Patty, he's not *my* cop."

"Sheila says that this guy…Farrell Riley, right? That he keeps to himself but everybody thinks he's terrific anyway. He's been cited for bravery twice. Her husband worships the ground he walks on. She says word is Farrell could be promoted, and Cal is afraid they won't be partners anymore.''

Gemma realized her heart was beating faster. She remembered this feeling of anticipation and excitement from high school. She thought she'd outgrown it, along with training bras and rock star posters.

She tried to ignore it. "He was very nice. He took a real interest in Mary.''

"I'm sure he'd like to know how she's doing. Maybe you ought to call him.''

"Apparently I don't need to. I'm sure you'll tell this Sheila everything, and she'll tell her husband, and he'll tell Farrell.''

"So you call him Farrell?''

"Patty…'' Gemma's tone was warning enough. "I've sworn off men. You know I have. I have the life I want and need. I'm happy.''

"Not every man is like Jimmy.''

"Maybe not. But what makes you think I could tell the difference? I was fooled once. Why not twice? Or as many times as I take a risk?''

"Jimmy was a salesman. He could sell sand in the Sahara, and probably did. All of us were fooled by his charm, but we learned. You most of all.''

Gemma had learned things that Patty didn't even suspect, but she wasn't about to go into them now. "Look, I'm happy. I took control of my life. I'm doing exactly what I want. I don't need complications.''

"What about sex? Do you need sex?"

Gemma was used to Patty's direct approach, but she could still feel her cheeks heating, not because of what Patty had said, but because of a sudden new image of Farrell.

And he wasn't walking the floor with a sick child.

"I thought so," Patty said triumphantly.

"I'm not going to get married just to have regular sex! And I'm not going to sleep around. It's just not my style."

"Then why don't you get married for love? You still believe in it, even if the prospect's a little tarnished right now. But pull it out and polish it up. You're too young to be a monk."

"Women can't be monks."

"You know what I mean."

"I *know* what you mean, and this conversation is finished. Got it?"

"If the cop's not really your style, John has a client who's—"

"Patty!" John, an investment banker, had already tried to promote romances for Gemma with several of his clients. John's idea of a perfect match was a healthy portfolio and an aversion to prenuptial agreements.

"You're such a prude." Patty wrinkled her patrician nose. "Well, I hate to do it to you, kiddo, but I've got to get out of here and make some dinner for the swarm. Give us a call if you're too tired to cope alone tonight. Better yet, give your cop friend a call. I bet he'd love to spend the night over here.''

Gemma stood and gathered Mary into her arms so that Patty could rise. ''Thanks for coming, if not for the conversation. Give my love to John and the boys.''

''If I can shout above the din.'' Patty gave Gemma a hug. ''Think about what I said.''

''No.''

''Oh, you will, no matter what you say.''

Gemma's response was interrupted by the doorbell.

''Expecting someone? Someone…interesting?'' Patty brightened considerably.

''No!''

''I think I'll go out the front door, just to be sure it's not a serial killer on the porch.''

''Your car's parked on the side.''

Patty smirked. ''I feel a need for exercise.''

The doorbell rang again. With Patty and Mary in tow, Gemma had no choice but to answer it.

Farrell didn't know why he was standing on Gemma's front porch. He'd had a long day, and just before going off duty he'd nearly had his head blown off by a teenager with a handgun. The kid had seemed almost as surprised as Farrell when the gun went off, and afterward, on the way to the station, he'd sworn that it wasn't supposed to be loaded. But who could believe a sixteen-year-old with a record as long as his daddy's latest prison sentence? The gun had been in the kid's possession, and the kid had made certain that the two men he robbed outside an automatic teller machine knew that he had it.

Hadn't there been a time when teenagers collected baseball cards instead of .44s and assault rifles?

The door opened, and Gemma stood on the threshold with Mary in her arms. Beside her was a woman who could only be Gemma's sister. The woman's coloring was different, but the features were much the same.

"Farrell…"

"I'm sorry. Did I come at a bad time?"

"Of course not. Patty was just leaving." Gemma turned toward the other woman. "Weren't you?" she asked pointedly.

"If I have to." Patty extended her hand. "I'm Patty Prescott, Gemma's sister."

He took her hand. "Farrell Riley."

"I figured."

"Patty…" Gemma sounded disapproving.

Patty grinned. "I live down the street from your partner. Sheila told me you and Cal were the ones to bring Mary here. I just put two and two together when I saw you."

Farrell thought that needed explanation. Did Gemma have so few men on her doorstep that the only possibility was the cop who'd dropped off Mary?

And if so, why?

"Come for dinner next Saturday, Gemma," Patty said. She turned to Farrell, and her eyes were dancing. "Since you like kids so much, Farrell, why don't you come, too? I have four little boys who'll change your mind. We'll invite Sheila and Cal, so they can see what they'll be getting into. Maybe Katy and her family can come, too. Katy's our little sister."

Farrell realized Patty had paused and was waiting for an answer. He avoided family get-togethers the way he avoided dark alleys and midnight strolls on Keller Avenue.

He found himself saying yes.

Patty patted his arm. "Oh, good. We'll do a barbecue if it's warm enough. I'll let Gemma know the time. We're always casual. Don't dress up."

Before anyone could say another word, Patty took off down the steps. At the bottom she waved before she disappeared around the side of the house.

"Well…" Gemma squared her shoulders and shook her hair back. "Hurricane Patty has blown over."

"How do you keep up with her?"

"She has to be that way. The boys are all under the age of nine. She's a Cub Scout den mother, and *she* wears the kids out." Gemma looked as if she didn't know what to say next.

"I don't know why I'm here. I just thought I'd check on Mary...and you."

"I'm glad you came. Come in. I promised you another cup of coffee, remember?"

He hadn't forgotten, although he'd tried.

He followed Gemma into the kitchen, trying not to notice the way her hips swayed gracefully in a blue dress that outlined her subtle curves.

"You must just have gotten off work. Have you had dinner?"

"No, but—"

"Good. Let me fix you something. Mary and I haven't eaten, either."

"I didn't come to beg a meal."

"Of course you didn't. You came to keep me company and hold Mary while I cook. She has a cold, and she hasn't been out of my arms for days."

"A cold? Are you sure that's all?"

"Absolutely. But on top of everything else that's happened to her, I guess she decided this was the last straw. She cries every time I put her down."

Gemma turned and held out the little girl to him. She had been dozing since his arrival; now she opened her pretty blue eyes, and they widened with pleasure. Before he could offer to leave, Mary pitched herself in his direction. All he could do was catch her.

"I hope she doesn't throw herself at men this way when she's a teenager," Gemma said.

Mary stroked Farrell's cheek. The exhaustion and frustrations of his job seemed to seep away with each childish touch. He was her captive. He couldn't make himself leave now.

Gemma opened the refrigerator. "What'll it be? Chicken? Fish? Are you a vegetarian?"

"I'll be a vegetarian when they sell soyburgers under the golden arches. Everything I eat comes straight off a fast-food grill or out of a can."

She peeked over the refrigerator door and made a face. "I'm going to make you something healthy, then, if you can stand it."

He tried to remember the last time anyone had worried about his diet. "Please don't go to any trouble."

"Trouble? This is sheer pleasure. Mary's appetite is good, but she's no gourmet. It'll be fun to cook for a grown-up."

"Anything will be fine."

"How about something to drink? Beer? Wine? I'm not much of a drinker. I don't have anything stronger."

"I'll take a beer." Farrell settled himself at the table and made Mary comfortable on his lap.

Gemma came over to the table with a bottle and a frosted mug. The beer wasn't something she'd picked up on sale at a convenience store. It was imported ale that was meant to be savored. He wondered what Cal and Archie would say.

"Here. Start on this." She returned with a plastic bag of fresh vegetables cut into thin strips. She arranged them on a plate and spooned something that smelled delicious into the center. "That's a spinach dip. You'll like it. Mary does."

As if to prove Gemma's point, Mary reached for a celery stick and lowered it into the spinach dip puddle. Farrell could do no less.

"Chicken breasts sound all right? I'll bake some potatoes in the microwave. I have fresh asparagus. Do you eat it?"

He didn't want to admit he'd never had the opportunity. "Sure. Thanks."

"Ummm... Good, I have mushrooms and red peppers. I'll do a sauce for the chicken. I know, I'll do pasta instead of potatoes. This is fun."

He had taught himself to remove frozen food from cardboard packages. Her plans were obviously on a different level. "You really don't have to go to so much trouble."

"Let me, please. I love to eat. Tell me about your day while I work. I'd like to know more about what you do."

He wondered what he could tell her. That until a sixteen-year-old tried to kill him, the rest of his day had consisted of traffic citations and faulty car alarms?

"There's nothing much to tell." He took a carrot stick from the plate. His stomach was rumbling, and he tried to remember if he and Cal had stopped for lunch.

Gemma filled a tall enamel pot with water and set it on the stove. "I'll bet you're good at defusing tough situations. You're so calm and reasonable. I bet you can talk people out of all kinds of crazy schemes."

"Not today." He clenched his jaw the moment the words were out. He'd had no intention of telling her what had happened to him, but Gemma was too perceptive to let that go unchallenged.

"No? What happened?"

He was left with a choice. He could be rude and refuse to answer, or he could spill his guts. And neither solution was in character.

She seemed to sense his struggle. "I'm sorry. I didn't mean to be nosy. I'm sure that sometimes you'd rather forget what you do for a living."

"Today would be one of those days." He found he wanted to tell her what had happened to him, wanted it more than he wanted his highly valued privacy. He didn't know how to start, but he took a stab at it. "I had a kid take a shot at me today. He wasn't impressed with how calm and reasonable I was. He was more impressed that I was about to arrest him."

Gemma dropped her knife at the word *shot*. "Farrell...that's horrible. Awful. But you're all right?"

"Fine." But he wasn't, which was why he'd ended up on Gemma's doorstep.

"How about the kid?"

"He's in jail. And not for the first time."

She hadn't gone on with her preparations. She stared at him, her forehead wrinkled, her face a paler shade. "You must have been pretty shaken up. You can't possibly get used to that kind of thing."

"Yeah, you do." He paused, then he shook his head ruefully. "No, you don't. Thank God it doesn't happen often enough for me to get used to it."

"Tell me what happened."

He found himself doing just that. She resumed her preparations, but she was listening intently. He couldn't remember anyone listening to him that way before, head cocked, eyes focused on his. She nodded as he spoke, and her soft blond hair fell forward over her cheeks and caressed her collarbone. He couldn't take his eyes off her, and somehow, he couldn't stop talking.

"I arrested him once before, a couple of years ago," he finished. "He was fourteen then. He hadn't graduated to handguns and ATMs yet. That time he stole a box of candy to give his mother for Mother's Day. Not that there was any guarantee his mother would have been around to eat it. She and his father are in jail more than they're out."

"I want to say poor kid. But he could have killed you."

"They'll put him away for this one, but he won't get any help. I think there's still something good in this kid, but it won't be there by the time he's free again.''

''I'm sorry.''

He liked that. No suggestions. No easy answers. Just a sincere statement of regret. ''Me, too.''

''You must see a lot of situations like that one.''

''More than I want to.''

She was chopping vegetables now, with an easy, practiced motion that sent them flying into neat little piles on the cutting board. Garlic sizzled in oil on the stovetop, and as he watched, the vegetables joined it. Next she sliced chicken and added it strip by strip until the smells were mouthwatering.

The water in the enamel pot began to boil, and Gemma added pasta. ''Well, it shouldn't be long now. I'll just do the asparagus, and we'll be ready to eat.''

Mary stirred restlessly, and Farrell realized she was beginning to whimper.

''Uh-oh. I was afraid this was too good to be true.'' Gemma washed and dried her hands. ''Shall I take her?''

''Why don't I try walking her a little?''

''She'd probably like that. But you must be dead on your feet.''

''Believe me, this is exactly what I need.''

She smiled her understanding. ''Good. And maybe she'll feel better if I can just get her dinner on the table.''

The equivalent of six blocks later, Mary reluctantly allowed him to set her in a booster seat at her very own place mat. Gemma served her plain chicken strips and canned fruit and one stalk of asparagus. The little girl sat stone-faced, staring at her plate.

"You know what? I suggest we eat quickly." Gemma took her own seat and motioned Farrell to his. "This may be the calm before the storm."

He didn't want to eat quickly. The food was delicious, even better than he had expected. And to his relief, the asparagus was edible, even if it looked like something Gemma had picked from an unmowed lawn. He was halfway through his meal when Mary began to cry in earnest.

Gemma was on her feet, sliding the little girl from her chair, before he could swallow. "You take your time," she said. "And that's an order. I'll entertain her a little, and when you're done, I'll finish my dinner."

He wondered if this was the way it was done in most families. Did mothers and fathers take turns comforting their children? Were there other women, like this one, who felt that a child's minor cold was enough of a reason to miss a meal? He couldn't imagine this kind of radiant goodwill, this attention to a child's needs. The world he had come from, the one he saw each day out on the streets, was a different one entirely. He felt as if he'd just been set down in the land of Oz.

And he realized he had no desire to find his way back to the land he was used to.

Gemma was murmuring softly to Mary, who was snuggled into her arms as if she'd been born into them. Something stirred restlessly inside Farrell, not for the mother or the child, but for the woman. She had strength that shone beyond the wide green eyes and delicate features. She believed in what she was doing. She wanted to make a difference in the lives of children like this one so that they didn't end up angry and desperate, like the teenager who had nearly killed him today. She was courage and wisdom packaged in a soft, shapely body that made his own ache with longing.

He wondered what it would be like to be loved by this woman, to lie with her in his arms, her body stretched the length of his. He knew better than to yearn for things he couldn't have. The lessons of his own childhood had taught him that.

But just for a moment, he wondered.

"Farrell?" She looked concerned. "Are you full already?"

Farrell knew he could never get enough of Gemma or anything she offered. He shook his head, and warnings flashed through his mind. He had a sixth sense that told him when he was in danger. Today he had dodged a bullet at exactly the right moment.

But somehow, he knew he was helpless to duck or dodge now.

Chapter Five

Gemma made potato salad for Patty's barbecue and a big chocolate cake with mocha icing. She had a feeling that Farrell liked chocolate. The night he'd stayed for dinner, he had eaten a bowl of chocolate chunk ice cream that was the equivalent of a week of desserts for her. She had shamelessly dragged out the meal that night because she had enjoyed having him there so much. If she could have followed up the meal with cheese and fruit in the European style, she would have. If she could have forced him to drink yet one more cup of coffee and followed it with brandy and cigars, she would have done that, too.

He had stayed for a while after the ice cream, anyway, patiently holding and walking Mary until the little girl finally gave in to sleep. Unfortunately, Farrell had put the little girl to bed, lovingly tucked covers around her sleeping body, then thanked Gemma for dinner and…left.

Gemma had been surprised at the disappointment she'd felt. She didn't want a relationship with Farrell Riley. But that night she had been sorry to see him go. She didn't know what she *had* wanted. But when he had walked out her door, she had felt a loneliness she couldn't pretend away. She had a full life, friends and more interests than she would ever have time to pursue. But the emptiness that had assaulted her after his departure wasn't something she could fill by sewing new curtains for the playroom or reading a novel by her favorite author. She had felt unwillingly connected to Farrell that night. She had been drawn in by his warm generosity with Mary and by his reluctant story of the day's events. She had been horrified to think that this man might have disappeared from her life before he had really entered it.

And, as before, she had felt the strong pull of sexual attraction between them.

She was almost surprised that he hadn't called to say he couldn't make today's barbecue. By leaving the moment Mary was in bed, he had made it clear that the child was their only tie. She thought that he felt the same physical tug that she did. Sometimes she found him looking at her with something close to desire. But clearly, Farrell didn't want a relationship any more than she did.

So why had he agreed to come to Patty's today, even to pick her up first? And why, given the opportunity, hadn't he changed his mind?

Gemma realized she was staring into space. Since there were no answers to her questions, she busied herself by tucking the potato salad and cake into a picnic basket. Mary, who had been contentedly piling wooden blocks into rickety towers in the corner, came to investigate. Gemma was convinced that Far-

rell had worked some sort of magic the night he had
lulled Mary to sleep, because the worst of her cold
was gone the next morning, and now she was
brighter and more cheerful than she had been since
arriving on Gemma's doorstep.

Mary favored Gemma with a huge smile, and
Gemma scooped her up for a hug. Mary hugged her
back.

Gemma's breath caught. She wasn't sure if she
had imagined the faint pressure. Mary was not un-
responsive. She listened, she watched, and Gemma
was sure that she processed everything around her.
But she was a child who had learned that she was
safest if she kept inside herself. Now she was discovering that people listened when she cried, and
tried to help her. And little by little she was learning
that no one would punish or ignore her if she had a
statement of her own to make.

A statement like a tentative little hug.

"You're very special, Mary." Gemma hugged her
again. "A very special little girl."

The doorbell rang, and Mary scrambled to get
down. Gemma's hands went to her own hair. Not that
there was much she could do with it. Fine, straight
hair did exactly what it pleased. Today she had
pulled it back from her face with a headband that
matched the soft gold of her skirt and blouse. But
the age-old impulse to primp before confronting an
attractive man won out over good sense.

Mary reached the door before Gemma did. She was in Farrell's arms the moment the door was unlocked. He lifted her and kissed her forehead. "How's my best girl today?"

Mary crowed with delight. "Yes!"

Farrell looked as startled as Gemma felt. Their gazes locked. "She's talking?" he said.

"A first." Gemma took a deep breath. She realized that in a matter of seconds she had nearly been reduced to tears.

"Well..." He looked down at Mary. "Definitely yes, sweetheart."

Gemma swallowed. "I bet she'd like to show you what she's been working on in the kitchen."

Farrell and Mary followed her inside. By the time they reached the kitchen, Gemma had her emotions under control.

Farrell set Mary on the floor, and Gemma watched the little girl run to the corner, making happy sounds. He made the appropriate fuss over her towers, insisting she was destined to become an architect. It was doubtful that she understood completely, but she beamed at the praise.

For those moments Gemma had the chance to watch Farrell undetected. He was dressed in dark jeans and a silver-gray sweater worn over a dark turtleneck. Men in uniform had a certain allure. This man still had it in casual clothing. The sweater stretched over shoulders broad enough to take on a thousand problems. The jeans hugged long, muscular legs and slim hips. No one looking at him could guess he was a cop, but even in civilian clothes he still retained a certain authority, a subtle unspoken announcement that here was a man to be reckoned with.

He looked up from Mary's blocks and found her watching him. For a moment their gazes locked, as they had when Mary had spoken. But this time something other than amazement passed between them. The air practically sizzled. His eyes drifted down her body, then up again.

"You look nice today." He didn't smile, but his eyes warmed.

"Actually, I was thinking that you do, too."

A few heartbeats passed, then a few more. Neither of them looked away.

"I'm glad you decided to come," she said at last. Not because she wanted to break the spell. She was not uncomfortable with Farrell, not even when neither of them knew what to say. She just wanted to be sure he knew she was glad he was there.

"I told you I would."

"And you never change your mind?"

"Not if I've made a promise."

She wondered if he knew how rare that was. Jimmy's promises had been worthless.

Her gaze dropped to Mary, and the spell was broken. "We have Mary and the picnic basket, and I packed a bag with Mary's toys, a change of clothes, a blanket…'' She paused, trying to decide if she'd forgotten anything.

''I'd be glad to drive, but I don't have a car seat. Would you like me to move yours to my car?''

''I can drive. It'll be easier. Unless you're one of those men who can't stand having someone else behind the wheel.''

''I have to put up with Cal's driving. I bet I can handle yours.''

She flashed him a grin and found he was smiling back at her. The fluttery feeling inside her was becoming an old friend.

Farrell liked Gemma's family. Patty was a brassier, louder version of her sister, but every bit as devoted to making the people around her comfortable. Katy, their younger sister, was a grown-up tomboy with short blond hair and a tendency to get down on the ground to roughhouse with her rambunctious nephews and her three-year-old son. Their husbands, John and Michael, obviously adored them, and although chaos had reigned from the moment Gemma and Farrell arrived, everyone pitched in and got along.

''Feel like you're trapped in the middle of a 'Brady Bunch' rerun?'' Cal leaned against a picnic table in the backyard and handed Farrell a beer. He and Sheila, his hugely pregnant wife, had immediately fit right in with everybody else, and now Sheila was lumbering after one of the little boys in an impromptu game of tag.

"'The Brady Bunch' was never this loud," Farrell said.

"My house was just like this. Lots of kids, lots of noise. We fought more, though. I figure we just yelled a lot to be sure we were heard." Cal took a swig of beer. "What about yours?"

He and Cal had been partners for two years, but Farrell had discouraged conversation about their respective pasts. He had come to terms with his life a long time ago, but he never thought of it as something to chat about.

"Nothing like this," he said.

"You're such a quiet guy. I always kind of thought you might be an only child."

"Good guess."

"I'm one of six, but I just want a couple of kids of my own. Sheila and I want to be able to spend a lot of time with them, you know?"

"You'll be a good dad."

"You think so?" Cal sounded pleased. "I get scared sometimes. What if I screw up?"

"Maybe you will. But kids are hardy, and you won't screw up often."

"Yeah? That's good to hear. What about you? You always say you don't want kids. Do you mean it?"

"I mean it."

"You're real good with Mary."

Farrell sought out the little girl with his eyes. She was safely ensconced in Gemma's arms. Mary seemed fascinated by the other children, but so far she had resisted all attempts to involve her in their play. Farrell couldn't blame her. Gemma's nephews were a high-speed, high-impact bunch.

"I'm not a family man," Farrell said.

"You'd have trouble convincing Mary of that. If she could talk, she'd tell you some stories about people who don't believe in family. The ones who had her, for starters."

Gemma must have seen them looking in Mary's direction. She smiled and started toward them.

"I'm going to make Sheila slow down. If this keeps up, I'll be a father before I'm ready." Cal strolled off and left Farrell to wait for Gemma alone.

"How are you doing?" Gemma settled herself and Mary at the picnic table beside where he was standing. "Is the noise getting to you yet?"

"I can take a lot of noise."

"Good thing. It's always like this, though. They aren't doing it for your benefit."

Farrell dropped to the bench beside her. Mary wiggled onto his lap and cuddled against him as if she was ready for a nap.

He stroked her hair. "She's pooped."

"I know, but she's enjoying this. I don't think she's seen many children."

Farrell was acutely aware of Gemma beside him. He hadn't purposely avoided her since their arrival at Patty's, but he hadn't sought her out, either. She had been busy with her family, and he had stayed on the sidelines.

Gemma lazily stretched her legs in front of her, shapely legs with trim ankles. The day was warm enough for sandals, and pink polished nails peeked out from crisscrossed leather straps. "John's just about to throw the burgers on the grill. Are you hungry?"

He turned to answer and found her face just inches from his. His heart slammed against his chest. He had thought about her constantly since the night he had stayed for dinner. And despite what he'd told her, he had strongly considered finding an excuse not to come today. In the end, he hadn't been able to lie to her or break his promise. But he had considered it, because he was fast getting in over his head.

"I am hungry," he said, but he didn't know which question he was answering. The one she had asked, or an unspoken one issuing from somewhere inside him.

"So am I."

Neither of them spoke. Neither of them looked away. He felt Mary sagging into sleep against him. He felt himself leaning toward Gemma. The space between them contracted. The air between them was charged with longing.

"Hey, Gemma," Patty called. "Come pour the drinks, would you? The swarm is thirsty and I'm up to my elbows in ground beef."

Farrell thought he saw disappointment in Gemma's eyes. He hesitated just an instant, then sat back against the table. "Go ahead. Mary's comfortable where she is."

Gemma's skirt swished against her legs as she went to join her sister. Farrell was powerless not to watch every step.

Farrell watched as Gemma pulled the door to Mary's room half-closed. She obviously wanted to be sure she would hear the little girl if Mary awoke during the night.

He spoke when she joined him on the stairs. "Poor little thing. She'll probably sleep a week."

"The boys wore her out, but she had fun. And she was holding her own there at the end. I think she really liked playing with Shawn."

Shawn was Katy and Michael's son, the closest in age to Mary and a shade less aggressive than Patty's boys. By the end of the evening, he had coaxed Mary out of Farrell's lap to play with trucks in the sandbox. Farrell had kept close watch over them, but Shawn had been careful not to hurt or frighten her.

"I know you can't eat another bite," Gemma said

when they reached the bottom of the stairs, "but would you like some coffee before you go?"

This was where he had made his exit the last time. Then he had known that the intimacy of sitting quietly over coffee with Mary sleeping upstairs would lead places that it shouldn't. Tonight he knew the same thing, but he couldn't seem to summon up the good sense to refuse her.

"You're probably tired." At the bottom of the stairs, Gemma stopped and faced him as she spoke.

The man who answered her was someone whose good sense had fled entirely. "You probably are, too. Do you really feel like making coffee?"

"Sure. After Mary goes to bed, I always sit and unwind a little."

"I'll tell you what. I'll make the coffee. You supervise."

She started to protest, then she seemed to catch herself. "I'm not used to being waited on. Thank you."

"You're welcome."

She made herself comfortable in her chair at the kitchen table. He could feel her eyes on him as he lifted the glass decanter from the coffeemaker. "I don't cook much, but somewhere along the way I did learn to make a decent cup of coffee."

"Good for you. I was married to a man who would have thought that was beneath him."

"Did he expect you to do all the cooking?"

She was silent long enough that he guessed she regretted mentioning her husband. "Jimmy believed in a division of labor," she said at last. "He did the division, and I did the labor."

This was the first inkling he'd had that her marriage hadn't been as happy as her sisters'. "Where do you keep the coffee and filters?"

"In the cabinet to the right of the coffeemaker."

He found what he needed without trouble. "The morning after I brought Mary here, you told me that you bought this house for the yard. Did you live here with your husband before he died?"

"No. We lived in Shore Haven, on the lake."

Shore Haven was an expensive housing development in the most exclusive suburb of the city. Farrell wondered if she regretted what was a noticeable move down in prestige. If so, the regret never showed.

"I like this better," she said, as if she'd read his mind.

"Do you?"

"We couldn't really afford that house. Jimmy worked on commission. I was never sure from one month to the next whether we could pay the mortgage. We had to have the right cars to go with the house, of course, and an interior that would impress anyone who made it through a security system sophisticated enough to protect Fort Knox." She smiled ruefully. "I don't have to keep up with anybody here. I can do what I please."

"And what you please is taking care of other people's kids."

"Yes."

Farrell switched on the coffeemaker, then leaned against the counter while the coffee brewed. "You must have had other options."

"I did. I could have kept my job at the preschool. And I'm certified to teach elementary school."

"I'm sure Mary's glad you made the choices you did."

She seemed pleased. "Do you think so?"

"She's happier every time I see her. And she seems more alert."

"I took her in for developmental testing on Thursday."

"Do they have results?"

"Not an official report, but the psychologist talked to me afterward. He says she's definitely behind. I knew that, of course, but I think she's already beginning to catch up. He's not as optimistic as I am that it's all environmental and that she'll make up for everything she's lost, but he seems to think that in the right kind of home, she'll continue to improve."

"A home like this one." It wasn't a question.

"Thank you."

"If she's too far behind, she'll be harder to place

for adoption. That is, if the courts ever get around to
making adoption a reality.''

''I guess we have to take it one step at a time.''

Farrell poured the coffee, which had just finished
brewing. He heard the sound of Gemma's chair sliding across the floor, but he was still surprised when
he turned and found her inches away.

''I was just getting the milk. I like…''

Her pupils grew larger and her cheeks stained
slowly with color. He knew he should move away,
that if he did, nothing would be altered between
them. He could still come and see Mary, still have
casual conversations with Gemma. Nothing he had
done today had changed anything. He and Gemma
were still practically strangers.

But she didn't feel like a stranger when he put his
arms around her. And she didn't taste like a stranger
when he kissed her.

Lord, she didn't taste like a stranger at all. She
tasted like heaven.

Her arms crept around his back as he pulled her
even closer. Her lips were soft, and they clung to his
with honeyed sweetness. Her body pressed so firmly
against his felt as real and as forbidden as the happy
life that had always been just out of his reach. He
knew, as he kissed her, that she was all the things
he had ever longed for and all the things he had been
denied until, one day, he had finally stopped reaching
for them.

And still, he couldn't let her go.

"Farrell, I didn't mean for this to happen." She whispered the words against his lips, not a protest but a confession.

He heard her words, but he felt the heat of her flesh continue to fuse with his. She wanted reassurance. He had none to give, but still, she didn't move away.

He kissed her again, and her lips parted under his. He brushed his hands over her hips, then under her shirt. Her skin was smooth and warm beneath his palms, and she sighed as his hands moved higher.

His fingertips lingered at the edge of her bra, the softest lace against the rough calluses. He hooked an index finger under the catch and realized that with one twist, the bra would give way. He could feel her hips melting gently against his, her body seeking its rightful place. Desire flared like fireworks in a night sky, and for that moment he gave in to it and ignored the insistent voice warning him that he should move away.

A car door slammed on the street in front of the house, and somewhere nearby a dog began to bark in protest. The ordinary neighborhood noises accomplished what a lifetime of caution had not. Farrell lifted his head and stared down at this woman who wasn't ordinary at all. No, Gemma wasn't ordinary, but she expected the world to give her ordinary things like love and family and happily-ever-afters. And how could he be the one to disappoint her?

"I didn't mean for this to happen, either." He clasped her close rather than look into her eyes. Her head rested against his shoulder.

"We can still go back to what we were," she said.

He shook his head, because he knew that nothing would ever be the same for him again.

Her voice deepened with emotion. "I've been in love once. I couldn't survive it again."

"I've never wanted to try love at all."

"So what do we do?"

His body was telling him in no uncertain terms what they should do. He had never felt desire this compelling. And he had never felt anything this close to terror.

"We don't do anything." His voice was gruff. "I leave."

Her arms were still wrapped around him. They remained that way. "And when do you come back?"

"It would be easier if I didn't."

"Yes. But we've already passed 'easy.'" She let her arms fall to her sides. "I'll settle for 'difficult,' if that means you'll stay around until we sort this out."

"*Is* this something we can sort out?"

She smiled sadly. "Not a chance."

He pushed a lock of hair off her cheek, and his fingertips lingered against her skin.

She covered his hand and held it against her cheek. "Go home and think about this, Farrell." She dropped her hand. "I'll think, too."

He knew he would think about nothing else. He left her standing in the kitchen, beside the coffee he had brewed for them both.

Chapter Six

Archie strolled by Farrell's desk in the report room, then backed up like a show horse being put through its paces. "Jeffries tells me you're checking some leads on that little girl's parents."

Farrell dropped his pen and leaned back in his chair. "We talked it over. He's in charge of the Keller Avenue investigation, but as long as I report anything I find, he doesn't mind if I snoop a little."

"He wouldn't. You know he's been shorthanded since Canfield moved over to homicide."

The day had been long, and Farrell's patience was uncharacteristically short. "Look, I'm doing this on my own time. I'm not working on this while I'm on duty, okay?"

Archie didn't address that. "You know we'll be promoting a patrol officer to detective to work in vice with Jeffries."

"Relax. I'm not bucking for the job, Archie. I'm just trying to find Mary's parents so her case can be settled."

"Isn't she doing okay where she is?"

"She's doing great."

"So?"

"A kid deserves to know where she's going to wake up every morning."

"What if you find her folks, they want her back, and the courts choose not to stand in their way?"

"I'm hoping that doesn't happen."

Archie rubbed the back of his neck. Obviously it had been a long day for him, too. "You know you're top of the list to make detective, don't you?"

Farrell didn't answer. He'd heard rumors, but he wasn't a particularly ambitious man. He liked his job; he would also like the move up to detective. In his professional life, as in his personal life, he didn't hope for the things he might never have.

When Farrell didn't respond, Archie went on, "Some people are going to think you're doing this to increase your chances. It could work against you."

"Then I'll take myself out of the running if I have to. But I'm not about to take myself off this case."

Archie nodded. "Just do it on your own time."

"I promise you'll get your usual pound of flesh."

"With you, it's always been a pound and a half." Archie rapped his knuckles on the desk, then turned and continued across the room.

Cal, who had been on the telephone a few desks south of Farrell, came over to see what Archie had said. Farrell shook his head. "He just wanted to know about the Keller Avenue raid."

"I just got a tip from a guy who lives over on Keller. He says he remembers some things about the

folks who set up shop in that house we raided. And
he thinks he saw one of them last night at a Laundromat over on Fifth Street, but he's not sure.''

Farrell regarded his partner. ''Who's the guy who
called? And why'd he call you?''

''Max is a schoolfriend of Sheila's. I'm the only
cop he knows. He was probably afraid if he called
and talked to just anyone, they might think he knows
more than he does.''

''You don't think he's involved?''

''No, he's a little eccentric, an artist or something,
but he's a good guy. He lives about half a mile farther down Keller, but he used to see the people at
that house when he walked his dog. Had a run-in
with one of them once when they almost backed a
car over him. He remembers a couple of faces, that's
all.''

The story seemed plausible enough, and it fit with
the little Farrell had been able to discover on his
own. If the man was really an artist, his description
might be good enough to be helpful.

In the days since the picnic at Patty's, he had put
in his time on patrol, then worked three or four hours
each evening on Keller Avenue, trying to see if he
could discover anything new. He had made a few
contacts, and last night a guy in a bar had been able
to tell him the street name of one of the men who
had lived at the drug house. But this was the best
break yet.

Cal looked eager to help. "Do you want to go talk to him? I'm done here."

"Yeah. I'll clear it with Jeffries."

"Hell, Jeffries would give you the case if he could. He's got a pile of files so high, he can't see over the top of his desk."

Farrell felt the thrill of the hunt, even though he schooled himself not to get his hopes up. "Let me finish my report, then we can get out of here."

Gemma heard the doorbell ring as she started down the stairs. She had just put Mary to bed for the night, and she was tired herself. She hadn't had a good night's sleep in a week, and she was beginning to feel the strain. For just a moment she was tempted to pretend she wasn't at home. Patty or Katy might be standing at her front door to start one more conversation about Farrell and her future, and she definitely wasn't in the mood.

The temptation waned. Marge Tremaine had planned to stop by earlier, and since she might be here now, despite the lateness of the hour, Gemma knew she couldn't really ignore the summons. She smoothed her hair behind her ears and opened the front door, only belatedly realizing that to be safe, she should have squinted through the peephole first.

"Do you open your door to just anybody?"

Farrell was standing on the front porch in civilian

clothes. He was scowling, which did nothing to diminish his appeal.

She was so surprised to see him that for a moment she didn't speak. Then she pulled herself together. "No lectures, okay? I realized I forgot to check as I was opening the door. I usually do."

"This isn't Shore Haven."

"You're right. It's a neighborhood for people with a whole lot less to steal." She opened the door wider and gestured him inside. She didn't even want to think about what she was feeling. "You just missed Mary. She almost fell asleep during her bath. By the time I tucked her in, she was out like a light."

"I didn't come to see Mary."

Gemma's heart beat a little faster. During the past week she had tried not to think about what had passed between them, about their mutual confusion and reticence, and the attraction that blinded them both to other things. But she had thought about those things anyway, in the darkest hours of night, and now she was paying the price.

"I came to talk to you about Mary's parents."

She lifted her chin. "I see." She didn't offer Farrell a seat or a cup of coffee. Not being hospitable was foreign to her, but Gemma was in no mood to pretend she was glad to be discussing business with this man.

"Let's sit."

Her shoulders drooped. She couldn't politely resist

his direct suggestion. She led him to the sofa and curled up against one end. "Have you heard something about Mary's parents? Have you found them?"

"No, but we're closing in. I just wanted you to know that I'm looking for them, Gemma. I didn't want you to find it out from somebody else."

"Is that your job?"

"No. But I've made it mine. I've been working on it in the evenings. And we're making some progress on the case."

"Why?" She crossed her arms in front of her. "Do you think she'll be better off with them than she is with me?" The words were out before she could withdraw them. She knew how stupid they were, but her exhaustion and insecurity were showing.

"That's what I was afraid you'd think." Farrell leaned forward. "You have to know that's not why I'm doing it."

"I'm sorry. Of course I do. It's been a long week, that's all."

The doorbell rang again before Farrell could reply. She shook her head in apology. "I don't know who that could be, unless it's Marge." At the blank look on his face she added, "Marge Tremaine. Mary's caseworker. She said she wanted to stop by at dinnertime, but she never made it."

This time she used the peephole and discovered that it was indeed Marge on the other side of the door. She opened the door, and the caseworker, a middle-aged African-American woman whose tastes ran to bright colors that glowed against her dark skin, greeted her warmly. The two women were fast becoming friends.

"I bet she's in bed, isn't she?" Marge said.

"I'm afraid so. I'm sorry you missed her. She's growing and learning by leaps and bounds."

"I got the psychologist's report. He's not as optimistic as you are, but we pay him to be cautious." Marge seemed to sense someone else in the house and glanced toward the living room.

Gemma filled her in. "Farrell Riley is here. He's the policeman who brought Mary to me that night. Come meet him."

Farrell got to his feet. Gemma made the introductions, then waited until Marge made herself comfortable in the rocking chair. "Can I get you anything?"

Marge waved her to the sofa. "Sit down, Gemma. You look beat. In a few minutes I'm going home to a good stiff drink and a hot bath. I just wanted to catch up with you first."

"Farrell has been telling me that there are some leads in the search for Mary's parents." Gemma sat back, hoping that the conversational ball would roll on without her. She didn't know what to think about Farrell's bombshell. He knew how well Mary was doing with her, yet he'd made it his mission to find the little girl's parents. Why?

"What kind of leads?" Marge asked, as Gemma had hoped she would. "Can you talk about it?"

"We've got a couple of detailed descriptions we didn't have before, and a possible sighting in the area. And if I can get a couple of people to look through mug books, we might even get some names. Anyway, we're farther ahead than we were this morning."

Marge nodded. "I guess I ought to be glad, huh? But I'm not. The minute Mary's folks are found, we have to start working with them. I don't know about you, but a mommy and daddy who leave a baby like Mary in an empty house just to save their own skins aren't my top candidates for reform. Sometimes people change. Sometimes there are circumstances. But my gut tells me this is not one of those times."

Farrell leaned forward. "Are you saying you don't want me to find them? Mary needs a permanent home."

Marge gave a wan smile. "Mr. Riley, this is the best home that little girl's probably *ever* going to have. Even if we get her parents to give up their rights, our Mary's not going to be tops on anybody's adoption list. She's a special-needs child. We don't know if she'll ever be normal. And by the time she's available for adoption, she'll be older and even harder to place. Having contact with her biological parents will confuse her more. By then she'll be thinking of Gemma as her mother...." Marge shook her head. "I'm sorry. It's been a long day. You're a cop. But I see stuff every day that would make even *your* hair curl."

"I'll tell you what makes my hair curl—a system that keeps children like Mary in limbo."

"I'm just saying there are worse things than an excellent foster home."

"Let me tell you what it's like to grow up in foster homes, Miss Tremaine." Farrell leaned even farther forward, and his eyes were the gray of thunderclouds. "I have some personal experience with it."

Gemma had been trying to think of a way to intervene tactfully, but now she couldn't have spoken if her status as a foster parent had depended on it.

Farrell didn't look at her. His eyes were on Marge. "Most of the time if you're a foster kid nobody ever takes the time to show you what a real home looks like. Still, you have dreams. You walk through each strange new door with those dreams intact, until you find out that the new place you've landed isn't a real home, either. You know because you have to keep your suitcase packed all the time, in case the people who gave birth to you decide they want you back, or until the judge and the social workers decide you're getting too comfortable where you are, maybe too attached to your foster parents."

He paused a moment, and Gemma held her breath.

She had never suspected that Farrell had been a foster child, or that his interest in Mary's case was anything more than his personal attachment to her. She heard him struggle to sound objective, and she heard him fail.

He shook his head, as if he were remembering something that even now had the power to hurt him. "One day you come home from school and somebody's waiting to move you to another home. Your third or your tenth, by then you've lost count. And this new home isn't real, either. These people are strangers, too, so you keep your bag packed again. You never enjoy the most basic feeling of security. You learn early that you can't even leave your toothbrush in the bathroom with everybody else's, because one time you were moved so suddenly you forgot to pack it. And the people at the new house punished you for not bringing a toothbrush with you."

Gemma felt tears stinging her eyes.

"I don't want Mary to grow up that way." He sat back, as if he were forcing his emotions to settle somewhere deep inside him again. "This may be the best home Mary will ever have, but unless we get her out of the foster care system, it may be the first of many. She deserves better."

Marge was silent for a few moments, and Gemma didn't know what to say. Finally Marge spoke. "It's different now than it was when you were a child, Mr. Riley. Mary can stay here until she's out of the system. We don't move children unless we absolutely have to.''

"But the minute she's old enough to realize what's going on, Mary will figure out that her life could change in a heartbeat. Even if it never changes, some part of her will always wonder and worry.''

He turned to Gemma, and the expression in his eyes was still fierce. "Gemma deserves this child. If she wants to adopt Mary, she should be able to. That can't happen if Mary's birth parents are still somewhere on the scene. And if they want her bad enough and prove they can take care of her, then they should have her back as soon as possible. Before Mary's torn apart.''

"Foster care is an imperfect solution, but it's the best we can offer in a lot of cases.''

"It's not the best solution in *this* case. Because at least two adults love this child and are willing to fight for her.''

Gemma was still so stunned by Farrell's revelations and the intensity of his response that she couldn't find the words she needed. But Marge didn't give her a chance to speak, anyway.

"Then she's already luckier than half the kids I see.'' Marge stood. "I'll leave you two alone. Will you let me know when you find out anything, Mr. Riley?''

"I'll be sure you know.''

Gemma rose and walked Marge to the door. In the

hallway Marge turned to her. "You know, he's his own worst argument."

Gemma didn't understand.

Marge smiled sadly. "The foster care system may not be perfect, but it produced one fine man when it chewed up and spit out Officer Farrell Riley."

Farrell's eyes were closed, but he heard Gemma come back into the room after saying goodbye to Marge Tremaine. He felt sick inside, as if he had laid himself open for examination and now he couldn't put himself back together.

He felt the sofa sag beside him. Gemma wasn't sitting at her own end of it anymore. She was close enough that he could feel the heat from her body and smell the faint fragrance of lilac.

"Don't tell me you're sorry about my childhood," he said at last.

"I'm not sorry."

Her voice was low and musical. He could feel her leg pressed against the length of his. He had tried not to think about her this week. He had nearly worked himself into oblivion just so he wouldn't have to think about her. Now he knew that underneath that frantic activity he had longed for her with single-minded intensity.

He could feel her leaning closer as she spoke. "How can I be sorry when your past made you the man you are? I wish it had been accomplished some easier way, but I wouldn't want the results changed even one little bit.''

He opened his eyes and turned his head, which was still resting against the back of the sofa. ''The man I am is more flawed than you can imagine.''

''Farrell...''

''I learned a long time ago that I'm better off alone. As a kid, I wanted a family so desperately, and every day that went by and I didn't get one, I discovered that taking care of myself was the only sure thing. But that knowledge came with a price, Gemma. I've been alone so long, I don't know how to be anything else. I have nothing to give, because I never learned how.''

''Oh, Farrell, none of that is true.'' She touched his cheek with her fingertips, then laid her palm against it.

''You just don't want to believe it. But I'm not the man for you. You need someone who wants the things you do. You need a man who knows how to love you the way you deserve.''

''I had a man like that, at least on the surface. I don't want another one.''

He wanted to push her away. He knew he should leave and never come back. But the same longing that had compelled him to seek her out tonight kept him in his seat.

She kissed him this time. With measured calcula-tion. The soft, womanly Gemma whom he had come

to know changed subtly. Her lips were as ripe and
sweet, but there was an insistence in her kiss he
couldn't ignore. Before, she had been hesitant; now
she was the aggressor.

He was lost from the moment her lips touched his.
His good intentions vanished. In that moment it
seemed to him that he had spent his whole life being
good in hopes that someday someone would reward
him. Now he knew that he wanted no reward other
than this night. If this was all he was ever given, it
would be enough.

He wound his arms around her and pulled her
closer. She made a sound of pure pleasure and
pressed her breasts against his chest. He was aware
of everything between them, of his wool sweater and
her denim jumper. He was aware that she had no
curtains in this room so that the daylight would shine
more brightly. He was aware that now, because it
was dark outside, a lamp glowed in the corner and
anyone who cared enough could see them in its reflection.

He was aware that all the bedrooms in the house
were upstairs. And he was aware that she had not
yet invited him to share one with her tonight.

"If this is only a kiss," he said, holding her just
far enough away to see her face, "then we have to
stop now."

"Is this my first warning, Officer Riley?"

"It's your only warning, Gemma."

"My bedroom's at the end of the hallway upstairs. If I stop kissing you, are you going to find your way upstairs or out the front door?"

She sounded faintly out of breath, and although she was trying to sound sure of herself, he heard the very real question behind her words.

"I'm going to find my way upstairs *while* you kiss me."

"It might take some time that way...."

"We have time, don't we?"

"We have all night."

They took a good portion of the night making their way upstairs. He could not imagine turning and moving away from her, not even with the prize that was waiting for him at the end of the journey. He couldn't seem to stop kissing her, or to stop holding her. He was hungry for the feel of her skin against his palms, for the swell of her breast in his hand, for the warmth of her breath mingled with his.

Her bedroom was large and comfortable, with heavy walnut furniture and filmy curtains billowing gently in the breeze. She took a moment to light three pastel candles sitting on a dressing table before she turned back to him. She rested her palms against his chest and lifted her head to kiss him again.

They took turns removing clothing. She tugged his sweater over his head and unbuttoned the shirt beneath it. He unzipped her jumper. She unbuckled his belt. He smoothed her panties over her hips.

Gemma was as beautiful as he had imagined. She did not have an athlete's body. She had a narrow waist, and full breasts and hips. It was a body meant to bear and suckle children, and he thought he had never seen anything quite so beautiful.

She turned back the covers as if they had always gone to bed together in this room, and he joined her under them. He felt no awkwardness; she didn't hesitate. She came into his arms as if she had done so every night for years. Her leg slid between his, her hand trailing over his chest and lower, until he was afraid he would explode with desire.

Her lips tormented his flesh. He explored her with the same relentless precision, with his hands and lips and the caress of his body. When he entered her, she moved against him as if she had been made for that alone.

He had not allowed himself to imagine the pleasure he might find. Only once did he break the silence that had fallen between them.

"If I had known that making love to you would feel like this, I would never have been able to stay away." He whispered the words against her neck, just before she arched against him in final fulfillment.

Later, as Gemma fell asleep in his arms, Farrell realized with a sinking heart what he had said. Worse, he knew that he had meant every word. He had never dared to imagine what loving and being loved by Gemma Hancock might mean. But now that he knew, he was sure he would never be able to walk away from her.

The lessons of his childhood had been hard won. But by falling in love with Gemma, he had failed his final test. He had not succeeded in locking himself away from dreams and hopes. Tonight he had given this woman the key to his heart.

Chapter Seven

"This guy, he comes in with two, three others."
The old man who owned a grocery store on Orchard
Avenue gestured excitedly with his hands, as if he
could sculpt images in the air. "I watch him, always.
He looks at things, this way." The man narrowed his
eyes, then glanced back and forth between Farrell
and the counter, as if he was watching to see if
his activities were detected. "He'd steal anything
not…" His voice trailed off.

"Nailed down," Farrell supplied. The old man's
English was excellent, but his command of the ver-
nacular was less so, since he had left his native Ku-
wait only a few years before. Farrell put the photograph back in his folder. Nearly a month after his
first conversation with Sheila's friend Max, Farrell's
persistence had paid off. Max had finally been per-
suaded to come down to the station to pore over mug
books. The photograph he had chosen was the one
Farrell had just shown the store proprietor. Now, not
only did the police have a name, the proprietor had
seen the man in the photograph last night.

"And he came in about this time last night?" Farrell said.

"Little later. Maybe ten. Every night almost. Right before I close."

In the past two evenings Farrell had shown this photograph at every small grocery store and service station within a two-mile radius of the Laundromat where Max thought he had seen the man. "Does he ever come in with a woman?"

"All the time." The old man made a face. "Dirty woman. Dirty clothes. I watch her, too."

"Anything else you remember about her?"

"Dark hair. Tooth missing here." He opened his mouth to show a full white set of his own and pointed to a bicuspid.

"I'm glad you're so observant."

"You going to stay and see if they come back?"

"First I'm going to call the station and tell them what's going on. Can I use your phone?"

The old man took him into a back storeroom and left him to make the call by himself. Archie was still at the station, and he listened as Farrell told him what he'd learned.

"Don't do anything until we get you some backup," Archie instructed. "I'll call Jeffries, then I'm on my way."

"Don't send anybody in uniform."

"You think I don't know how to do my job?"

Farrell hung up. He wondered if he was about to encounter Mary's mother at last. For a moment he tried to imagine what Gemma would think when she found out.

His thoughts these days were almost always of Gemma. Since the night they had become lovers, she had inhabited his thoughts, his dreams, his plans for the future. When he wasn't with her, he was planning what they would do when he was. They maintained the illusion of separate lives, but the time they spent apart was only preparation for the time they could spend together.

Farrell and Gemma had talked at length about his quest to find Mary's mother, as well as a million other details of their lives. He thought she understood his obsession with finding a permanent home for Mary, but he didn't know if she would ever forgive him if this turned out badly. If he had done this work only to have Mary taken from Gemma's loving care and returned to abusive parents, then he wasn't sure he would be able to forgive himself, either.

He returned to the front and spoke briefly to the proprietor, instructing him on how to act. Then he went to one of the outside aisles and began to methodically examine canned goods.

The door opened, and a large man in casual clothes strolled in. Archie directed one quick gaze in Farrell's direction before he continued his stroll to the other side of the store and began to examine cereal boxes. Ten minutes later Jeffries, a thin man with less hair than savvy, entered the store and devoted himself to an intent study of the freezer case.

Farrell knew that impromptu stakeouts like this one rarely bore fruit, but he prayed that this one would prove the exception.

Half an hour passed, and ten o'clock drew nearer. Farrell had progressed to fresh vegetables and was weighing mushrooms in a hanging scale when the door opened again. He didn't investigate immediately, and when he did, only his head turned, as if in idle curiosity.

Two men and a woman sidled into the wide center aisle. The face of one man was familiar, although without a mug-shot scowl he was slightly better looking. The woman was overweight, with long unkempt hair and lifeless eyes, but even though she was a complete stranger to Farrell, he recognized her immediately. The woman had a daughter who strongly resembled her. And when she spoke to the man in the photograph, and Farrell saw that she was missing a tooth, he knew for certain he was looking at Mary's mother.

He caught Archie's eye, then Jeffries's, too. As a unit, the three men moved toward the door. In moments, and with only a short scuffle, the three shoppers were escorted to Jeffries's car.

"Sally?" Farrell closed the file folder he'd been examining. Jeffries stood against the door, his arms folded. He had agreed to let Farrell talk to Mary's mother, but he was going to observe the process. "May I call you Sally?" Farrell asked politely.

"Like I care what you call me."

He didn't let her ruffle him. "Then Sally it is."

"You don't got nothing on me. You got no reason to arrest me."

"You're just here to answer some questions." Farrell smiled politely.

"I got nothing to say to you. I don't have to talk to you unless I got a lawyer."

"You're right about that. But I thought you might want to find out about your little girl."

Sally didn't blink. "What little girl?"

"Sally, let me remind you that your daughter has a birth certificate. And now that we know your name, we can track it down and tie you to her like that." He snapped his fingers.

Sally, who according to identification in her purse was Sally Margaret Matthews, twenty years old and born and bred in their fair city, shrugged. "So?"

"Aren't you interested in what happened to Mary?"

Sally gave up pretending. "I read the papers."

"So you know she's okay."

She shrugged. "I figured."

"Can you handle this without me?" Jeffries asked Farrell.

"No problem."

Jeffries left, and Farrell took a seat on the other side of the table from Sally. He knew Jeffries—and Archie, too—would be watching through a two-way mirror, but Sally probably didn't.

"I was there the day the house was raided," he said in a conversational tone. "As a matter of fact, I was the one who found Mary in the closet."

"I didn't put her in no closet."

"Didn't you?"

"I wasn't even there that night. Someone else was taking care of her."

Farrell nodded, as if he believed her. When she relaxed a little he added, "Of course, you were *seen* there that night by one of the neighbors, so we know that's not quite true."

Sally slumped. "I didn't put her in no closet. She was asleep on the bed last I knew. I had to leave fast. I didn't have time to get her."

Farrell nodded again, as if in his world, that happened all the time. "She was badly frightened."

"Well, I didn't frighten her, did I? You were the ones that broke in while she was sleeping."

"The courts don't look kindly on mothers who abandon their children. You've never called to ask about her, have you? You haven't tried to find her."

"So?"

"She's a beautiful little girl." He cleared his throat. "I've spent some time with her since I found her."

Sally looked as if she wondered what this had to do with her.

Farrell let his emotions shine through in his voice. "I'd do almost anything to make sure she isn't hurt again."

Sally suddenly seemed interested. "That so?"

"Yeah." He shook his head ruefully. "I don't have kids of my own. Mary's almost like a daughter to me."

"That so?" Sally tossed her dirty hair back over her shoulders.

"Does her father spend time with her?"

"I don't know." She grinned.

Farrell cocked a brow in question.

"I don't know who her father is," she said triumphantly, as if she'd told a wonderful joke.

"Oh." He nodded. Under the table, his hands balled into fists. "She needs a father."

"Maybe she does." Sally was still grinning, but her eyes narrowed. "Maybe I ought to find her one, you know?"

He waited, not quite holding his breath.

"Am I in big trouble?" she asked, in what seemed like a change of subject.

"I'm afraid so."

"Can you help me?"

"How could I do that, Sally?"

"Well, you and me, we could come to an understanding, right?"

He felt sick inside, but this was exactly what he'd been hoping for. "What kind of understanding?"

"Mary needs a daddy, and it sounds like you might want her."

"And?"

"And I got the right to give her away, but I got to get something in return...."

"In other words, you'll give me Mary if I do you a favor?"

Sally looked cagey. "Yeah, something like that."

Farrell sat back and closed his eyes.

Farrell put his arm around Gemma and brought her to rest against his shoulder. He didn't know why he hadn't told her about finding Mary's mother. He had come to Gemma's house late, well after his interview with Sally Matthews. Jeffries had come back into the room, and together they had explained that in addition to everything else, she was now in serious trouble for having offered Farrell her daughter in exchange for his help. Selling a child, no matter what the currency, was against the law.

He hadn't told Gemma, although that had been his conscious purpose in arriving at her doorstep. But once inside, he had taken her in his arms instead, and now they were upstairs in her bedroom after passionately making love. She was snuggled against him, and he knew that soon she would be asleep.

His heart was overflowing with emotion. A long

time ago he had given up his childish hopes of ever loving or being loved by anyone. Gemma had come into his life accidentally, and he had very nearly lost her before he found her. But there had been a spark inside him that a childhood of neglect and alienation hadn't been able to extinguish. And Gemma had fanned it into flame.

He loved this woman with a passion that was grander because he hadn't believed it possible. He wanted to tell her, but he had never had any practice. Still, he wanted to tell her....

"Gemma?"

"Hm...?"

"I didn't know I could be this happy."

She made a soft sound of pleasure. "Me either."

"I didn't want any of this."

"You just didn't *know* you wanted it."

"Maybe..." He stroked her hair. "I don't want it to end."

She was silent, but she didn't move away.

He didn't know how to tell her what he was feeling. She could talk openly about her emotions; he had spent a lifetime learning to repress his.

Instead, he started with what had happened that night. "I came to tell you something. I didn't come for this."

"Are you apologizing?"

He laughed. "Are you kidding?"

She touched his face. "I like it when you do that."

"What?"

"Laugh that way."

"I do it a lot more often than I used to."

"That you do."

"I do have something to tell you, Gemma. Are you awake enough to listen?"

He could feel her body tense. "Go ahead."

"Mary is going to be freed for adoption."

She sat up and looked into his eyes. "What?"

"We found her mother tonight. And she's agreed to relinquish her rights."

"Why?"

He had hoped to avoid this, but he had guessed that Gemma would want to know it all.

Gemma listened without saying anything until he had finished. "She tried to exchange Mary for her own freedom?"

"She had nothing else to bargain with."

"What if she changes her mind?"

"She doesn't want Mary, Gemma. That part was crystal clear. And since three cops heard her offer to give me Mary if I helped her out, she can't really change her mind."

"What's going to happen to her now?"

"She has a record, but so far it's mostly minor offenses. She abandoned Mary, but if it looks like she's trying to do the right thing now by giving Mary up for adoption, the judge will probably be lenient. Unless she's linked directly to activities at the drug house, she'll probably be put on probation...until she's arrested for something else.''

''Mary's really safe? You're sure?''

''I talked to Marge Tremaine and told her what happened. She says the paperwork will start immediately. She also said that you can apply to adopt Mary.'' He paused and took a deep breath. ''Or that we can.''

''We?''

Farrell had dodged bullets, chased criminals on foot through rush-hour traffic, handcuffed and hauled in men twice his size, but nothing compared with the difficulty or danger of his next words.

''I know we've only known each other a little while....''

She didn't answer. She wasn't going to help him in this.

''Gemma, I never thought I wanted to marry or have children. I didn't think I could offer a woman or children anything. And it's hard to believe, I know, that being with you and Mary could change how I feel so quickly. But one of the things I learned in all those foster homes was to grab what I needed when it came around, because if I didn't, it might never come my way again.''

''Farrell, I—''

He rested a finger against her lips. ''I want to spend my life with you. I want to spend it with Mary, and the children we have together. I know this is sudden. I know it's too soon to speak, but circumstances, Mary's adoption, make it necessary. You probably don't trust—"

This time she was the one to put her finger on his lips. "Farrell, no. Please, you've got to listen to me now."

She looked as if she wanted to cry. Everything inside him froze. In the weeks they had been lovers, he had misunderstood. He had believed that the passion they had found together was more than it was. He had seen love when there was only attraction. He had moved too quickly....

She sat up and moved away from him. In a moment she got up and pulled her robe off the chair and slipped it on. Then she sat back down on the edge of the bed and turned to face him.

"I've never told you much about my marriage to Jimmy."

"It's never mattered to me."

"I have to tell you. You have to know, so you'll understand...."

He didn't want to ask her what he had to understand. She was going to say no to marrying him and adopting Mary together. That was as clear as anything in his life.

His voice was hollow, the voice of the man he had been before falling in love with her. "You don't have to make excuses. If you don't want to marry me, that's good enough."

She pulled the robe tighter around her. "Do you remember the day you told Marge what it was like to be a foster child?"

"What does that have to do with anything?"

"The only way you could make us understand how you felt about Mary's situation that day was to tell us why it mattered so much to you. I have to do the same thing."

He didn't want to hear this. Her relationship with her dead husband had nothing to do with him, but he was powerless to tell her so, because he didn't want her to stop talking. When she stopped, where would they be?

"I married Jimmy the summer after my last year of college. He was bright, good-looking, charming in every way. It was a small school. If we had voted for Most Likely To Succeed, Jimmy would have won hands down. I thought I was the luckiest girl in the world. Everyone loved him, and I thought I did, too."

"So you were living a fairy tale. I don't understand what this has to do with me."

She continued as if he hadn't spoken. "A year passed, then two, and I began to see what I'd been too young and immature to realize at first. Everyone loved Jimmy, but Jimmy loved himself most of all. The world revolved around him. He knew how to get anything he wanted, and he did, regularly. If he couldn't get it in the usual ways, he'd manipulate others until he had what he wanted. He wasn't above lying or wearing people down. Just as long as things went his way."

Farrell watched her. She wasn't quite looking at him. She was looking at her past, and she didn't like what she saw.

Gemma continued. "You know, I was raised to take care of people. My mother was a stay-at-home mom, and I adored her. She took such good care of my sisters and me when we were growing up, and I wanted to be just like her. She and my father were so happy, and when I married Jimmy, I wanted us to be just like them. So even though I began to see things about him that disturbed me, I closed my eyes."

He interrupted. "I don't know what this has to do with me. Do you think I'm like him?"

"No!" She shook her head so hard he couldn't doubt what she said. "You're nothing like him. We were married for five years before I realized that he'd been leading me on about wanting a family. I wanted children, and Jimmy had always promised that we'd have them. Somehow, though, he always came up with an excuse why we had to wait. By then I was beginning to see him for what he really was and to have serious doubts about our future together. My parents had moved to Florida, so I made arrangements to go and visit them to think about what I was going to do. I was twenty-seven, and it was clear to me that I'd married a man who wanted things, not people, in his life. I think Jimmy realized that I might leave him. He was sales manager for a conservative company that strongly promoted their family image, and divorce would have been frowned on. One day while I was away, his boss took him aside and asked him about his plans for the future. Jimmy decided that children would be good for his career.''

"He told you this?''

"I figured it out later. Jimmy was too smart to admit something like that. He realized that if I knew what he was thinking, I'd never agree to stay with him, much less bring children into the marriage. No, he knew me too well. He came down to Florida, cried like a baby and told me that he couldn't live without me. He asked me to go into counseling with him. I was ecstatic. I came home. We went to counseling for a few months, and Jimmy fooled me and the therapist. At the end he told me he was ready to have children, and I believed him because I wanted them so badly.''

"But you didn't have them?''

"I got pregnant quickly, but it was a tubal pregnancy.'' She looked straight at him. "I didn't want to admit anything was wrong, and I waited too long to see my doctor. I lost the baby and my chance to have another. I can't have children, Farrell. I had an emergency hysterectomy.''

"Gemma...''

She shook her head, warning him not to say anything. "I wasn't as devastated as you might think. I mourned terribly, but I knew that even if we couldn't have children of our own, Jimmy and I could still adopt. But Jimmy had other ideas. He waited until I got out of the hospital, then he informed me that he wanted a divorce."

Farrell couldn't remain silent. "That doesn't make any sense. If he didn't really want kids, he had the perfect excuse. And his job..."

"No, it made sense to Jimmy. You see, he had a new job by then, and no one was asking questions about his personal life anymore. But even though he wasn't sure if he'd ever want children, he *was* sure he wanted a wife who could have them. For Jimmy, adoption was out of the question. He felt it was his duty to pass on his own exceptional gene pool. Jimmy wanted everything he owned to be perfect, and in his eyes, I wasn't perfect anymore."

She had tried to finish as if she were telling a story about somebody else. But now she looked at him, and he saw the misery in her eyes. "He moved out. For months I just sat at home, frozen with grief. I had always wanted children, and now I couldn't have them. I had wanted a man like my father, and instead I'd married a man without an ounce of integrity. Jimmy didn't sit at home, of course. He found a young woman who worshiped him, one who could probably bear a dozen babies. Then, the night before his attorney was going to file the divorce papers, Jimmy ran a stop sign, and that was that. On the last day of his life, he couldn't stop long enough to let someone else have the right of way, and it killed him.''

She shook her head. ''Jimmy wasn't much for details. He hadn't gotten around to changing his will. I was still the beneficiary for his insurance policies, his pension. He bought insurance the way he bought everything else. Only the biggest and the best. It's the ultimate irony, isn't it, that Jimmy left me enough money so that I can spend my life raising other people's children?''

Farrell knew that the words he said now would be the most important of his life. He wished that he knew how to put his feelings into words. But all he could do was try.

''I'm sorry. I know how badly you were hurt.'' He wanted to reach out to her, but he knew better than to touch her yet. ''He was a bastard, Gemma.''

''That he was.''

''But you told me you know I'm nothing like him.''

''You're not, Farrell. Jimmy could talk about everything. What he was feeling, what he was supposed to be feeling, what he wanted me to think he was feeling.'' She shrugged. ''He could charm anyone until they couldn't see which end was up. Even my family was fooled, until the truth was right in front of them. Jimmy would say anything I wanted to hear. You tell the truth whether I want to hear it or not. And believe it or not, that's what I...'' She shook her head, as if she couldn't finish.

''I can see why you might have trouble trusting a man again.'' He was making his way carefully, like a man in a pitch-black room.

''I trust you.''

''Then what does this have to do with us, Gemma?'' he asked gently. ''After everything that happened, are you afraid? Do you need more time? I can give you all the time you need, even if it makes the adoption trickier. I can—''

''Farrell, I can't marry you, no matter what I feel. Don't you see? I was married to a man for almost seven years. I gave him everything. And in the end, he tossed me right out of his life because I couldn't give him children.''

''Do you think that matters to me?''

''Yes!'' She took a deep breath. ''A while ago you said something about the children we would have together.''

''Give me some credit here. I didn't know you couldn't have children. Do you think I would have said something like that if I did?''

''No. I know you wouldn't have. You're a good man. An honorable man. You'd marry me anyway, and just tuck that away. But sometimes, when you saw other people with their newborns, you'd wish, just a little, that you were holding your own child in your arms.''

''No, that's not—''

''Farrell, you have never had a family of your own! Never! And I can't give you one. If you married me, you would never have biological ties, not to one person on the face of this earth. Don't you think I know how important that is? I have family. I have nephews. Mark's hair is the color of mine. Shawn looks like my baby pictures. I don't have to bear children to see family all around me. I can love my nephews. I can love Mary. I can love the other children who come into my life. But I can't love you, because I know that in the end, you'll resent me for depriving you of your own babies.''

He couldn't find a thing to say. He was struck by two things simultaneously. One, that she believed every word she was saying, believed them so vehemently that her mind would not be changed tonight. The second was that she didn't *want* to believe them. But if he couldn't find a way to change her mind, they had no future together. In the very center of Gemma's heart was a place so bleak, so damaged by her ex-husband, that it would take a very special kind of healing to make her whole again.

She had healed him, or, at least, she had begun the process. Now he had to find a way to do the same for her. And he thought he knew what it might be, although the thought of it made him feel sick inside.

"You're wrong about everything," he said quietly. He reached for her hand and clasped it.

"I don't think so." She let him hold her hand, but hers was limp inside his, as if she were already schooling herself to let him go.

"We've talked enough tonight." He squeezed her hand, then turned away from her to find his clothes. "Keep tomorrow night clear for me, Gemma. I'm coming over after dinner. We'll finish this then."

"It's finished now, Farrell."

"No, you had your say. I get a turn. That's only fair."

"Nothing you can say will change my mind."

"I'm not going to say anything. I just have some things to show you."

She didn't answer.

"But there is one thing I didn't say tonight because I haven't had any practice." He zipped his pants and reached for his shirt; then he faced her again.

"Don't, Farrell, I—"

"I love you, Gemma, and I think you love me. I know this happened quickly, and that you don't trust it yet. But I never expected it to happen at all, so I'm going to fight hard to keep you. Nothing you've told me changes the way I feel. And nothing changes my intention of making a family with you. A real family."

She shook her head mournfully.

He came around the bed and pulled her head to rest against his belly. "Go to sleep. Don't think about this now. Just go to sleep. We'll settle this tomorrow."

Her cheek was wet against his skin. He smoothed her hair and prayed that tomorrow he would have the courage to make her understand the truth.

Chapter Eight

Gemma watched Mary running through the back-yard with Shawn right behind her. Katy had a doctor's appointment, and she had asked Gemma to baby-sit Shawn for the afternoon. The two children had played together several times since the picnic at Patty's, and they were well suited. Whenever Shawn visited, Mary seemed to evolve right before Gemma's eyes, as if she had just needed a role model so that she could learn how a child was supposed to act. On the other hand, Shawn was learning how to behave with a younger child, which was good, since Katy had told Gemma over lunch that she was pregnant again.

Right now the little boy was holding himself back, as if he were afraid that if he really caught Mary, the game would be over. Mary stepped into the rope net that webbed the skeletal pirate ship and began to climb, giggling as she crept higher and higher.

Gemma held her breath, but her foster daughter didn't stop or even falter until she had reached the top. It was a new milestone in Mary's development. This was not the child who had clung so pathetically to Gemma and Farrell. This was a child growing confident, a child who was growing in all the important ways.

A child who might one day be Gemma's very own.

Gemma dropped to the picnic bench and watched Mary begin her descent. She suspected a new game would ensue now. Mary would climb up and down until she tired of this new achievement, and Shawn would find some way to work this strange behavior into his own game. In years to come, would Shawn continue to adapt for this girl cousin? In ten years, or fifteen, would they still be friends, or would the rivalries and passions of adolescence separate them until they were adults again?

Whatever happened, it seemed that Gemma would be there to watch Mary grow, to suffer the pangs and joys of growing up with her. Thanks to Farrell Riley.

The grass was warm against her bare feet, and she wiggled her toes, taking her eyes off the children for a moment. Toes were as good for contemplation as belly buttons, and there were more of them. But more didn't change a thing. She could contemplate all day and well into the night, and nothing was going to change. She could not bear children. One man had already left her because of her infertility, and she could not ask another to give up having a family of his own.

Last night she hadn't gotten any sleep after Farrell left. She had tried to convince herself she was wrong, that her inability to bear children wasn't a good enough reason to destroy her future happiness. But as many times as she had gone over it, she hadn't changed her mind. When Jimmy had left her, she had sworn she would never be that vulnerable again. She would rather be lonely than pitied or resented.

Tears stung her eyes, and she took a deep breath. She loved Farrell Riley. She knew that she had never really loved Jimmy. She had loved Jimmy's image, the glow that surrounded him, the man he pretended to be. But the Farrell Riley she loved was the man inside the human shell, the passionate, sensitive, yearning man. The man who deserved the biological ties, the family he'd never had.

"Ma..." Mary ran full tilt in Gemma's direction and threw herself into her lap. She clasped Gemma around the neck and buried her face in Gemma's shoulder. And again she used the word she had heard Shawn use with Katy. "Ma..."

Gemma hugged her until the little girl began to wriggle in protest. There were no breaths deep enough to keep tears from sliding down Gemma's cheeks. "Oh, Mary."

"Ma..." Mary touched her cheek and frowned.

"I'm just happy," Gemma explained. And she was. Mary was going to be her real daughter now. In the ways that mattered, she already was. Gemma hadn't even dared to dream this might happen so soon. Yet even while she stroked Mary's hair and murmured her name, the tears continued to slide down her cheeks.

The box under Farrell's arm was as heavy as lead. His heart was nearly as heavy. He had taken the afternoon off work, and he had spent it digging memories out of his attic. He hoped he never spent another afternoon exactly the same way. He would rather take his chances on the worst streets of Hazleton than dig through his past. But if this was what it took to convince Gemma that he wanted her forever, then he would do it every day without flinching until she saw the truth.

He hadn't told her when he would be coming, and he hadn't called before he left the house. He imagined he was catching her at dinnertime, which was what he had hoped for. He wanted to see Mary. If he couldn't make his case tonight, he didn't know how often he would see the little girl in the future. The thought of losing Mary, like the thought of losing Gemma, was something he couldn't contemplate.

As a child, he hadn't been able to fight for what he wanted.

But he was not a child anymore.

He knocked and waited, looking around as he did. The pansies in planters flanking the front steps were wilting in the late-afternoon sun, as if Gemma had forgotten to water them. Mary's plastic tricycle lay turned on its side next to the front door, and dried leaves huddled against the morning paper, which had never been taken inside.

Gemma appeared at the front door, a Gemma without a smile or one trace of makeup. Her eyes widened. "I thought you'd be by later."

His other reason for coming at dinnertime was to throw her off guard. He could see he'd succeeded. "I was hoping you'd feed me. I brought dessert." He held up a bakery box containing a fresh apple pie. "If you don't have enough, I could just eat the pie."

She smiled, almost as if she couldn't help herself. Then she sobered. "Don't you think we should do this after Mary goes to bed?"

"Absolutely. I'll wait."

She shook her head, but she let him in. And once inside, he had no intention of leaving until this was settled in his favor.

Mary covered the awkward silence in the hall by dashing into Farrell's arms. Gemma grabbed the pie just in time, and he lifted Mary with one arm, protecting the box under his other arm.

"Can I take that, too?" Gemma asked.

"I'll put it in the living room." He didn't explain. He carried Mary with him, setting the box on a table out of her reach.

In the kitchen, he watched Gemma open the refrigerator and peer inside. She didn't look at him. "I was just going to cook a hamburger patty for Mary.

I have some carrots from last night. I hadn't even thought about what I'd make for myself.''

"Why don't I order a pizza?"

The suggestion seemed to startle her. "Pizza?"

"Yeah, you know, crust, sauce, pepperoni. No work for anybody except dialing the telephone.''

"I never order pizza."

He suspected there were a number of things she hadn't learned in her first marriage that she would learn in her second. He was not marrying her to be taken care of. He was marrying her to share her life.

"Sit," he ordered. "All you have to do is think about what toppings you want.''

"I don't care.''

"Then I'll get a supreme, and you can take off whatever you don't like.''

She sat, almost as if she were in a trance. He grinned at her, forcing a confidence he didn't feel, and picked up the telephone. He knew the number by heart, since pizza was a cop's best friend. When he hung up the phone, she was still sitting and staring at him as if he'd just been transported to earth from a spaceship.

"Okay, where's the hamburger? Our little girl may like this pizza just fine, but she needs something healthier to start her off.''

"Oh." Color rose in Gemma's cheeks, and she started to get to her feet.

"Sit," he ordered again. "And stay there. You look beat. Just tell me where to find everything."

She didn't argue. With her supervision, he found and unwrapped a hamburger patty and started it sizzling in a small frying pan. He found the cooked carrots next and slipped them into the microwave; then he poured Mary a plastic tumbler of milk and set her in her high chair with a slice of bread and jam.

By the time the hamburger and carrots were on a plate in front of Mary, he had found two ice-cold beers and poured them for himself and Gemma. Mary filled the strained silence with comments on the food in front of her, some of them amazingly close to standard English. As soon as she started putting sounds together in a slightly different order, Farrell's little girl was going to be quite a linguist.

The pizza arrived before the silence between the two adults stretched too thin. Farrell retrieved it and paid the deliveryman. Then, back in the kitchen, he dished it up, with a small piece for Mary, too.

He joined Gemma at the table. "You've given me a good taste of your life. You need a taste of mine. That way, when you marry me, you'll know exactly what you're getting."

"Farrell—"

He shook his head. "Eat up before it gets cold."

Mary was an instant pizza convert. She gobbled her slice, then a slice of apple pie, fretting when she couldn't have another. Farrell made the disappointment up to her by giving her a horsey ride around the house while Gemma cleaned the kitchen.

Gemma rescued the little girl after a good long gallop and took her upstairs for a bath, but Farrell was the one who read her a good-night story and tucked her into bed. Mary pointed at pictures in the simple storybook, as if she was memorizing the names of every animal and object. Just as soon as she had the vocabulary she needed, Farrell's little girl was going to be quite a reader.

He left the door open, just in case she needed anything, but one last peek in her direction convinced him she was falling asleep. He stood at the top of the stairs for a moment, girding himself for what was to come; then he went down to find Gemma.

He found her in the living room. "Do you want your pie now? I could make some coffee to go with it."

She shook her head. "I couldn't eat another thing."

"Then we'll save it for later."

She looked as if she wasn't sure there would be a later. In fact, she looked as if she was sure there *wouldn't* be. "She adores you."

"She knows it's mutual."

"You're so good with her. You're a natural with children."

"Who would have guessed it?"

She didn't ask him to sit beside her, but he did, anyway. "I had some news this morning."

"Oh?"

"I'm moving up to detective."

"That's wonderful." For the first time that evening, her eyes lit up. "That's really wonderful.... Is it a dangerous job?"

He smiled, because she hadn't managed to keep the concern out of her voice. "No more so than any other job on the force. And I'll be spending a lot more time on investigations. The hours won't be as regular, and I'm sorry about that. But if I work long hours one week, I can take time off the next."

"I'm proud of you."

He wondered what else he could say about the promotion. He wanted to keep talking about other things. He would have been happy to talk about almost anything to keep from discussing what he'd come for. But the time had arrived.

"Farrell, I—"

"Gemma, I—"

They both stopped. Gemma flushed. "I've given this a lot of thought, Farrell. That's all I've done. And I still—"

He held up his hand. "I have some things to show you. Can I do that first? Then you can tell me what you think, and I promise I'll listen. I promise I'll always listen to you. But this time, I need to go first."

She looked doubtful, but she nodded.

He stood and retrieved the box from the table where he'd set it; then he brought it over to the sofa. "Come sit beside me. You can see better."

She scooted closer. "What is it?"

"It's my childhood, Gemma. My life."

He had been very careful about how he had placed things in the box. Now he opened it, spreading the cardboard flaps so that the contents were in view. He lifted out a worn scrapbook with a padded plastic cover. The cover was torn, but it had been neatly taped. One of his foster mothers had discovered the scrapbook in the destructive hands of a foster brother, and she had helped Farrell repair both the cover and some of the inside pages. She had been one of the important people.

He was not a man to make speeches, but now he knew he was about to make the longest speech of his life. "I've told you a little about the way I grew up. But not enough."

"I thought it was something you probably didn't want to talk about."

"You were right. But you need to know me better." He balanced the scrapbook on his knees and opened it to the first page. Dust filtered through the air. The scrapbook had been stored away for years, and although he had carefully wiped off the cover, he hadn't touched the inside pages.

The photo on the first page had been imprinted on

his brain from hours of staring at it as a child. He hadn't seen it for a long time, but he hadn't needed to.

"This is my mother. Her name was Noreen, Noreen Wakefield. She grew up on a small farm in Iowa. Wakefields owned that farm for five generations."

"She was lovely." Gemma touched the edge of the photograph. "You look a little like her."

"I've been told that before." He did resemble the woman in the photograph—the same dark hair, the same straight nose. But his mother was smiling with the exuberance of youth, and he had never felt that kind of joyful abandon.

He touched the edge of the photograph. "She was seventeen when this photograph was taken. Just out of high school. She moved to Des Moines right afterward. She moved to bigger and bigger cities after that to escape her roots. She did a good job of it."

He turned the page. "These are her parents." The snapshot, probably taken with an ancient box camera, was faded and unfocused. It showed two people in front of a small frame house. An old pickup was parked beside them. "I never met my grandparents. A great-aunt, my grandfather's stepsister, sent me this photo when I was in high school. She would write me occasionally. She was very old and unwell, but even though we weren't related by blood, she tried to stay in touch with me. Her name was Hattie.''

He turned the page again and pointed to the first of two photos. ''That's Hattie.'' The snapshot was slightly more focused then the one of his grandparents. Hattie was a prim-looking woman, with the weathered face of someone who had worked hard and seldom pampered herself.

''This is Hattie's sister, Clara. I never met her. I think she died before I was born.'' The photo was similar to the one of Hattie, and he moved on to the next page.

There was no photograph here, just a small plastic bag filled with dirt. ''This is soil from the family farm. When I got out of high school and the state of Illinois couldn't tell me what to do anymore, I hitch-hiked to Iowa. Hattie was dead by then, but I wanted to see where my family had lived. The farm is still in cultivation, but it's owned by a huge conglomerate now. The house is used for hay storage.''

Gemma gazed up at him. ''What happened? Didn't anyone in your family want it anymore?''

''It was auctioned to pay off debts back in the seventies.'' He turned the page to one showing two young men, standing with cocky indifference under a large oak tree. ''These are my mother's two brothers, Alfred and Gary. I lived with Gary once for a few months, until the state stepped in and put me into a foster home.''

"Why?"

"Let me show you the rest of the album first."

She looked puzzled, but she nodded. "Okay."

He turned the page and revealed a stack of letters. "These are Hattie's letters. I kept every one of them."

He turned the page again. "This is my father, Paul Riley."

The man in the photograph didn't resemble Farrell in any way. He had a wide face and curly blond hair. He was dressed in a cheap polyester suit, and his shirt was unbuttoned to show a substantial portion of bare chest and three gold chains. "And *this* is my father," he said, turning the page.

The second picture was a fading newspaper photo of the same man, but this time he wasn't wearing a sly smile. He looked surly and mean. The headline beside it read Local Man Arrested In Robbery.

Farrell turned the page again without looking at Gemma. "This is the transcript of a hearing dated just after my birth. I filed for and got this when I was twenty-one."

"A hearing?"

"My mother tried to get child support from my father, but he claimed that I wasn't really his son. For all I know, he may have been right. I saw Noreen on and off through the years before she died, just often enough to keep the state from severing her parental rights, but she never would tell me if Paul

Riley was my real dad. The court seemed to think
he was. They told him he had to pay support for me,
but it didn't really matter, because he never had any
money—at least, none that he could claim on his
income tax.''

He turned to the last page. It was a collection of
short newspaper articles, all detailing the conclusion
of criminal trials or subsequent sentencing. Paul Riley was the subject of them all.

Farrell closed the scrapbook. ''I had similar articles about my mother, Gemma. I tore them out and
threw them away the last time I looked through this.
I'm not sure why. Noreen wasn't any better than
Paul, although at least she admitted I was her child.
She and her brothers left the farm in Iowa and never
looked back. She wanted the good life. She told me
once that she didn't want to end up like her mother,
bitter and depleted, so she went looking for something else. Only, she didn't take any of the values
she'd learned in church as a child. She stole and lied
and used her body to get whatever she could from
men. She got pregnant with me and tried to use me
to get money from Paul. When that didn't work, she
gave me to the state to raise.''

''What about your grandparents? Didn't they try
to help you?''

''I was born late in my mother's life. My grandparents were old, and they had washed their hands
of all their children by the time I was born. Alfred

and Gary had turned out like my mother, using whatever they could to get whatever they wanted. My grandparents had mortgaged the farm to help their sons out of one jam or the other. In the end, they were so deeply in debt they couldn't recover."

"But none of that was your fault, Farrell. How could they take it out on you?"

"In one of her letters Hattie said that my grandparents were rigid people who only saw the world a certain way. They thought that anything that didn't fit into their views was no good. My mother was obviously no good, and so, in their eyes, I couldn't be, either. And a child born out of wedlock didn't fit into their picture. They never even wrote to me."

"Maybe your mother turned out the way she did because of them."

"Maybe she did. And maybe I was better off not having them in my life. Unfortunately, like I said before, I had one of my uncles for a while. Gary took me in when I was seven. He looked good on paper, I guess. He had a wife, a job. He'd been in trouble with the law, but the court thought that he'd cleaned up his act. They didn't know he wanted me because he needed a child to stand watch for him."

"Stand watch?"

"His talents ran to burglary. He set me up with an ice cream cone and a puppy he got from the pound, and the puppy and I would walk back and forth, up and down the block, while he broke into houses. If

I saw a police car, I whistled. Unfortunately, Gary was cockier than he was smart. He got caught on our third trip out. I got sent back to foster care, and the puppy went back to the pound.''

"Farrell..." Gemma laid her hand on his arm. "You're breaking my heart. Why are you telling me this?"

"Those are the people I came from, Gemma. They're my blood, the stuff that I'm made from. At the worst they were criminals. At the best they were rigid and bitter, with no joy or love in their souls for their only grandchild. I thought you should know.''

"Why? Do you think it matters to me what your family was like? You're *you,* and you're nothing like them!"

He let that sink in a moment. He wanted her to think about what she'd said. "I'm not," he said quietly. "You're right. I'm the man I am because of some people I met along the way. Not because of the people whose bloodlines I carry.''

Gemma watched Farrell's face. He had not shared this story of his family often. She knew him well enough to know that. But he wasn't ashamed. She knew that, too. Farrell had grown past the family who had given him life. He knew who he was and what was in his own heart. He knew which side of the law he stood on, and he was a proud, confident man.

Gemma couldn't think of anything to say in response to what she had learned about him. Farrell's family was as different from hers as the county jail was from Shore Haven. She understood what he was trying to say, and she wanted to accept it, to reach out to him and tell him that they could make a different kind of family together. But she was still so tied up in her own misery, her own failures, that the words wouldn't come.

Farrell seemed to understand. He reached inside the box for a second album. This one was stuffed full. He opened it before she could speak. "I had ten foster homes. Six of them didn't make it into this album. Four of them did."

He opened the album to the first page. "These are the Jensens. I was only with them a year, but Sarah taught me to read. She wasn't a warm, welcoming woman, but she took her job seriously. I was a shy seven-year-old. I'd been moved twice in first grade. At the beginning of second grade I went to live with Gary, and he didn't send me to school. By the time the Jensens got me, I was so far behind that the schools decided I was slow. Sarah wouldn't have that. No child in her care could possibly be slow. So she drilled me every night until I was in tears. But she taught me to read, and I never had trouble in school after that, no matter how many schools I attended. Sarah made me understand I could do anything I wanted if I just tried hard enough."

He smiled at the picture of the Jensens. It wasn't

a photograph, but a childish drawing of two blond and overweight adults. He turned the page to a yellowing school paper printed neatly on wide lines. "My first A. Sarah's doing. She's the one who bought me this scrapbook." He turned the page again. "My first good report card. Sarah smiled when she saw it. It might be the only time she did."

Gemma put her hand on his arm. "You don't have to go on, Farrell."

"I think I do." He continued showing her mementos of the other homes where he'd learned the things he needed to become an adult. She listened to him tell about the Watkinses, who had taught him to take care of himself with older, rougher boys. The Petersons, who had given him music lessons and bought him exactly the right kind of clothes so that he would fit in with the other thirteen-year-olds at his school. The Lamberts, who had attended every school conference and even every football game the year he had warmed the bench for junior varsity.

He ran his finger along the snapshot of a nondescript older woman. "Mrs. Lambert was the one who helped me repair that first scrapbook. When the county tried to move me in my senior year, she and her husband threatened them with a lawsuit. She was there when I graduated from the police academy, too, although she was in the last stages of cancer. Through the years I started to think of those four families as 'the important ones.' They weren't my families by blood, but they gave me the things I needed to become a man.''

He closed the second album with its collection of photographs and pictures, its school papers and report cards.

He set it back in the box, then turned so he could see Gemma's face. Her eyes were clouded with tears, and she couldn't speak.

He did. ''You were right when you said I needed my own family, Gemma. You were right, because I *do* have things I need to pass on to my children. I need to teach them that they can do anything if they try hard enough, just the way Sarah Jensen taught me. I need to teach them to take care of themselves and not to be afraid, the way Sam Watkins did. I need to show them I understand how important it is to explore new parts of yourself and to fit in, the way the Petersons did. And I need to show them that I care what they do and what they feel, the way the Lamberts did.''

He took her hand. His was warm and strong, a hand that wrapped around hers protectively. ''Those are the things I need to pass on to my children, Gemma, the very best parts of myself. Not my genes. Not my heritage. The man I am *despite* that heritage. You've come to terms with your inability to bear children. Now you have to come to terms with my acceptance of it.''

''Farrell...''

He spoke the next words slowly. "I don't care where my sons and daughters come from, Gemma, but I do care desperately who their mother is."

Tears flowed down her cheeks—healing, renewing tears. She hadn't meant to cry. It seemed wrong, when her heart was so filled with hope and with love for him. He lifted her hand to his lips and kissed it. "Marry me. Share my life. Let's make a real family together."

She moved into his arms as naturally as if she had never moved out of them.

He kissed her, and she kissed him back. As he held her, in her mind she saw the family they would make, a family filled with love and warmth and laughter.

She pulled away at last, and he wiped the tears off her cheeks with his thumbs.

"I love you," she whispered. "I will forever. When we have grandchildren and great-grand-children—"

"Ma?"

Gemma turned and saw Mary standing in the doorway. Her thumb was firmly in her mouth and her blanket was trailing behind her. Mary, the first of the children they would raise and love together. Farrell put one arm around Gemma and held out the other. Mary flew across the room and scrambled into his lap.

Farrell Riley enclosed his family in his arms.

*   *   *   *   *

Dear Reader,

I was so pleased when Silhouette® invited me to be a part of this tribute to mothers. 'Mother's Day Baby' is a story that is especially dear to my heart.

Like my heroine, Christina Richards, I also travelled to China to adopt a beautiful, three-month-old baby girl I named Autumn. I was a single mother with three grown daughters, while Christina was experiencing the miracle of motherhood for the first time.

Through Christina's journey, I relived my wonderful memories of the people of China, the fabulous White Swan Hotel, the scenic tours and shopping in the marketplaces.

I actually wept tears of joy as I wrote the scene in the orphanage when Christina saw and held *her* Autumn for the first time, as that was how it happened with me and *my* Autumn.

But Christina Richards had an added ingredient in her adventure in the form of handsome Daniel Shay. He was the last thing she expected to find halfway around the world.

Daniel, too, was very surprised to have his life become so complicated when he took a temporary assignment in the American consulate in Guangzhou.

You'll follow Christina and Daniel down the bumpy road to love, and watch their Autumn blossom into a happy, heart-tugging little girl.

I hope you enjoy 'Mother's Day Baby.' I am delighted to have the opportunity to share Christina and Daniel's romance with you, have you get to know their Autumn and, in a way, introduce you to my daughter, as well.

Warmest regards,

Joan Elliott Pickart

MOTHER'S DAY BABY

Joan Elliott Pickart

For my fourth daughter,
Autumn Joan Pickart
Born: June 21, 1995
Nanjing, China
Home: September 27, 1995

Chapter One

Christina Richards stared intently out of the window of the van, attempting to memorize every detail of what she was seeing.

The driver of the van was leaning on the horn, but the loud, insistent noise had little effect on the cars in his path, nor on the multitude of people riding bicycles in the midst of the surging, congested traffic.

Guangzhou, China, Christina thought incredulously. She was really here. After all the months of paperwork, of hurry-up-and-wait, of having no idea as to when this journey would actually take place, she was truly here. It was unbelievable.

Guangzhou, she mentally repeated. She must remember to pronounce it correctly, picture in her mind the phonetic spelling of the foreign word that she'd practiced saying. *Gwuan-joe.*

"It's quite a sight, isn't it?" a woman said.

Christina turned to smile at her seatmate, Libby Duling.

Libby was the representative from Little Hands Overseas Adoptions, who was accompanying Christina and four other couples on this eagerly anticipated trip. An attractive woman in her early fifties, Libby was the steadying force among the excited travelers, making certain that everything went as smoothly as possible.

"It's incredible," Christina said. "There are so many people out there. Those who are riding bikes are certainly brave souls. They're right in the middle of the maze, demanding their place in the traffic flow."

"I know," Libby said, laughing. "The first time I made this trip, I kept closing my eyes so I wouldn't see what I was certain would be a bicyclist struck by a car. But this is my seventh time in Guangzhou and I've yet to witness an accident. That's organized chaos out there, I guess." She turned slightly in her seat. "How's everyone doing?"

Libby's question was answered by smiles and nods.

"If we lived here," one woman said, laughing, "I'd be set on automatic No when Hannah asked if she could go outside and ride her bike."

Everyone laughed, and Libby settled back again in her seat.

"Hannah," she said, looking at Christina again. "That's a lovely, old-fashioned name they've chosen for their new daughter. Let's see. We're to have a Hannah, Emily, Kaylee, Kate and, of course, your Autumn."

"Autumn Christina Richards," Christina said with a wistful sigh. "Oh, Libby, I'm not sure I believe I'm really here in China, in Autumn's birth country.

It's all been a hope, a dream and a prayer, for so many months and..." She stopped speaking and shook her head.

"You're having a perfectly normal, butterflies-in-the-tummy reaction," Libby said, patting Christina's knee. "Want to add some more butterflies? If everything stays as scheduled, this very afternoon you'll be seeing and holding your three-month-old daughter for the first time."

"Oh-h-h," Christina said, pressing one hand on her stomach. "That did it. Another flock of butterflies swooshed right in with those already there."

Libby laughed in delight, then announced that she needed everyone's passport so she could register them all at the White Swan Hotel, where they would be staying for the next ten days.

Christina retrieved her passport from her huge tote bag, gave it to Libby, then looked out the window again.

Autumn Christina Richards, her mind echoed. In a few hours she might very well be holding her daughter. In a few hours she, Christina Richards, also known as Auntie Ann to those who read the children's books she wrote, would have the official title of Mother.

Pure and wondrous joy swept through Christina like a warm waterfall, filling her to overflowing.

The decision to become a single mother had not been an easy one to make, she mused. She'd written a long list of pros and cons, weighed and measured, sifted and sorted, wanting, *needing,* to know she was doing the right thing, not only for herself but for a child, as well.

Finally after weeks of thinking, thinking, thinking, the inner peace had come, the serene feeling of rightness about moving forward with her dream.

She'd filed an application with Little Hands and the paper trail had begun. She'd taken it step-by-step—getting a physical examination; obtaining a copy of her divorce decree with a court seal; filling out a packet containing seemingly endless questions about her childhood, her career, her views on parenting.

A social worker had conducted a home study to make it possible for Christina to obtain the certification to adopt that she needed in Maricopa County in Arizona.

On and on it had gone. This document, that document, requesting the signature of the secretary of state, having everything translated into Chinese, to finally produce a completed bundle that was labeled her dossier.

Little Hands sent the dossier winging its way to the powers that be in Beijing, China. Then the silence. Then the waiting. Then the emotional roller coaster as days turned into weeks, with no report of an approval from Beijing for her dossier and the heartfelt request to adopt a Chinese baby girl.

There were days, Christina remembered, when she began to doubt that it would really happen, that a baby named Autumn was waiting for her somewhere in China, waiting for Christina to come and take her home.

And there were days she did believe that Autumn would be a reality. As she prepared the pretty nursery done in pale yellow and mint green and stood next to the empty crib, she could clearly envision a baby sleeping there, *her* baby, her daughter.

Then two weeks ago the telephone had rung. Christina had been working on her new book and had almost let the answering machine pick up the call. Deciding she needed a break, she'd lifted the receiver just before the machine clicked on.

"Hello?" she had said, rather absently.

"Christina? This is Libby Duling from Little Hands. How are you today?"

"Hello, Libby. I'm fine, just fine," Christina replied, very aware of the increased tempo of her heart.

"Well, Mother," Libby said, "would you like to know how old your daughter is?"

"Oh, dear heaven," Christina said, pressing one hand to her forehead.

"Autumn Christina Richards," Libby said, "is two and a half months old. We received from Beijing, five matches of babies to parents, and our group will be traveling to Guangzhou, China, in two weeks.

So, your Autumn will just be turning three months old when you get her.''

"Oh, dear heaven," Christina repeated. "Oh, Libby, I... Oh, my, I just..." Christina sniffled as tears filled her eyes. "Oh-h-h."

Libby laughed. "That's a very appropriate and familiar reaction you're having. Go right ahead and cry. After all, this is the telephone call you were convinced at times would never come.

"The pictures of the babies should be arriving soon, and we'll be having what's called a travel meeting to instruct everyone on the do's and don'ts of being a visitor in China. I'll speak with you soon, Christina. Oh, and congratulations. Bye.''

Christina smiled as she continued to look out the window of the van.

But the pictures of the babies had never arrived, she thought. They had gotten lost in the mail somewhere between Beijing, China, and the Little Hands office in Phoenix, Arizona.

All any of them knew about their daughters was the date they were born. Well, that was fair. After all, Autumn didn't know what her mommy looked like, either.

The van whizzed its way into a short, dark tunnel and Christina was suddenly staring at her own reflection in the window.

Do I look like a mother? she wondered. Yes, she supposed so. Mothers came in all shapes, sizes, ages and nationalities. She was an average-appearing woman of thirty-five, five feet six inches tall with short, curly black hair and blue eyes.

She was a tad too thin, she'd decided years before, but no amount of eating changed her weight. According to those around her, her eyes were her best feature. It was very striking, friends said, to have blue eyes, fair skin and black hair.

The van emerged on the other side of the tunnel and Christina was once again looking at bustling Guangzhou.

What difference did it make what she looked like? What was important was who she was inside, how she felt about Autumn Christina Richards in the section of her heart that had yearned for so very long to be a mother, to hold her child in her arms. She loved Autumn, sight unseen. Autumn was her daughter, and soon, very soon now, she'd see her baby for the first time.

The van came to an abrupt halt, jarring Christina from her thoughts.

"The White Swan Hotel," Libby sang out. "This is the finest hotel in Guangzhou, and it's where the presidents who visit this city always stay. Collect your luggage, please, from the back of the van and stay together in the lobby while I get us all registered. Off we go."

In a flurry of activity the excited, chattering group claimed their suitcases. They'd all gasped in shock during the travel meeting when they'd been told they could take only one suitcase and one carry-on bag into China.

"Pack for your baby," Libby had said. "That suitcase needs to hold about eight dozen diapers, formula, bottles, baby clothes and blankets. Take about three changes of clothes for yourself and use the hotel laundry service, which is excellent."

"I bet we won't ever want to see those three outfits again," one of the woman had said, smiling.

Libby had laughed. "That's a given."

They entered the lobby of the White Swan and everyone stopped speaking as they walked slowly forward, awed by what they saw.

There were large, intricate sculptures of sailing ships, pagodas, dragons and Buddhas carved out of jade, coral and ivory on display. The tall hotel was built in an atrium style, with a waterfall cascading at the far end.

A small bridge crossed the water beneath the waterfall on the lower level and fish swam about lazily in the pond. A throng of people were taking pictures of each other on the bridge with the majestic waterfall as a backdrop.

"It's all so beautiful," Christina said as they gathered by a railing to wait for Libby. "In all my travels I don't remember ever seeing anything quite this breathtaking."

"I know I haven't," a young woman said, laughing. "I haven't been anywhere."

"Bill and I have traveled a great deal," another woman said, "but this tops anything we've seen. Don't you agree, honey?"

"I sure do," Bill said. "Did you see the detail work on the ship carved out of jade? It's unbelievable."

Christina let her gaze sweep over her traveling companions, knowing there was a special bond between them. They were all in China to fulfill their dream of having a child, of becoming parents. Their ages ranged from mid-thirties to late forties and they'd all been matched with babies under a year old.

"Christina—" one of the woman said quietly as the others continued to exclaim over the exquisite sculptures and the unique waterfall.

"Yes, Kathy?" Christina said, smiling.

"I'm suddenly terrified. I'm about to become a mother, for heaven's sake. What do I know about being a mother of a five-month-old baby? Nothing, absolutely nothing. I've been reading books on parenting for months now and I swear I've forgotten every word."

"I'm no expert, believe me," Christina said. "All we can do is love our daughters. Beyond that, wing it."

"You're so brave to be taking this on all alone," Kathy said.

"Or out of my mind," Christina said, laughing. Her smile faded. "I'm just grateful that the Chinese government allows single mothers to adopt."

"I'm not sure I believe we're really here after all these months."

"I know what you mean," Christina said. "And later today, hopefully, we'll see and hold our daughters. We're in the midst of a miracle, Kathy."

Daniel Shay entered the White Swan and headed for the registration desk, a suitcase in each hand.

Snazzy place, he thought, glancing around quickly as he got in line at the desk. He'd heard that the White Swan was something to behold, but it went far beyond what he'd expected.

Well, good. Maybe staying at a ritzy hotel would brighten his dark mood. Then again, he'd been in such a lousy frame of mind for the past month, the opulence of the White Swan probably wouldn't even dent his gloom.

Daniel sighed and set his suitcases on the floor as he heard the woman in front of him tell the clerk she was checking in her entire group.

She was probably a tour director, accompanied by a slew of people who were thrilled out of their socks to be in China. Judging from the woman's accent, she was an American, was from the good old U.S. of A. The tourists with her would enjoy their adventure on the other side of the world, then when the trip was over be glad to be once again at home.

Home. After a dozen years of living overseas as a high-ranking official in American consulates in Paris, London and Moscow, he was going home. He'd received his new assignment of Washington, D.C., a month ago, with the usual wind-down procedure, and had been frowning ever since.

Home, Daniel's mind echoed again. Small word. Big problem. He didn't *have* a home. There was nothing, and no one, waiting for him in the States. Nothing except memories. Painful memories.

His request for another overseas assignment had been denied, the big boys in charge having decided that Daniel Shay was long overdue to reconnect with his country, the people, the workings of the government, in order to perform his duties efficiently. Damn.

Well, he'd delayed the undesired inevitable for another couple of weeks. The employees of the consulate in Guangzhou had been hit hard by the flu, the remaining people unable to carry out all the duties required of them. So here he was, Shay to the rescue, zooming in to take charge and save the day. Big deal.

Tired of his own rambling thoughts, Daniel tuned out his brain and tuned back in to the conversation between the woman standing in front of him and the attractive Asian woman behind the desk.

"There you are, Mrs. Duling," the clerk said.

"The keys and the passports. The cribs are already in the rooms, as you requested in your cable. The attendants on your floor have been notified that you'll be bringing in babies soon, and they are ready to assist you in any way possible."

"Thank you so much," Libby said. "Everything is perfect, per usual, which is why we always stay here at the White Swan when we make these wonderful trips. If we're able to go to the orphanage this afternoon, we'll be bringing the babies to the hotel tomorrow."

"We'll be ready," the clerk said, smiling.

Libby scooped up the keys and passports, then turned to see a tall, handsome man standing behind her.

"Daniel Shay," he said to the clerk.

"Yes, sir," the woman said.

"Excuse me," Daniel said to Libby.

"Yes?"

"I couldn't help overhearing what you were just saying. You're in China to adopt babies?"

"Yes," Libby said, smiling. "I'm Libby Duling, one of the agency representatives from Little Hands Overseas Adoptions. I've brought in a group from America—Phoenix, Arizona, to be precise—to adopt and take home five precious little girls."

Daniel matched her smile. "That's nice, very nice. I'm the man who will be issuing visas for those babies. I'm Daniel Shay, and I'm on temporary assign-

ment here at the consulate because they've been hit
by a flu bug. I'm sort of stopping off on my way
from Moscow to the States—Washington, D.C., to
be exact.''

"How marvelous to meet you," Libby said.
"Why don't I introduce you to my group? We won't
have completed all the red tape and be ready for your
services for almost ten days, but I think it would be
lovely for them to feel connected to you and those
coveted visas early on.''

"Sure thing," Daniel said. "Just let me finish registering.''

Daniel proceeded with checking in by rote as he
mentally shook his head.

Brother, he thought. He had just oozed diplomatic
charm ad nauseam. He didn't have to be hit by a
brick to realize how sick he was of his own lousy
company. He'd put off going to his room by agreeing
to meet a bunch of starry-eyed parents-to-be. Lord,
he was in worse shape than he'd realized.

After requesting that his luggage be taken to his
room, Daniel pocketed his key and passport and produced his best, albeit phony, smile for Libby Duling.

"All right, Mrs. Duling," he said. "Lead on.''

"Oh, call me Libby.''

"And I'm Daniel.''

"Daniel, it is. My people are across the lobby
there by the railing.''

Libby started off at a brisk pace and Daniel fell in step beside her.

"My goodness," one of the woman said, "look what they gave Libby at the registration desk. Talk about a yummy souvenir."

"You can't have one of those," her husband said, laughing. "I'll buy you some chopsticks, though."

Everyone in the group turned in the direction the couple was looking.

To say "my goodness," Christina thought, was putting it mildly. The man coming their way with Libby was, without a doubt, one of the most attractive members of the male species she'd ever seen. He was the epitome of the age-old cliché of tall, dark and handsome.

He was, oh, maybe thirty-eight or forty, had thick, dark hair and rugged features, with a square jaw and a straight blade of a nose. Wide shoulders, long legs, custom-tailored suit that fit him to perfection and, well, my goodness, Libby did, indeed, know how to select her souvenirs.

"Everyone," Libby said, beaming as she halted in front of the group, "this is Daniel Shay."

Christina listened to Libby's explanation as to who Daniel Shay was while she finished her mental inventory of him at the same time.

There were a few strands of gray at his temples, she mused, that were going to result in his looking even more distinguished when they multiplied. The gray, plus the tiny lines by his eyes, pushed him closer to forty. His eyes were very dark, his teeth were pearly white and as straight as a row of Chiclets. Yes, indeed, he was poster perfect. Except for the fact that his smile was as phony as a three-dollar bill.

She'd had to produce her share of plastic smiles when she was exhausted to the bone during book-signing tours, so she recognized one when she saw it.

Well, she wouldn't fault Daniel Shay for his mannequin smile. In diplomatic school, they probably took a class in how to create them.

"And this is our single mother-to-be," Libby was saying, "Christina Richards, also known as Auntie Ann."

"Pardon me?" Daniel said, frowning slightly.

"Christina is a well-known author of children's books," Libby said, "and writes as Auntie Ann. Her characters have been used in board games, made into puppets, dolls, all kinds of wonderful things for the kiddies."

"Oh, I see," Daniel said. "I'm not familiar with them, I'm afraid. I've been out of the loop, having lived overseas for a dozen years."

"But now you're going home to Washington, D.C.," Libby said. "You must be so delighted. Well, say hello to Christina."

Daniel shifted his gaze to the woman in question and immediately felt his pulse quicken.

Christina Richards, he thought, was absolutely lovely. She wasn't stunningly beautiful, nor voluptuous, by any means. Yet there was a delicate, feminine aura about her that would definitely turn men's heads when she entered a room.

Her short, curly dark hair appeared silky, beckoning to him to sift his fingers through it. Her sapphire blue eyes were a dramatic contrast to that dark hair, and her skin was as exquisitely fair as a porcelain doll.

Christina certainly didn't look like any "auntie" he'd ever had while growing up. She was, perhaps, in her early thirties, and was tall and slender. He usually preferred a more well-endowed woman, but Christina had struck a sensual cord within him. The flash of heat that had coiled instantly low in his body was proof of that pudding.

"Ms. Richards," he said, nodding.

"Christina," she said, smiling, "and I guess everyone in our group is going to call you Daniel. After all, you play an intricate role in our journey. You'll issue the visas that will make it possible for us to take our new daughters home."

"Yes. Yes, I will," Daniel said, unable to tear his gaze from Christina's compelling blue eyes. "You're going to be raising your baby alone?"

Christina lifted her chin a notch. "Yes, I am. Autumn and I will be a wonderful team. My office is in my home and I'll be able to work around her schedule while she's tiny. When she's more active I'll either have someone come in to watch her while I'm busy, or take her to day care, where she can interact with other children.''

''You said tiny,'' Daniel said. ''Just how old is your Autumn?''

''She'll turn three months this week.''

''Whew,'' Daniel said. ''You really are taking on the whole nine yards of motherhood, aren't you? How will you write on a given day if you've walked the floor all night with a fussing infant?''

''I'll manage.'' Christina cocked her head slightly to one side and frowned. ''I'm getting the distinct impression that you don't quite approve of single women adopting babies, Mr. Shay.''

''I didn't say that, Ms. Richards. I was merely remarking on the fact that you're embarking on a tremendous undertaking.''

''I assure you that I'm aware of that,'' Christina said coolly.

''Well...um...let's get organized, shall we?'' Libby said, her eyes darting nervously between Christina and Daniel.

Christina looked at Daniel for another long, glaring moment, then directed her attention to Libby. Libby handed out the keys and passports, then instructed the group to go to their rooms, unpack and stay put.

"I'll need to know where you are after I speak with the head of the orphanage," she said. "Keep your fingers crossed that they'll be prepared for us to visit this afternoon, as planned."

"Fingers crossed," a woman said. "Toes crossed. Elbows crossed. Eyes crossed. I want to meet our Kaylee."

Everyone picked up their suitcases, and Libby pointed in the general direction of the elevators. Kathy walked close by Christina's side.

"Christina," Kathy whispered, "sparks certainly were flying between you and Mr. Hunk-of-stuff. That man is so gorgeous, it's sinful."

"He's pompous and overbearing," Christina whispered back. "How dare he question my ability to care for Autumn on my own?"

"Maybe he was just trying to make conversation."

"Then he needs a lesson in how to chitchat," Christina said with an indignant little sniff.

"Well, even I said you were terribly brave to be planning on raising Autumn alone. Remember?"

"I realize that, Kathy, but Daniel Shay was passing censure. How could I possibly work if I'd been up in the night with a baby? The nerve of that man. I do *not* like Mr. Shay."

Kathy sighed. "What a shame. He's so handsome. It would be so romantic if—"

"Kathy, please," Christina interrupted, rolling her eyes heavenward.

"Okay, okay. I'll concentrate on hoping we'll be able to go to the orphanage this afternoon. Our Emily is only miles away. Oh-h-h, I'm getting terrified again."

Christina laughed and smiled warmly at Kathy as they all moved into the elevator. Daniel joined them and leaned against the back wall of the crowded enclosure.

Shay, you're a jerk, he admonished himself. He'd managed to alienate Christina Richards within moments after meeting her. What had happened to his smooth Shay charm, his years of diplomatic expertise? They sure hadn't been front row center when he'd spoken to Christina.

Ah, hell, what difference did it make? He wouldn't see Christina again until she showed up at the consulate in about ten days with baby in tow to get her Autumn's visa.

Why, he wondered in the next instant, wasn't a woman like Christina married? And why would someone who was as successful in her career as she was, who could travel the world, go first class all the way, tie herself down to a limited existence of diapers, bottles, sticky fingers and chicken pox?

Christina Richards, also known as Auntie Ann—which was a tad corny—was an intriguing woman.

Within that delicate, feminine aura was a feisty temper, which had caught him off guard.

There were many layers to Ms. Richards. She was challenging, and represented a delectable, mysterious package just waiting to be unwrapped.

No, forget it. He wasn't interested in attempting to know Christina better. What was the point? She lived in Phoenix, Arizona. He was headed for Washington, D.C. And he sure as hell didn't want anything to do with a woman who was encumbered with a baby.

But then again, if he spent some time concentrating on the enigmatic Ms. Richards, it would be that many fewer hours he'd be dwelling on how much he didn't want to return to the United States.

What the heck, Shay, he decided, go for it. He certainly didn't have anything better to do.

"Libby," he said as the elevator bumped to a stop, "I'm not scheduled to report in to the consulate until tomorrow morning. I'd be honored if you'd allow me to accompany you to the orphanage if you go this afternoon."

"We'd all be delighted to have you," Libby said, beaming.

Delighted? Christina thought crossly. Thrilled to pieces to have Daniel Stuffed-Shirt Shay tagging along? Not in this lifetime.

Chapter Two

Any lingering thoughts of Daniel Shay, good, bad or in-between, that Christina might have had vanished the moment she stepped inside her room and saw the Portacrib that had been set up next to the double bed.

A soft smile formed on her lips as she set her tote bag and suitcase on the bed, then stood next to the crib. The sheet and puffy comforter were a matching set done in bright blue and white flowers.

Christina ran one hand over the marshmallow-soft comforter, mentally envisioning Autumn sleeping peacefully in the pretty crib.

Ten months ago, she thought, she'd made the momentous decision to adopt a child, and now the dream was about to come true.

"I'm here, Autumn," Christina whispered, still gazing at the empty, waiting crib. "Very soon now, my precious, we'll be together. Mommy is here at last. I've come to take you home."

A warmth suffused her and she wrapped her hands around her elbows as though to hold it within her, savor it, knowing that her arms would soon be cradling her beloved daughter.

"Unpack, Christina," she told herself, pulling her mind from the blissful place it had floated to.

The room was large and had a balcony that overlooked a wide river with barges chugging in both directions. Small fishing boats bobbed in the water, appearing to be dangerously close to the bigger vessels.

The busy traffic on the river reminded Christina of that on the streets of Guangzhou. The fishermen seemed determined to have their share of space, just as the brave bicyclists were.

Christina opened her suitcase and began to transfer the multitude of diapers to the dresser drawers. Next came tiny undershirts, sleepers, bibs and a crocheted bonnet her agent had given her.

At the travel meeting held in Phoenix, Libby had said they would be having a celebration dinner the evening before leaving Guangzhou. It was a tradition on that night to dress the babies in red, the Chinese color for good luck, happiness and prosperity.

Christina's parents had asked if they might be the ones to buy Autumn the special red dress. Christina had agreed, and the dress had arrived from Florida, where her parents lived in a retirement community.

Having no clue as to what Autumn weighed, they'd sent a size for a three-month-old infant, along with white booties and a sweater.

Christina lifted the dress from the tissue paper she'd folded carefully around it and held it at arm's length in front of her. It had a white yoke with a row of perky red teddy bears marching across, and the skirt was velvet with white lace trim.

She spread the tissue in a drawer and placed the dress gently on the paper, nestling the booties and sweater next to it.

Formula, bottles, wipes and diaper-rash ointment were lined up in exacting order on the table.

She then tended to her own clothes, which didn't take long due to their limited number, and put her cosmetic bag on the bathroom vanity. The suitcase was pushed into the closet, her purse retrieved from the carry-on tote bag, and that was that.

Christina sat down on the edge of the bed, only to rise again an instant later. Pacing restlessly, she stopped finally and attempted to concentrate on the activity on the river. She soon turned from the sliding glass door with a sigh of frustration.

She couldn't relax, she thought, wait calmly to hear from Libby whether they could go to the orphanage today as planned. If the trip was postponed for whatever bureaucratic reason, she'd blow a circuit in her busy brain.

"Today, today, today," she said aloud, resting crossed fingers on her cheeks. "We *will* be going to the orphanage today."

The telephone rang and Christina gasped in surprise as the shrill noise sliced through the quiet room. She hurried to snatch up the receiver.

"Hello?"

"It's Libby. Dr. Yang, our liaison with the orphanage officials, is already out there. They're ready for us to come. The van is waiting out front, so hustle down to the lobby and gather by that railing where we were standing before."

"Yes. Yes, I'm on my way," Christina said breathlessly. "Bye, Libby."

Christina dropped the receiver back into place, grabbed her purse and left the room, the wild tempo of her heart echoing in her ears. Not seeing others from the group anywhere in the hallway, she dashed for the elevators, arriving just as the doors to one were closing.

"Hello, hello. Hold the elevator, please," Christina called.

The doors swished open again and Christina ran into the enclosure, coming to a teetering halt in front of Daniel Shay.

"Hello, Christina," he said, smiling as he pressed a button on the panel.

"Hello," she said, then drew a steadying breath. "I must have looked like I thought the building was on fire. It's just that I'm so excited, so…" She waved one hand in the air. "Never mind. If I try to explain how I'm feeling at the moment, I'll probably just babble like an idiot. Ignore me."

"You're not an easy woman to ignore." Daniel paused. "Listen, we got off on the wrong foot, I'm afraid. I sincerely apologize if I offended you in any way earlier. That certainly wasn't my intention. Could we start over, Christina?''

"Oh. Well, certainly. Yes, of course, no problem." Christina splayed one hand on her heart. "I'm a nervous wreck."

"That's understandable. This is a big day for you and the others."

"It's a dream-come-true day," she said, smiling up at him.

"Dreams are an enviable commodity."

"Don't you have any? Dreams?"

Daniel shook his head. "No, not really."

"That's very sad, Daniel. Maybe…well, maybe you could look a little deeper within yourself to see if there isn't a dream hiding from your view, waiting to be discovered."

"No wonder you're a writer. You have a lovely way of expressing your thoughts." He nodded. "I'll think about what you just said."

"Good."

They continued to look directly into each other's eyes. Their smiles faded as a crackling *something* began to weave around them, then into them, with an incredible swirling heat.

Of its own volition, it seemed, Daniel's hand floated upward, fingertips tingling as he reached toward the dark, silky curls fanning Christina's face.

The elevator bumped to a gentle stop and Daniel

snatched his hand back as though he'd touched something hot. The doors swished open and Christina hurried out of the enclosure, hoping to the heavens that her cheeks weren't as flushed as they felt.

Another elevator arrived moments later, spilling forth the remainder of the group. Christina merged quickly with her chattering, excited friends, leaving Daniel to bring up the rear.

Daniel shook his head slightly to dispel the last of the sensual haze hovering over him, then frowned.

What was that woman doing to him? he inwardly fumed. During a very brief ride in an elevator she'd managed to turn him inside out, had caused heated desire to coil painfully low in his body.

This was crazy. Things like this didn't happen to him. He'd long ago perfected the ability to maintain total control over his body and emotions in regard to women.

He set the pace. *He* walked away when he was ready to go. A little slip of a woman, who spent half of her life in the silly persona of Auntie Ann, wasn't going to push *his* buttons.

"Everyone is here," Libby was saying as Daniel joined the group. "Splendid. The van is waiting for us out front. It will take about thirty minutes to drive to the orphanage. Try to relax and enjoy the new things you'll be seeing on the way."

Libby laughed.

"There, I've said it, but I know from experience

that you won't relax one iota. Daniel, I want to dou-
ble-check this mound of paperwork I'm carrying, so
why don't you sit with Christina and chat, try to
make the time pass more quickly for her?''

"Oh, but…" Christina started.

"Off we go," Libby said, not having heard Christina speak.

They all trailed after Libby as she marched briskly
across the lobby, which was congested with people.
Two by two they went, in couples, Christina and
Daniel at the end of the line.

Like little ducks all in a row, Christina thought,
swallowing a giggle that held the hint of near hysteria. *Oh, Christina, please, get a grip.*

The episode in the elevator had been absurd—un-
settling, yes, but positively ridiculous. Daniel Shay
had pinned her in place with those fathomless dark
eyes of his and she'd practically melted into a puddle
at his feet like ice cream on an Arizona summer day.

Well, all right, her overreaction to Daniel was understandable…sort of. She was far from being her
usual steady, sensible self. She had jet lag far greater
than any she'd dealt with before. Plus, she was in a
highly emotional state. She was half an hour away
from seeing and holding her daughter for the first
time.

There. She'd figured it all out and felt better for
it. And another thing was crystal clear—it was never
going to happen again. While she was in this weak-

ened state, per se, she would stay on red alert in regard to the oh-so-sexy Mr. Shay. Even better, she'd just totally ignore him.

When everyone was seated, the driver of the van started off, immediately pressing on the horn at regular intervals. No one spoke, as thoughts turned inward. The couples held hands. Christina clasped hers in her lap.

Hurry, she mentally directed the driver. *Autumn is waiting for me, so please, please hurry.*

Daniel slid a glance at Christina, seeing the tight grip of her hands, the unnaturally pale hue of her fair skin. Her blue eyes looked big and beautiful as she stared straight ahead, her back ramrod stiff.

He couldn't even imagine what Christina was thinking and feeling, he realized. She appeared scared to death, so alone and vulnerable, and he had to fight the urge to slip his arm across her shoulders, pull her close, comfort her.

He turned slightly to sweep his gaze over the others in the van.

Lord, he thought, they were all impersonating stone statues. They looked like a van-load of people about to have six root canals each, instead of parents-to-be who were within miles and minutes of meeting their daughters for the first time.

Daniel leaned forward to speak to Libby, who was busily shuffling papers in the seat directly in front of him and Christina.

"Libby," he said quietly, "I'm not sure your group is breathing. They're frozen in place, or something. Aren't they supposed to be happy and excited?"

"This is perfectly normal, Daniel," Libby said, her voice hushed. "This drive is usually made in complete silence. It never fails. You have to understand that these people have waited months for this moment. They're attempting to comprehend that it's finally here."

"Weird," he whispered.

"Wonderful," Libby said, smiling. "You're going to witness miracles in that orphanage. It's all very moving, very humbling. I've yet to get through the first meeting of the babies and the moms and dads without weeping buckets. You won't ever forget what you'll see there today, Daniel, believe me."

Daniel nodded, smiled pleasantly, then leaned back in his seat.

Libby Duling, he thought, was projecting her womanly emotions onto him and they didn't fit, not by a long shot. He wasn't the sentimental type, wouldn't succumb to the emotional atmosphere that was apparently going to prevail at the orphanage.

He was a step removed from what was going to take place, was, literally, just along for the ride. He'd chosen to accompany Christina and the others for the self-serving reason that he hadn't wanted to spend

the afternoon alone in his hotel room, nor wandering
around the streets of Guangzhou on his own.

Daniel frowned as he looked at Christina again.

He probably shouldn't have come, he thought.
This trip was not sounding like a good time. To be
trapped in a room with crying adults and probably
wailing babies was not his idea of a great way to
spend the next few hours.

Well, it was too late now. He was stuck for the
duration.

Daniel folded his arms over his chest and scowled
into space as he made a mental list of ten places he'd
rather be than where he actually was.

The minutes and miles ticked slowly by.

"There's the orphanage up ahead," Libby said finally, bringing everyone to attention.

"Oh, my," Christina said, "it's so big. It's one,
two…seven stories tall."

"And filled to overflowing," Libby said. "The
government's decree that a family can only have one
child, and the tradition of the Chinese culture to want
a boy, who will care for his parents in their old age,
has resulted in a multitude of homeless little girls.
This is only one of thousands of orphanages."

"Emily is in there," Kathy said. "Oh, my gosh,
what if I faint? No, I'm fine. No, I'm not."

"Easy does it, Almost-a-Mommy," her husband
said. "You can't faint, because I'm going to."

Everyone laughed, breaking the nearly palpable

tension that had built in the van during the drive. They began to chatter like magpies. Christina placed one hand on her heart, drew a deep breath, then let it out slowly.

"How are you doing?" Daniel asked quietly.

"Butterflies," Christina said, not looking at him. "My stomach is holding a convention of butterflies that is being very well attended."

Daniel chuckled, once again tickled with Christina's charming way with words.

The van came to a screeching halt in front of the orphanage and they piled out, Libby shaking hands with an Asian man who appeared to be in his middle thirties.

"Everyone," Libby said, "this is Dr. Yang, the man you've been hearing about for so many months."

"Hello," Dr. Yang said, smiling. "I understand the match pictures of your daughters never arrived. I mailed them myself, but…" He shrugged. "Who knows where they ended up? I assure you that your babies are beautiful. But you'll see that for yourself very soon now. Shall we go inside?"

"I'm definitely fainting," Kathy said.

"Shh," her husband said.

The orphanage was obviously very old, but appeared spotlessly clean. They were transported to the seventh floor in a minuscule elevator that creaked and groaned and moved with maddening slowness.

It took three trips to get them all upstairs, where they were escorted into a fairly large room made to appear like a living room. The furniture was faded and worn, the green paint on the walls was peeling and the carpet on the floor was nearly devoid of color due to wear.

"Sit down, please," Dr. Yang said. "Libby, if you'll come with me? You have the paperwork?"

"Yes, right here," she said. "We won't be long," she added, smiling at everyone.

Christina sank onto a love-seat-size sofa. Daniel sat next to her and glanced around.

"It's not exactly cozy, is it?" he said.

"What?" Christina said. "Oh, no, it's rather stark. They do well to have enough money to buy food for the children. There certainly aren't funds left over for decorating."

"I understand," Daniel said, nodding, then paused. "So, tell me, Christina, do you live in Phoenix itself, or in one of the surrounding cities?"

"I live in Scottsdale." She looked up at Daniel. "Thank you, Daniel. I know you're doing your best to help me relax as we wait, and I appreciate your efforts." She laughed softly. "It's not working, but it's the thought that counts."

Daniel matched her smile. "The butterflies are still arriving at the convention?"

"In droves. I—"

"Oh," Kathy gasped, across the room.

A smiling Libby and Dr. Yang reentered the room, then stood to one side to reveal two women, each carrying a baby wrapped in a pink-and-white flowered blanket in the crook of each arm. A third woman could just barely be seen behind them.

This is it, Christina's mind hummed. Oh, dear God, this is it. Which baby was Autumn? Which one of those precious little miracles was her daughter?

Without realizing she was doing it, Christina grasped one of Daniel's hands as she stared intently at the unforgettable scene in the doorway.

Daniel blinked in surprise as Christina grabbed his hand, then realized she probably didn't know she had done it. He covered her hand with his free one.

The color had drained from Christina's face again and her hand was ice-cold. Well, Daniel thought, this *was* a momentous moment in her life. It wasn't every day of the week that a woman became a mother, met her new daughter for the first time. Under the circumstances, he might very well have a convention of butterflies swooshing around in his stomach, too.

None of the parents-to-be moved or spoke, and they hardly breathed. All eyes were riveted on the babies in the matching blankets. Libby and Dr. Yang spoke in low tones as they looked at the papers in Libby's hand, then the babies. Libby finally placed one hand on a baby.

"Emily," she said.

"Go get our daughter, sweetheart," Kathy's husband, Jack, said.

Kathy burst into tears and nearly ran across the room to lift Emily from the caregiver's arm.

"Hannah," Libby said, touching another infant after Kathy had resumed her seat next to her husband.

Christina's hold on Daniel's hand tightened as each baby was claimed.

Then the two caregivers moved aside to make room for the other one to step forward. She carried one little baby in her arms.

"We didn't forget you, Christina," Libby said, beaming. "Here is your Autumn."

"Oh, God," Christina whispered. "My legs are trembling so badly I'm afraid I can't stand up."

Daniel slipped his hand free of Christina's and wrapped his arm around her waist. He helped her to her feet and smiled at her.

"Your daughter is waiting for a hug from her mother," he said.

"Yes," she said, nodding. "Yes."

With unsteady steps Christina crossed the room, not aware that her arms were already extended to receive the miraculous gift she was about to be given. The caregiver smiled and placed the bundle in Christina's arms.

And there she was.

Autumn Christina Richards.

Instant tears filled Christina's eyes as she stared at

her daughter, who was staring back at her, a very serious expression on her little face.

"Hello, Autumn," Christina said, a sob of happiness catching in her throat. "Hello, my darling daughter. You're so beautiful."

Autumn blinked, her expression remaining extremely stern. She had a cap of silky black hair, dark almond-shaped eyes, a button nose and an exquisite, rosebud mouth. Her skin was fair and looked as soft as velvet, and her tiny fists were tucked beneath her chin as though she was ready for battle.

From where Daniel stood he could clearly see Christina and Autumn. At the moment when the baby had been placed in Christina's arms and he'd witnessed the emotions visible on her face, a strange and foreign warmth like nothing he'd experienced before suffused him. His gaze remained riveted on mother and daughter, and his heart thundered.

Christina walked slowly toward him, smiling and talking to Autumn.

"Oh, Daniel," she said, stopping in front of him, "look at her. Isn't she wonderful? So beautiful?"

You are beautiful, Christina, Daniel's mind yelled. Her blue eyes were glistening with tears, making them appear like sparkling sapphires. The pure joy on her face was breathtaking, so very real it could never be captured totally by an artist's brush.

Daniel tore his gaze reluctantly from Christina to look at the baby nestled in her arms. Another jolt of the strange warmth surged through him as he found himself being stared at by eyes as dark as his own.

"Hi, Autumn," he said.

Was that his voice? he thought incredulously. It was gritty, ringing with emotion, and sounded like a man who was fighting against tears he refused to shed. His throat felt achy and tight and... *Lord, Shay, get it together.*

"Let's sit down," he said quickly. "Don't new mothers like to count all their baby's fingers and toes, or something?"

Christina laughed and Daniel nearly groaned aloud as the musical resonance hit him like a physical blow in the solar plexus.

The entire room was overflowing with happy chatter, laughter, sniffles as tears were wiped away, and cooing baby talk directed at new daughters.

Christina settled back onto the sofa and placed Autumn on her thighs. Daniel sat next to them and watched as Christina unwrapped the pink-and-white blanket. Autumn was wearing a faded yellow cotton nightie, and Christina lifted the hem to reveal tiny feet and a diapered bottom.

"Toes," Christina said, wiggling them. "You have ten little piggies." She smoothed the nightie back into place, then tiptoed her fingertips up Autumn's tummy. "One, two, look at you."

Autumn flung her hands out from beneath her chin, drew a wobbly breath and then...

And then…

Autumn Christina Richards smiled.

And her mommy burst into tears.

Daniel Shay swallowed a very large lump in his throat.

"Oh, my Autumn," Christina said with a funny hiccuping noise, "thank you so much. I will never forget that smile. Never."

Nor would he, Daniel thought. That little handful of humanity was turning him into a sentimental, soggy mess. Autumn was a heart stealer, all right, and her mother was no slouch in that department, either.

Be very careful, Shay, he ordered himself. This feminine duo was dangerous to his peace of mind and sense of self. He wanted no part of the world they represented, not even close.

"What do you think of my daughter, Daniel?" Christina said, turning to look at him.

"She's very special, really cute. She's also extremely fortunate to have you for a mother. You look perfect together, Christina, you really do."

"We're a match made in heaven," she said with a decisive nod.

Libby came bustling over to them, dabbing at her nose with a tissue.

"Well?" she said, smiling. "Is everything all right here, Christina?"

"Oh, yes, it is, Libby. Isn't Autumn beautiful? She

smiled at me. You should have seen that smile.'' Christina laughed. ''I can't describe how magnificent it was.''

''Then you're officially accepting the child you've been matched with?'' Libby said.

''Autumn is my daughter,'' Christina said softly.

''Bless you both,'' Libby said, then hurried away to check on the next couple.

''You have ten more minutes,'' Dr. Yang announced from the doorway.

''Oh, no,'' Christina said. ''I have to give Autumn back to the caregivers.''

''You'll sign documents this evening,'' Dr. Yang went on, ''and tomorrow you'll return and take your daughters to the hotel.'' He laughed. ''Then the fun will begin.''

''Then our future together will begin, Autumn,'' Christina said. ''It will be just the two of us, and we're going to be a wonderful team.''

Daniel stiffened and frowned as a chill swept through him. He had a mental flash of his own future and shook his head slightly to dispel the disturbing image.

Forget it, he fumed. This emotionally charged scenario he'd been caught up in in this room had gotten to him for a moment, that's all. He was erasing from his memory what he'd just felt, chalking it up as unimportant.

He refused to dwell on the fact that for an icy-cold instant he'd been consumed by a foe he'd fought and defeated a decade before.

Its name was loneliness.

Chapter Three

Christina sat cross-legged on the bed in her hotel room, examining with great pleasure the purchases she'd made during the afternoon shopping spree. Autumn was snoozing peacefully in the pretty crib.

Setting aside the rattle she'd bought for Autumn, Christina began to fold the gorgeous, pure silk blouses and shirts she'd found for her friends and family. Each had been hand-embroidered with delicate flowers, or traditional dragons.

As Kathy had pointed out gleefully, as they used up the multitude of diapers, space was being made available in the suitcase for the wonderful and unique items that were in abundance in Guangzhou.

After packing away the gifts, Christina propped the pillows against the headboard on the bed, settled back and wiggled her toes.

Her feet were crying for mercy, she thought with a smile. That morning they'd trudged four blocks to a clinic, where the babies had been given a quick and rather strange physical examination. The endeavor had resulted in the necessary medical-release document being signed by a doctor, who spoke very little English.

After lunch at the hotel and naps for the little ones,

they'd all set out to shop. This, the sixth day in Guangzhou, was the first one that hadn't included a fascinating tour arranged by Libby and Little Hands to take place after the scheduled paperwork step.

Christina sighed with contentment.

Everything was going so perfectly. She and Autumn were doing beautifully, with the mommy already recognizing the meaning of the daughter's various squeaks and cries.

Autumn smiled now when she saw or heard Christina, each wondrous smile causing Christina's heart to feel as though it was overflowing with love.

Christina frowned slightly as she glanced toward the crib.

To her annoyance, she'd found herself thinking about Daniel Shay at the oddest moments. It was due, of course, to his having been with her when she'd held Autumn for the first time and had witnessed, with her, that very first smile produced by her daughter.

When Autumn had stuck her tongue out at Christina yesterday, she'd had the sudden wish that Daniel could see the baby's cute antics.

During Autumn's first bath, when the baby had kicked and splashed, drenching her mother, Christina had decided that Daniel would say the baby looked like a slippery little fish in the water.

Such nonsense, Christina thought, to have lingering images, memories of a man who had touched her life so briefly. She'd see Daniel once more at the consulate when they went there to obtain the babies' visas, and that would be that.

But, she knew, because she would never forget that day at the orphanage and the fact that Daniel had shared it all with her, she'd never totally erase the man from her memory bank.

Well, so be it. Daniel would simply be one more memory in the treasure chest in her heart and mind that she'd be taking home from China.

A knock at the door brought Christina from her thoughts and she slipped off the bed to pad barefoot across the plush carpeting. She opened the door, fully expecting to find someone from the group with a suggested plan for having dinner.

Instead she found herself staring wide-eyed at Daniel Shay, while having the irrational thought that she'd conjured him up by thinking about him.

"Hello, Christina," Daniel said.

"My goodness, this is a surprise," she said, smiling. And, my goodness, wasn't she glad that Daniel couldn't read her mind, or hear the sudden increased tempo of her heart? He was even more gorgeous than she remembered. He was so tall and solid, and just so incredibly *male.* "How are you, Daniel?"

"May I come in?" he said, smiling, "or would I be compromising your reputation by being with you in your hotel room?"

"A scandal in Guangzhou." Christina laughed.

"Now there's a title for a book." She stepped back to allow him to enter the room. "Come in."

As Christina closed the door behind him, Daniel went directly to the crib. Christina slipped her shoes on.

"Autumn has grown," Daniel said, smiling as he looked at the sleeping infant. "She really has. Her cheeks are fuller and she…I don't know, she just appears bigger."

Christina walked to Daniel's side and peered into the crib.

"Do you really think so?" she said.

"Absolutely. Is she still smiling?"

"Oh, yes, all the time," Christina said, shifting her gaze to Daniel. "My heart gets all fluttery whenever she smiles at me. She recognizes me now, too. She's eating well, adores her bath and has been a real trouper about being toted all over Guangzhou." She stopped speaking and laughed. "Listen to me. I sound like an obnoxious new mother who won't quit talking about her child."

"No," Daniel said, no hint of a smile on his face, "you sound like a proud and happy new mother and that's fine, really great." He paused. "You have a lovely glow about you, Christina. Motherhood becomes you."

"Thank you, Daniel," she said softly, then reminded herself to breathe.

Dear heaven, she thought, the heat, the sudden

burst of heat thrumming throughout her was like a raging fire burning out of control.

She had to move, break the sensuous spell that Daniel was casting over her.

But Christina *didn't* move. She was held immobile by the mesmerizing depths of Daniel Shay's obsidian eyes; eyes that were changing, were now radiating a message of raw, earthy desire.

Daniel framed Christina's face in his hands and at last, *at last,* wove his fingertips through the silky curls fanning her cheeks. Heat coiled low in his body, tightening, consuming him with want and need.

"I thought about you a great deal during the past few days," Daniel said, savoring the feel of the curls entwined around his fingers. "There was a tremendous backlog of work piled up at the consulate and I've been getting back here to the hotel too late at night to disturb you."

"Oh," Christina said, then for the life of her couldn't think of one more intelligent thing to say.

"Did you have a kind thought or two about *me*, Christina?"

"Well, I...well, yes, I did. More than two. What I mean is..." Christina drew a wobbly breath. "Daniel, please stop fiddling with my hair. I can't think straight when you do that."

Daniel's hands stilled. "There. I stopped. I'll do something else, instead of fiddling with your hair."

And with that Daniel lowered his head and kissed her.

Oh, yes, Christina thought, her lashes drifting down, this was much, much nicer than hair fiddling. This kiss was ecstasy. This kiss was long overdue. This kiss was Daniel, and she was so very glad that he was here.

Christina's hands floated upward to encircle Daniel's neck, and he deepened the kiss. Tongues met in the sweet darkness of Christina's mouth and passions soared.

Daniel dropped his hands from Christina's face and wrapped them around her slender, womanly body, nestling her to him.

Somewhere in the sensual haze consuming his mind, he marveled at how perfectly Christina fit the contours of his body, as though she'd been custom made just for him.

He lifted his head a fraction of an inch, drew a quick, rough breath, then slanted his mouth in the opposite direction, claiming Christina's lips once more.

Christina, what are you doing? her mind whispered, then shouted at her in the next instant. *Stop! This is wrong. Very dangerous and very, very wrong.*

She broke the kiss and splayed her hands flat on Daniel's chest, pushing gently but definitely relaying the message that he was to release her. He dropped his arms to his sides and she took a step backward.

"No." Christina's voice trembled slightly and she clasped her hands around her elbows. "That shouldn't have happened."

"Why not?" Daniel cleared his throat when he heard the raspy sound of his voice. "We both wanted it to happen, Christina. You can't deny that."

"I don't intend to deny it," she said, lifting her chin, "nor claim that I'm not attracted to you." She shook her head. "But it's more complicated than that. You were with me at the orphanage when I saw and held Autumn for the first time. It's impossible for me to erase you from the memories of that day."

"That has nothing to do with my desire for you, Christina," Daniel said, his voice rising. "Yes, I was there when you and Autumn were united. It was a very special event. It moved me emotionally to the point that I was stunned by my own reaction to what I felt privileged to have witnessed."

He raked a restless hand through his hair.

"But that's separate and apart from the fact that I haven't been able to get you off my mind, and separate from the kisses we just shared. Do catch that word, Christina. Shared."

"Yes, all right. I believe it's all intertwined and you don't. It really doesn't matter either way. What's important is that there will be no more kisses *shared* between us."

"Why the hell not?" Daniel yelled.

Christina narrowed her eyes and planted her hands on her hips.

"Daniel Shay, I may not have been a mother for very long, but I have learned one of the rules that has been etched in stone since the beginning of time. Anyone who wakes a sleeping baby is a dead person."

"Oh." Daniel glanced quickly at the crib where Autumn was still sleeping peacefully. "Sorry. She didn't even flicker, though."

"Well, Autumn is used to a noisy environment because of being in the orphanage. So far, she seems quite capable of sleeping through just about anything."

"Of course," he said, nodding. "I knew she was extraordinary the minute I saw her. It's her eyes. There's a wisdom there that's hard to define. When she looked at me I felt as though she could see my very soul. She…" He stopped speaking as he saw the rather perplexed expression on Christina's face. "What?"

"I'm just surprised, that's all," she said. "Autumn really has gotten to you, as the saying goes, hasn't she? I guess I was so wrapped up in myself and what I was feeling, I wasn't aware of what you were experiencing that day at the orphanage."

Daniel shrugged. "I probably had on my pleasant, albeit blank, diplomatic face."

Christina laughed. "Oh, I see."

"Christina, look," he said, serious again, "let's get back to the subject, shall we? I'm not attempting to hustle you into bed. I just want to spend some time with you, be together. There's nothing wrong with that, is there?

"We certainly don't have to make a list of ground rules like no kissing, no touching. We're mature adults who are free to do whatever feels right at the moment."

"Well, when you put it like that, Daniel, I do seem a bit foolish for verbally stamping my foot and acting like a Victorian maiden."

"Good. Now we're on the right track. Will you have dinner with me tonight?"

"Don't you mean will Autumn and I have dinner with you?" Christina said, raising her eyebrows.

"Well, I imagine that a top-notch hotel like this one has a baby-sitting service."

"Oh, now wait just a minute, Daniel. I didn't travel halfway around the world to get my daughter so I could leave her with a stranger while I'm wined and dined."

"You've got to have a balance in your life, Christina. You can't forget that you're a woman just because you've become a mother."

"I know who I am, Daniel Shay," she said, none too quietly. "That balance, as you put it, will fall into place once Autumn and I are home and settled into a routine. But while I'm in Guangzhou? Where I go, Autumn goes.''

Damn it, Daniel thought, he was taking second seat behind a ten-pound baby, who, despite her diminutive size, was calling all the shots.

And he didn't like it, not one little bit.

His ''I'm in control here'' was being shot to hell, and he was definitely bent out of shape about it. That fact was not very flattering. What had he become during the past decade? A self-centered, machismo-is-my-middle-name jerk?

''Okay, you win,'' he said, raising both hands. ''Will you and Autumn do me the honor of being my guests at dinner tonight?''

Christina smiled. ''We'd be delighted. I'd prefer to eat in one of the restaurants here in the hotel, though. Autumn has been wonderful about being toted here, there and everywhere, but she can become very vocal when she has had enough of being jostled around. I'll be able to whisk her back here to the room if she starts to cry.''

''Wonderful,'' Daniel muttered.

''Do you have a problem with the plan?''

''No, no, it makes perfect sense. I'm just not used to a tiny baby being so in charge of everything.''

Christina laughed. ''You're catching on, Mr. Shay. That's exactly how it is when they're this small.''

The telephone rang and Christina hurried across the room to pick up the receiver.

"Hello?"

Daniel tuned out Christina's side of the telephone conversation as he shifted his gaze to a still-sleeping Autumn.

Autumn looked so peaceful, he thought, considering all the upheavals she'd experienced in her young life. Maybe she knew that she was safe now, had a mother who loved her beyond measure, would be a cherished daughter in a home overflowing with love. Yes, maybe wise little Autumn somehow knew all that.

Oh, how those dark eyes of hers would sparkle when she took her first steps, realized she was maneuvering in her world on her own. That would be a sight to behold, no doubt about it. It would be as momentous as that first smile that he'd witnessed.

Daniel frowned slightly.

He wouldn't know when Autumn took her first steps, cut her first tooth, said her first understandable word, nor would Autumn have any idea that he even existed. She'd be with Christina in Scottsdale, Arizona, while he was stuck behind a desk in Washington, D.C.

Damn it, what was the matter with him? Christina and Autumn were in his life for a handful of days. He knew that and would not, in fact, want it any other way. He was *not* a hearth-and-home, wife-and-baby man.

That dream had died years before.

*Maybe you could look a little deeper within your-
self to see if there isn't a dream hiding from your
view, waiting to be discovered.*

Christina's words echoed suddenly in Daniel's
head and he turned from the crib to glare at Christina
where she was talking on the telephone.

Not a chance, Auntie Ann, with your fancy
writer's way of speaking, he fumed. He didn't have
a hidden dream. He was a realist, who operated in
the now, the moment at hand.

He was standing in that room at the White Swan
for no other reason than that he was attracted to
Christina Richards, and her company would make his
brief stay in Guangzhou more enjoyable. End of
story.

"Do keep me posted," Christina was saying into
the receiver. "Autumn and I will be having dinner
with Daniel Shay here in the hotel. I'll check in with
you later this evening.... Fine. Goodbye, Jack."

Christina replaced the receiver and turned to look
at Daniel, a troubled expression on her face.

"What's wrong?" Daniel said, more than happy
to direct his attention away from his own jumbled
thoughts.

"That was Jack, Kathy's husband. Both Kathy and
the baby woke up from their naps with temperatures.
Kathy has the chills and an upset stomach, and Emily
is very fussy."

"Uh-oh," Daniel said. "That sounds like the flu that hit the employees at the consulate."

"I hope it isn't serious. Jack is going to track Libby down to find out what the situation is regarding a doctor, in case one is needed."

"Libby probably has that information from previous trips," Daniel said. "If not, I'll see what I can do through the consulate's resources."

"Thank you very much, Daniel. I told Jack that I'd be checking in with him later. I'll relay your message to him then. I—"

Autumn suddenly stirred, snuffled, squeaked, then began to cry.

"Oops," Christina said. "Someone is hungry."

"She sure has a good set of lungs," Daniel said. "Hey, Autumn, dinner is on the way. Okay?"

"And her reply to you," Christina said, laughing, "is 'Yeah, right, buster. Promises, promises.' She wants a bottle, not a speech."

"No joke." Daniel sat down on one of the chairs at the table to get out of Christina's bustling way. "Go for it, Mother."

Christina scooped Autumn from the crib, placed her on the bed and changed her diaper with an economy of motion. She lifted the wailing infant to one shoulder.

"Oh, this is a treat," Christina said. "I can prepare her bottle with two free hands."

She went to where Daniel was sitting and plopped Autumn into the crook of one of his arms.

"Oh, wait a second here," Daniel said. "I've never held a baby in my life, let alone one who is doing an impersonation of an air raid siren."

"She won't break." Christina measured dry formula into a bottle, then picked up a tall jug. "Oh, drat, I forgot to get more hot water. I knew there was something I was supposed to do." She started toward the door, carrying the jug. "I'll be right back."

Daniel's eyes widened. "Christina, stop. Halt. Whoa. You can't leave me alone with Autumn. Listen to her. She's crying even louder. Her face is getting all red and... Christina!"

"Talk to her," she said, then snatched her key from the top of the dresser and left the room.

"Talk to her?" Daniel repeated to the empty room. "She'll never hear me over the racket she's making." He shifted his frowning gaze to the furious infant. "So, Autumn Christina Richards, how's life?"

Autumn's volume kicked up a notch.

"Got it. Your complaints have been noted and will be acted upon at the earliest possible moment." Daniel wrapped his arm more securely around the unhappy bundle and jiggled her a bit. "There, there, don't cry."

But Autumn continued to cry, and two tears slid down her tiny cheeks.

"Oh, man, that's not fair," Daniel said with a groan. "Come on, kiddo, don't add tears to the soup. Grown men have been known to crumble into pieces at the sight of female tears. I bet baby girls have that programmed into their brains before they're even born. Right?"

Daniel got to his feet slowly, holding the baby as though she was a bunch of very fragile eggs. He crossed the room, then turned to retrace his steps.

"Talk to her. Okay, here goes. Autumn, I'm Daniel Shay, but you already know that. I was there when your beautiful mother saw and held you for the first time. You should have seen her face, Autumn. It was awesome, really something. I'll never forget what I witnessed in that room in the orphanage, believe me."

Autumn cried on and on.

"Your mom says I should look deep inside myself to find out if I have a dream hiding someplace. I don't have a dream, I know that, but if I did? If, say, I found out that I wanted a wife and baby? Well, I would be one very proud daddy to have a daughter like you.

"The thing is, I had that dream a long time ago and it blew up in my face. I figure it's one to a customer in that arena, and mine is long gone."

Autumn drew a wobbly breath, then stuck her fist into her mouth as far as it would go. Blessed silence fell over the room. A huge grin broke across Daniel's face.

"Well, now," he said, sounding extremely pleased with himself, "check this out. I'm obviously doing something right. We're a pretty good team, kiddo.

"You're staring at me again, Autumn, with that I-can-see-your-soul bit. Not much there, is there? That's where the dream would hide if there was one.

"Dreams, Autumn Richards, are for very special people like your mom. She had a dream that was you, and she didn't stop until she'd gotten what she was determined to have.

"You're a lucky little girl to have Christina for a mommy. But you know what? Christina is very fortunate to have you as a daughter, too. I won't forget the two of you, not ever."

The door opened and Christina whizzed back into the room.

"I'll feed Autumn," she said, "and then we can go have dinner."

"No," Daniel said, sitting back down with Autumn.

"No?" Christina set the jug on the table and looked at Daniel questioningly. "You've changed your mind about our having dinner together?"

"No, but I think we should have room service deliver our meal up here."

"Why?"

"Because the flu bug has hit the White Swan,

that's why. We can't take Autumn into one of the restaurants in the hotel. For cripes sake, Christina, there are germs out there. Think about it, will you?''

What she was thinking, Christina thought, tearing her gaze from Daniel and proceeding with preparing a bottle of formula, was that Daniel looked very right and very special while holding her daughter.

What she was thinking was that Daniel's declaration that Autumn wasn't to be exposed to the germs lurking in the shadows at the White Swan was one of the sweetest things she'd ever heard.

What she was thinking was that little by little Daniel was staking a claim on her heart and she must *not* allow that to continue.

When she arrived back in Scottsdale with her new daughter, she did not want one of the souvenirs she was bringing home from China to be a broken heart caused by Daniel Shay.

Chapter Four

*E*nchanting.

That was the word that kept floating through Christina's mind as she and Daniel ate dinner.

Having finally convinced a skeptical Daniel that Autumn had already been exposed to Kathy and Emily's menacing germs after spending the day with the ailing pair, they'd left the room.

Daniel had suggested that they eat at the patio restaurant a level above the waterfall so they could thoroughly enjoy the beauty of the cascading water tumbling into the pond below, where the goldfish swam.

They'd been seated near the railing, affording them a marvelous view of the beautiful spectacle. Autumn was placed on an extra chair pulled close to Christina's and the baby was enthralled by the multitude of overhead lights.

The sweet and sour pork they ordered was delicious. The waterfall made Christina feel as though she'd been transported to a private island. Daniel was charming and attentive.

It was all, Christina decided yet again, totally enchanting.

"Have you ever been married?" Daniel asked, refilling Christina's small cup with tea.

"Yes, very briefly, years ago," she said. "It was soap opera awful. I caught my husband in flagrante delicto on the sofa in his office with his secretary. We'd been married less than a year. No, correct that. *I* was married, he wasn't. I came away from that experience vowing to never marry again."

"Is that fair?" Daniel pushed his empty plate to one side and folded his arms on top of the table. "One crummy apple doesn't necessarily mean the whole barrel is rotten. There *are* some decent, trustworthy men in this world, Christina."

Christina shrugged. "I suppose, but I'm not convinced I can tell the good guys from the bad. I've never regretted my decision to remain single."

"Don't you get lonely?"

"I don't have time," Christina said, laughing. "My career has kept me extremely busy, I date several different men, have wonderful friends, and terrific parents, who have retired to Florida. The only thing missing from my life was a child." She smiled at Autumn, who was staring at the fascinating invention known as her hand. "And now? Well, there she is, Autumn Christina Richards, my daughter."

Christina propped her elbows on the table and laced her fingers loosely beneath her chin.

"What about you, Daniel? Why are you footloose and fancy free?"

Nice going, Shay, he thought with self-disgust. He'd been so curious as to why Christina wasn't married, he'd walked right into a tit-for-tat dialogue where he was now expected to divulge what he'd long ago chosen never to discuss.

"The bachelor life suits me just fine," he said. "More tea?"

"No, I've had plenty, thank you. You've never been married?"

Daniel leaned back in his chair and frowned. "It's old news."

"So was my marriage, but I shared the grim details with you." Christina raised her eyebrows. "Well?"

Daniel's frown deepened. "My wife was killed in an automobile accident a dozen years ago. She was on her way to meet me at a restaurant, where we were going to celebrate our second wedding anniversary. I waited and waited, but she never arrived."

"Oh, Daniel, I'm so sorry."

"I put in for overseas duty and haven't been back to the States since."

"You…well, you ran away from the painful memories," Christina said softly.

"Yes, frankly, that's exactly what I did. I was very happily married, had a career that was on the upswing, we were talking about buying a house and starting a family. In one split second it was gone, erased. I had two wonderful years, which is more than some people have, I suppose."

"You don't believe that you could be happily married again?"

"No. How many chances does a person get to have what I did? One. I had it. It's gone. End of story."

"Wait, wait," Christina said, waving one hand in the air. "Let me make certain I understand your philosophy. Because my marriage was a disaster, I should consider trying again? Because yours was bliss, you're not eligible for round two? Have I got it right?"

"I've never spelled it out quite like that in my mind," Daniel said, "but, yes, I guess I'd have to say that's my theory."

"Daniel, Daniel," Christina said, shaking her head, "that is so lopsided it's a crime. Can't you see that, now that you've actually spread it out and examined it?"

"Christina, Christina," he said, producing a small smile, "we are now changing the subject before we get into a rip-roaring argument on the issue."

"But..."

"Do you have your camera in your purse?"

"Always."

"Let's go down to the lower level and I'll take your picture with Autumn on that bridge crossing the pond. From what I've observed, that is the traditional place to take pictures to best remember the White Swan."

"All right, but, I'll never forget the White Swan, or Guangzhou, or China or one minute detail of this trip."

"And me?" Daniel said quietly, looking directly into Christina's eyes. "Will you remember me, Christina? Not because I was with you when you met Autumn for the first time, but because of us, the woman, the man, what *we've* shared."

"Is it important to you that I remember you, Daniel?" Christina said, unable to tear her gaze from his mesmerizing dark eyes.

"Yes. I don't know why but, yes, it's important to me. I've experienced quite a few surprises about myself since I met you. One was my emotional reactions that day at the orphanage. When I saw you hold Autumn for the first time I... Well, I was deeply moved."

Daniel reached across the table and covered one of Christina's hands with his own.

"And there's Autumn herself," he went on. "She's a heart stealer, that's for sure. I'd like to keep in touch with you so I know how she's doing."

Christina jerked her hand free and shifted her attention to Autumn.

"Certainly," she said stiffly, staring at the baby. "We'll exchange Christmas cards every year. I'll write you a note and bring you up to date on Autumn's activities during the past months."

"Why are you suddenly angry, Christina?"

Christina snapped her head around to glare at Daniel.

"I'm not angry," she said. "I'm confused, muddled up, and it's your fault. You hold me, kiss me, Daniel, make it clear that you want me. I respond to you, admit to myself that I desire you, too. You talk about emotions, your separating the mother from the woman, viewing me in regard to you, the man.

"This is how relationships begin, Daniel, the slow, steady building, one emotional brick at a time. I don't want to be part of a serious relationship. Yet when you speak of being pen pals, per se, it disturbs me, makes me feel sad and troubled that I'll never see you again."

Daniel nodded. "That pretty well sums up a lot of what I'm going through myself." He smiled. "I do believe, Auntie Ann, that we're the president and vice president of the newly formed Confused-to-the-Max Club."

"That's not funny." In the next instant Christina laughed. "Yes, it is. For supposedly mature adults we're acting like adolescents with hormone rushes. Oh, forget it. Autumn and I will be leaving Guangzhou in a few days and that will be that."

Daniel's smile disappeared. "And in the meantime?"

"Well, I'm not going to hop into bed with you, Mr. Shay. That would be tacky, very tacky, because

I know our paths won't ever cross again. I don't do one-night stands.''

"I didn't believe for one minute that you did. You're a very classy lady, who has an equally classy daughter.''

"True.''

Daniel laughed. "You are also the most refreshingly honest woman I've ever met. I like you as a person, Christina Richards, I really do.''

"Thank you, Daniel.''

Their smiles matched, as did the thrumming heat that was growing hotter and hotter within them. Desire radiated from eyes as dark as night and eyes as blue as a summer sky.

The confusion was pushed aside by passion's heat, causing hearts to race and all that was around them to disappear into the sensual mist encasing them.

"Boo,'' Autumn said.

Christina and Daniel jumped at the sudden noise and returned to reality with a thud. Christina scooped Autumn up and nestled her into the crook of one arm.

"Boo?'' she said, laughing. "You're a genius who can talk at three months old?''

"Ba. Boo. Ba,'' Autumn babbled, waving her tiny fists in the air.

"Would you like to have your picture taken on the bridge in front of the famous White Swan waterfall, my sweet?'' Christina said.

Keep jabbering to Autumn, Christina told herself.

Do not look at Daniel Shay again, not yet. Get a grip on yourself, Christina.

Daniel *knew* she desired him, wanted to make love with him. It had been written all over her face, Christina was certain of it, and had probably been very visible in her eyes as well, just as his want of her had been crystal clear.

Oh, she wished she'd never met Daniel Shay. He was complicating her life at a time when she was already on emotional overload because of Autumn. Why couldn't he have just gone straight home to Washington, D.C., instead of stopping off in Guangzhou, China, to turn her into a muddled mess?

Home to Washington, D.C., her mind echoed.

There was the key, the truth she'd hold on to to keep herself sane and from doing something very foolish in regard to Daniel that she'd regret for the rest of her life. She had no intention of taking any negative memories with her when she left China, and making love with Daniel would be very, very wrong.

Okay, she was fine now, in control of herself, focused first and foremost on her daughter. She would enjoy Daniel's company while in Guangzhou, then bid him a pleasant adieu.

Christina looked at Daniel again and lifted her chin. "Shall we go down to the bridge?"

"Sure," he said, signaling to the waiter for the check. "Just let me settle up here."

"Thank you for a lovely dinner. It was delicious.

Why don't I wait for you by the outer railing over there?''

"Fine."

Christina collected her tote bag, which was doubling as a diaper bag and purse carrier, and walked quickly away, Autumn peering at Daniel over Christina's shoulder.

Daniel watched them go, then sank back in his chair.

Lord, that woman was dangerous, he thought. Christina could turn him inside out with a look, a smile, the sound of her lilting laughter.

And Christina thought *she* was confused? She ought to be dealing with the tangled maze in *his* mind. He was a walking, talking, six-foot mass of contradictions.

Become involved in a serious relationship with a woman, any woman, let alone one who had a child? No way.

Face the reality that he'd never see Christina and Autumn again once they left Guangzhou? The mere thought caused a cold fist to tighten in his gut.

"You're a wreck, Shay," he muttered. "Pay the check and go take some dumb pictures. And keep your hands off Christina Richards."

The noise of the tumbling waterfall was so loud that while standing on the bridge people were required to shout at each other to be heard.

Daniel used hand signals to direct Christina to
where he wanted her, then motioned to her to lift
Autumn higher in her arms. He took several pictures,
then felt someone tap him on the back. He turned to
see a smiling Chinese man.

"Would you like me to take a picture of you with
your wife and baby?" the man yelled. "It would be
a nice remembrance for you."

"They're not my…" Daniel started, then stopped
speaking, deciding it was ridiculous to holler the explanation of not being husband, nor father. "Yes.
Thank you."

Daniel handed the camera to the man, moved next
to Christina and encircled her shoulders with one
arm. She looked up at him questioningly.

"Just smile," he said. "It's too noisy to explain
it all."

The man took pictures from three different angles,
then returned the camera to Daniel. A shouted
"thank you" and "you're welcome" were ex-
changed, then Christina, Autumn and Daniel left the
bridge and the roar of the water. Daniel gave Christina the camera and she slipped it into the tote bag.

"Want to browse through some of the shops here
in the hotel?" Daniel said.

"Yes, all right, for as long as Autumn lasts."

"Let me carry her. I'm a real pro at this now, you
know." Daniel lifted Autumn from Christina's em-

brace and tucked her securely in the crook of one arm. "There you go, kiddo."

"Boo," Autumn babbled happily.

"Boo to you, too," Daniel said, laughing.

Hours later Daniel stood on the balcony outside his room, staring at the river below. He'd been unable to sleep, had tossed and turned until he'd uttered several earthy expletives and left the bed.

It was two-thirty in the morning, he fumed, and there he was, wide awake with his mind set on overdrive, one jumbled thought tumbling into the next.

Why?

Because Christina Richards, the ever-famous Auntie Ann, refused to budge from his brain space. The image of her in his mind's eye was so vivid, so enticingly real, it was as though she was standing right there next to him on the balcony.

And as if Christina wasn't enough to drive him over the edge of sanity, there was also Autumn Christina Richards chipping away at the wall around his heart.

Would you like me to take a picture of you with your wife and baby? It would be a nice remembrance for you.

Cripes, Daniel thought sullenly, even perfect strangers were out to get him. The words spoken by the man on the bridge were echoing over and over.

Wife and baby. *Your* wife and baby.

"Damn it," he said, shoving both hands through his tousled hair.

He strode back into the room, yanked the rumpled sheets into semi-order, then stretched out on the bed, determined to get the sleep he needed.

Boo, a taunting little voice whispered in his mind, and was followed by the sound of Christina's laughter.

"Get out of my head, Christina," Daniel said aloud, "and take your kid with you."

He rolled onto his stomach, punched his pillow into a ball and lowered his head.

Sleep, Shay, he ordered himself. *Don't think. Sleep.* Why Christina had such power over him he had no idea. If he didn't know better, he'd think he was showing symptoms of a man who was falling in love.

"Ridiculous," he mumbled. "Not a chance. No way."

At last he slept, but when the alarm shrilled at dawn he awakened with a groan, realizing his restless slumber had been accompanied by continuous dreams of Christina.

Showered, shaved and dressed in his consulate uniform of suit and tie, Daniel was about to leave the room in search of breakfast when the telephone rang. He snatched up the receiver.

"Hello?"

"Daniel? This is Libby Duling with Little Hands."

"Good morning, Libby."

"No, it's a terrible morning. The flu bug hit me in the middle of the night and I feel rotten. I have two moms, a dad and three babies down with it at last count. Dr. Yang is coming in today to look us over."

"I'm very sorry you and the others are ill," Daniel said. "Are you confident about Dr. Yang's abilities as a doctor?"

"Oh, yes, he's wonderful. I do need your help, though, Daniel. The group is scheduled to go to the Department of Welfare this morning at ten to sign papers. Luckily, only one parent is needed and the babies don't have to be there. The van will be out front at nine forty-five. I hate to send my families off alone. Is there someone from the consulate who would be free to go with them?"

"Yes, of course. I'll take care of it, Libby. You just rest and get better."

"Oh, thank you, Daniel. You're a dear. Good-bye."

"Goodbye."

Daniel replaced the receiver slowly, his eyes narrowed, his mind racing.

After the night he'd just spent, he thought, he definitely needed to put some distance between himself and Christina. He'd have breakfast, go to the consulate and send one of the staff to the White Swan in time to accompany the group to the Department of Welfare. Fine. Excellent plan.

At nine forty-five a so-disgusted-with-himself-he-could-spit Daniel Shay sat down on the seat in the van with Christina and Autumn and instructed the driver to head for the Department of Welfare.

Two hours later the driver of the van redeposited his cargo in front of the White Swan.

"Have a nice day, Christina," Daniel said, not looking directly at her. "I'll talk to you later...or whatever." He turned and started away.

"Daniel," Christina said, "wait a minute."

He slowed his step, then halted, looking at her over one shoulder.

"Yes?" he said, raising his eyebrows.

Christina watched until the others in the group had entered the hotel, then marched forward and around Daniel to stand directly in front of him. Autumn was sleeping peacefully in Christina's arms.

"Would you care to explain, Mr. Shay?" Christina said, with no hint of a smile.

"Explain?" Daniel said, an expression of whatever-do-you-mean on his face. "Explain what?"

"Oh, nothing much," she said, her voice ringing with sarcasm. "Only the fact that you've spoken about five grumpy words maximum to me all morning. It's a tad difficult to understand your mood, considering that before we parted last night you kissed the living daylights out of me and said you were looking forward to seeing me at some point today.''

''Shh.'' Daniel glanced quickly around. ''You don't have to broadcast our private kisses to the world, for Pete's sake.''

''At the moment, Mr. Shay, I don't give a rip who knows about those kisses. You didn't strike me as a game player, but apparently I read you wrong. Heaven knows I have a lousy track record as far as being able to determine accurate data regarding men.''

Christina lifted her chin and executed an indignant sniff she was extremely pleased with.

''Good day, sir,'' she said, then moved around Daniel and started toward the entrance to the hotel.

Daniel stared up at the sky for a long moment, shook his head, muttered ''Oh, hell'' and caught up with Christina just inside the lobby.

''You win,'' he said, falling in step beside her. ''And you're right, you deserve an explanation for my behavior this morning.''

''Do tell,'' Christina said, continuing toward the elevators.

''Would you stop a minute so I can talk to you?''

''No. Autumn needs a dry diaper. I'm going up to my room.''

''Fine. I'll come with you.''

"Don't you have a consulate to run?"

"Hey," Daniel said, "you worry about your kid and I'll worry about my consulate. Okay?"

"Sounds fair to me," a man said as he passed them.

"Oh, good grief," Christina said, bursting into laughter.

They stepped into an empty elevator, and Daniel pressed the appropriate button, then dragged both hands down his face as the elevator started upward.

"For a private person," he said, shaking his head, "I'm certainly advertising my personal business all over the White Swan."

"Look at the bright side," Christina said, still smiling. "We're both leaving town soon. No one will remember that we were even here."

"*I* will," Daniel said quietly.

Christina's smile faded. "So will I. I'll never forget... Well, we've talked about that."

The elevator bumped to a gentle stop and the doors swished open. The trio walked down the hall in total silence, then entered Christina's room.

She changed Autumn, who blinked then went back to sleep. When the baby was tucked into the crib, Christina turned to Daniel.

"You have the floor, Mr. Shay," she said, striving for a light tone that didn't materialize.

Daniel sat down on the edge of the bed and extended one hand toward Christina.

"Come here," he said. "Please."

Christina closed the distance between them, placed her hand in Daniel's and sat next to him. Daniel cradled her hand between both of his and looked directly into her eyes.

"I—" he started, then stopped and cleared his throat. "I behaved very badly toward you all morning and I apologize for that. I was attempting to emotionally separate myself from you, Christina, but it really didn't work."

"Why did you want to do that?" she said softly.

"Because whatever this is that's happening between us is powerful, is consuming my mind…hell, maybe even my heart, I don't know. It has thrown me off-kilter, out of control."

"And?" she asked, hardly breathing.

"I don't like feeling this way. Christina, look, even if I was receptive to a serious relationship, which I'm not, we still wouldn't have a prayer of having a future together. I assume you're very settled in Scottsdale, wish to raise Autumn there."

Christina nodded.

"I'm assigned to Washington, but I'll put in for overseas duty again as soon as possible."

"I see."

"Do you? Do you see, understand, that there's something building, growing between us?"

"Yes," she whispered.

"We're walking straight into heartbreak, Christina, and we have to stop. We'll have a brief meeting at the consulate when you come with the others to apply for the babies' visas. Beyond that? I'm out of your life as of this moment.''

An achy sensation seized Christina's throat and she fought desperately against sudden tears.

Daniel brushed his lips over hers. ''Goodbye, Auntie Ann. Thank you for… Well, it's a long list.'' He got to his feet. ''I'll never forget you, Christina.''

''I'll remember you, too, Daniel,'' she said, her voice trembling.

Daniel walked to the crib and looked at the sleeping baby.

''Boo,'' he said. ''You're a winner, Autumn Christina Richards, and you've got yourself one fine mom, the best. I hope you know you've stolen a piece of my heart, kiddo.'' He looked at Christina again. ''And so have you. Goodbye, Christina.''

''Goodbye—'' a sob caught in Christina's throat ''—Daniel.''

Daniel left the room, closing the door behind him with a quiet click.

Autumn whimpered in her sleep.

Two tears slid down Christina's pale cheeks.

Chapter Five

The remainder of the day seemed endless.

Christina went to lunch with some of the others in the group, but they all agreed that the flu hitting their "family" was making them apprehensive about venturing out of the hotel. Everyone planned to spend a quiet day in their rooms.

By late afternoon Christina felt as though she'd been cooped up with her own warring thoughts for an eternity.

A part of her knew that what Daniel had said and done was the sensible thing to do. They were most definitely headed for possible heartbreak, and it was best not to be in close proximity to each other. Pure and simple.

But another section of her being was a muddled mess. At one point she was angry, mentally fuming that Daniel had had no right to make such a major decision for them both without thoroughly discussing it with her first.

Then she'd bounce from mad to sad; missing Daniel, wanting to be held and kissed by Daniel, wishing he'd march into that room, pull her into his strong arms and kiss her senseless.

Back and forth her mind went. Back and forth.

"Your mommy is a cuckoo, you poor baby," Christina said to Autumn as she fed the infant her night bottle. "There's a song about leaving a heart in San Francisco. Well, I lost my mind in Guangzhou, China. What do you think about that, sweet daughter?"

Autumn was more interested in consuming the offering in the bottle.

At 3:00 a.m. Christina was awakened from a restless sleep by Autumn's crying.

"Hungry," Christina mumbled, then snapped on the light next to the bed. "Mommy's coming, Autumn."

When she got to the crib, Christina gasped in shock. Autumn had been sick to her stomach, the curdled, sour formula covering her sleeper and blanket. Christina placed her hand on the wailing baby's forehead.

"Oh, no," she whispered. "You have a temperature. Oh, Autumn, you've got that awful flu."

Stay calm, Christina, she ordered herself. *You must stay calm.*

Twenty minutes later Christina began to walk the floor with a crying Autumn cradled against her shoulder. The baby was in fresh clothes, the crib had been cleaned and Christina had coaxed Autumn into taking about an ounce of water.

Christina sang a lullaby as she paced, but nothing soothed the unhappy baby.

Time ticked slowly by.

At dawn an exhausted Christina telephoned Libby.

"Hello?" Libby said, sounding half asleep.

"This is Christina. I'm sorry to disturb you so early, Libby, especially since you're not feeling well, but Autumn has the flu. She has a temperature and is upchucking. What has Dr. Yang been doing for you and the others?"

"Another sick baby?" Libby said. "The numbers are growing. Dr. Yang said the flu has to run its course. There's really nothing he can do. Keep offering Autumn liquids, give her tepid baths to bring her temperature down and watch for signs of dehydration."

"Yes, all right."

"I wish I could come help you, Christina, but I can't even keep dry toast down. I hate the thought that you're tackling this alone."

"I knew I'd face times like this as a single mother," Christina said. "I just didn't think it would be so soon. You go back to sleep, Libby. I'll follow the instructions you gave me."

"I'll talk to you later and see how you two are doing. Goodbye, dear."

"Goodbye."

Christina replaced the receiver and took a steadying breath.

Okay, she was on her own, she thought. Fine. Autumn was dozing at the moment, so…

Christina collected her clothes and headed for the bathroom for a quick shower.

She'd have breakfast delivered to the room, she thought, and order a large pot of coffee with it. She'd eat every bite of the food to keep her strength up, and the caffeine in the coffee would jolt her from her blurry, need-of-sleep state.

She could handle this.

Single mothers all over the world faced dilemmas like this one every day.

She'd do whatever was necessary to see Autumn safely through this illness.

Yes, of course, she could handle this.

She had to.

"Daniel?"

Daniel looked up to see one of the women on the staff of the consulate standing in the doorway to his office.

"Yes, Pam?" he said.

"I just had a call from Libby. They were supposed to come here to the consulate today to apply for visas for the babies they've adopted. Their scheduled appointment would have given us enough time to get the visas processed before their departure date."

"And?" Daniel said, raising his eyebrows.

"As you know, we have to actually see the parents

and babies. Libby said that another parent and baby just got sick, and because there are so many down with the flu they can't possibly get over here.''

Daniel's heart began to thunder and he forced himself to maintain a bland but somewhat interested expression.

''Did Libby happen to mention which family that was?'' he asked.

''She said the latest victim was a baby named…'' Pam frowned. ''Darn it, it's on the tip of my tongue. Summer? No, no, Autumn.''

Daniel lunged to his feet. ''Autumn has the flu? How sick is she? Is Christina…is Autumn's mother all right, or is she sick, too?''

Pam's eyes widened in shock at Daniel's sudden outburst.

''Goodness, Daniel, I don't know anything other than the baby's name,'' she said. ''I know you've taken that group to some official meetings. You've become very emotionally involved with them, haven't you?''

''Well, I… What I mean is…'' Daniel cleared his throat and sat back down. ''They're very nice people, that's all. So, Libby said they can't get here to the consulate?''

''No, not all of them. We had this happen with another adoption group about a year ago. I simply took the visa applications to the White Swan and met with each family individually. I can do that again, then you can add your signature to the forms when I bring them back.'' Pam laughed. ''The last time I was so helpful I caught the flu from the sick babies.''

''Well, we can't have that, can we?'' Daniel said. ''Your catching the flu is above and beyond the call of duty. You're one of the few who didn't get it when it swept through the consulate. You prepare a packet with the necessary documents and I'll go to the White Swan myself.''

Pam shrugged. ''You're the boss. Your wish is my command.'' She turned and hurried away.

He'd settle for his mind following his directives that well, Daniel thought dryly.

He shook his head and dragged both hands down his face.

Lord, he was tired. He'd had only snatches of sleep last night, had tossed and turned and thought about Christina for hours.

No amount of orders shouted to his weary brain to close the file on Christina Richards, to push her into a dusty corner of his mind, did the least bit of good.

He knew, damn it, *he knew* he'd done the right thing by telling Christina they were not to see each other again, except on official business.

But all the knowing-he-was-right in the world didn't diminish his longing to see her, touch, hold and kiss her. Heated desire rocketed through his body at the mere thought of her.

It wasn't just physical want and need that kept Christina in the front of his depleted mind. He missed the sound of her laughter, the sparkle in her big blue eyes. He envisioned her with Autumn, seeing the glorious picture they made as mother and daughter.

Autumn, Daniel thought, stiffening in his chair. That sweet little kiddo was sick with the flu. How ill was she? How was Christina coping with what had to be a frightening situation? Christina was all alone, tending to a sick baby. All alone.

"Well, not anymore, she's not," he said, getting to his feet.

He came from behind the desk, strode halfway across the room, then stopped.

Whoa, Shay, he told himself. What was he doing? What had happened to his firm resolve not to see Christina again, except for when she applied for Autumn's visa? Where was his sensible reasoning, the knowledge that staying away from Christina was the prudent thing to do?

"That's all on hold for now," he said aloud, "because Autumn changed the rules temporarily by catching the damnable flu."

Fine. That made sense. Didn't it? It was a sound analysis. Wasn't it? He was zeroing in on the word *temporarily,* had himself focused on his mission to help a single mother tend to her sick child. Right?

Yeah, right, he thought, rolling his eyes heavenward. He didn't know squat about what to do for an ill infant. His mad dash to the rescue wasn't worth diddly.

Then again...

He was an expert at holding Autumn now. Sick kids liked to be held, didn't they? That baby knew who he was, was calmed by his voice. That ought to be worth something.

"Ah, hell, forget it," he said. "I'm on my way to the White Swan, and that's that."

Christina Richards was *not* going to be alone with her sick daughter. Not while Daniel Shay had a breath left in his exhausted body.

The consulate was only about three blocks from the White Swan, and Daniel's long legs covered the distance in short order. People scurried out of the way of the tall American carrying a briefcase, who was obviously intent on getting where he was going as quickly as possible.

In the lobby of the hotel Daniel telephoned Libby and explained that he had come to meet with the group on an individual basis to fill out the visa applications.

Libby thanked Daniel profusely and assured him that everyone was staying in their rooms, sick or well, awaiting instructions as to how the problem of getting the documents processed on time was to be solved.

Daniel scribbled names and room numbers on a piece of paper as Libby rattled them off.

"Okay, got it," Daniel said. "Have them do a calling-tree system, Libby, with each telephoning the next to tell them I'll be there eventually. That way you won't have to use up your energy. You don't sound well at all."

"I think I died, but my brain hasn't gotten the message yet. This flu is nasty, Daniel. I hope you don't catch it by visiting my sick people."

"Don't worry about me. Just take care of yourself, and I'll talk to you later. Bye."

Daniel replaced the receiver and headed for the elevator.

Yes, he thought, he'd see everyone on the list, and the necessary documents would be completed. But his first and most important stop would be at the room where Christina and Autumn Richards were registered.

In less than five minutes Christina would no longer be alone.

Christina walked slowly across the room with Autumn in her arms. The baby was crying and Christina was humming. She'd long since given up on singing lullabies and was now just making what wasn't proving to be a soothing sound.

A sharp knock at the door caused Christina to stop her trek.

The marines have landed! she thought with a slight edge of hysteria. Wasn't that super-duper? A whole platoon of those guys was going to march in there and take turns walking the floor with Autumn.

The knock came again.

"Oh," Christina said. "Well, let the troops in, Christina. Oh, just shut up, Christina."

She shifted Autumn to one arm and crossed the room to fling the door open.

"Daniel?" she said, her eyes widening. "Oh, it is not. I'm seeing things, because I'm a total, exhausted wreck. Goodbye." She started to close the door.

Daniel's hand shot out to grip the edge of the door to keep it from being slammed in his face.

"Christina?" he said, frowning. "What's wrong with you? It's me. Daniel. I'm really standing here."

"Well, fancy that," she said with a strange little giggle.

"May I come in?"

"No, no, you can't. Autumn has the flu, so we're under quarantine in here. Nope, you must not enter this germ-laden room. Goodbye."

"Would you quit saying goodbye?" he said, pushing gently on the door. "I'm coming in there."

"Whatever," Christina said, taking several steps backward. "Do note, however, that you do so at your own risk. Don't come crying to me if you get sick. Crying. Autumn has been crying for hours and absolutely nothing I do helps her."

Daniel shut the door and set his briefcase on the floor next to the wall.

"I've given her tepid baths," Christina went on, "and offered her plain water and sugar water, and I've sung every song I've learned since the day I was born, and I've walked twenty-two miles around this room and—"

"Christina…"

"But Autumn is so unhappy, so miserable." Christina sniffled. "I'm doing the best I can, the very best I possibly can, but—"

"Christina—"

"My poor little baby is sick." Two tears slid down Christina's pale cheeks. "I can't fix it, her, the flu. Oh-h-h, this is terrible, just awful." Two more tears joined the others.

"That cooks it." Daniel lifted a wailing Autumn from Christina's arms and cradled her up against one of his shoulders. "Christina, sit down. No, stretch out on the bed. You're completely exhausted."

"But—"

"Do it!"

Christina opened her mouth to protest, realized she didn't have the energy to argue, then flopped onto the bed. She rolled onto her back and drew a wobbly breath.

"Why are you here, Daniel?" she said. "You made it perfectly clear that we weren't going to see each other again."

"This doesn't count. I'm here because Autumn is ill and…well, you need help, you need *me*."

"I'll have you know, Mr. Shay, that I'm a single mother who is perfectly capable of taking care of my child on my own, thank you very much."

"Fine. I'm sure you could handle this situation without any assistance. The fact that I chose to lend a hand isn't going to diminish your role as Autumn's mother, nor does it insinuate that I feel you're not capable of coping."

"Oh."

"I'll take that as meaning you understand and accept what I just said. Close your eyes and your mouth, and get some rest."

"You're a very bossy person," Christina said, glaring at him.

"Yes, I am, when I have to be. Put a cork in it, Christina."

"Well, I'll rest my eyes for a minute. I'll just close my eyes and…rest for a second…or two, then…"

"Your mommy just conked out, Autumn," Daniel said to the crying baby. "Okay, kiddo, it's you and me now." He began to walk across the room. "Hey, there was this time in Moscow when a big, ole wild blizzard blew in. I was supposed to be attending a fancy reception deal, so I started out, and snow was swirling like crazy and…"

Christina stirred, opened her eyes, glanced at the clock, then shot bolt upright to a sitting position.

She'd been asleep for more than two hours, she thought frantically. Where in heaven's name was her baby? Why wasn't Autumn crying?

Christina shook her head slightly to chase away the sleepy cobwebs, then looked at the expanse of bed next to her.

"Oh, my," she whispered.

Daniel was on his back, suit coat and tie removed, his head on the pillow. He was sound asleep, and tummy-down on his chest was a sleeping Autumn, one of Daniel's hands resting protectively on her tiny back.

A soft and gentle smile formed on Christina's lips as she drank in the sight of her daughter and the man...

Her smiled was replaced by a frown and an increased tempo of her heart.

The man, her mind whispered, she...loved?

No! Oh, no, no, she wasn't in love with Daniel. She couldn't be, wouldn't be, mustn't be. She had *not* succumbed to the tangle of emotions plaguing her; the desire, the yearning, the wondrous joy of being with Daniel Shay.

No! Absolutely, positively not.

Shaking her head, Christina slipped off the bed and headed for the bathroom.

She'd freshen up, she decided, put on a dab of makeup and a clean blouse. The nap had helped immensely. She was still weary, but not exhausted to the bone and a breath away from bursting into tears as she'd been when Daniel had arrived at her door.

She was also *not* going to give one more second of thought to the disastrous notion that she might very well have fallen in love with Daniel. To ignore the idea was to avoid an inner dialogue with herself regarding her true feelings for him.

"You're a coward, Auntie Ann," she muttered as she closed the bathroom door.

The sound of running water woke Daniel with a start. He stilled immediately when he realized that Autumn was asleep on his chest. Easing himself upward, he cradled one hand on the baby's bottom, the other on the back of her head.

Moving very slowly and carefully, he left the bed, crossed the room and placed Autumn in the crib. The baby wiggled, quieted, then continued to sleep.

He'd put on his tie, combed his hair and was just slipping into his suit coat when Christina emerged from the bathroom.

"Hi," he said, smiling slightly. "I have to get going here. I'm seeing members of the group individually in their rooms to fill out visa applications. It's the best way to handle it, due to half of the outfit being sick." He paused. "Oh, Autumn drank about two ounces of water."

"Thank you for everything," Christina said quietly.

"No problem. I'll have you fill out your visa application later."

"Yes, all right."

Daniel retrieved his briefcase from the floor next to the wall, then stopped in front of Christina.

"Look," he said, "I intend to see you through this situation with Autumn, and I'd appreciate it if you wouldn't argue about it. I need and want to do it."

Christina nodded as she met Daniel's gaze.

"As for us?" he went on. "We've covered that issue before. There's no point in attempting to discover what this is that's happening between us, because there's no way we could have a future together. Neither of us is interested in being involved in a serious relationship. Plus, we live a couple of thousand miles apart back in the States."

There were two cowards in this room, Christina thought. Count them. One. Two. So be it.

"We'll work as a team to get Autumn over the flu, but those are our roles, Christina. We're two people tending to a sick baby, nothing more."

"You're being bossy again," she said.

"Have you got a better idea?"

Christina sighed. "No. I don't wish to address this—" she waved one hand in the air "—whatever it is between us, either."

"Fine. Then the ground rules are set and we agree on them. I think you should move Autumn to my room."

"Why?"

"Because I have a suite with a separate living room. We can take turns caring for her and the person not on duty can sleep without being disturbed. I'll explain the rationale to Libby so she won't think we're engaging in a torrid affair."

"Well, I..."

"Here's my key. Call housekeeping and have them help you transfer the crib and Autumn's supplies. I'll meet up with you in my suite later."

Daniel stepped around Christina and left the room.

"Very, *very* bossy," she said aloud. "But what can I say? Taking advantage of a suite makes sense under the circumstances."

Christina went to the crib and wrapped her hands around her elbows as she watched Autumn sleep.

If everything was so *sensible,* she thought, why wasn't she registering a sense of peace and the comforting knowledge that things were as they should be?

Why was she consumed, instead, by a foreign chill that she knew, just knew, was loneliness?

Chapter Six

At 1:00 a.m. Christina made no attempt to stop the tears of joy and relief that spilled onto her cheeks.

Autumn's fever had broken.

The baby had eagerly consumed four ounces of formula an hour before, and the midnight dinner had stayed put in the hungry little tummy. She was sleeping peacefully in the crib in the living room of Daniel's suite, oblivious to the fact that she'd managed to thoroughly exhaust and worry the two adults tending to her.

Christina glanced heavenward. "Thank you," she whispered. "It's over. Thank you."

As Christina dashed the tears from her cheeks, Daniel entered the room wearing only a pair of jeans. In the glow of the one lamp that was turned on, he saw the glistening tears on Christina's face and moved quickly to stand in front of her.

"What is it?" he said, frowning. "Is Autumn worse? I'll track down Dr. Yang. There has to be something he can do."

"No, no," Christina said, smiling. "Autumn is fine. Her fever broke and she has kept down formula, instead of just water. We did it. You and I—together—saw her through this crisis and she's on the mend. Oh, Daniel, we did it.''

''Awright!'' Daniel punched one fist high in the air, then wrapped his arms around Christina. ''We're the dynamic duo, the terrific two, the—''

''Stop,'' Christina said, laughing. ''If I fall apart laughing, I'll probably end up in a crying jag out of heartfelt relief.''

Daniel chuckled. ''I might just join you. Man, what an experience this has been.''

''How can I ever begin to thank you, Daniel, for all that you did?''

''You don't. I wanted to be with you and Autumn through this. I don't know why it was so important to me, but...

''I should thank you for putting up with me while I was in my bossy mode. We'll celebrate our victory over the germs in the morning with a huge breakfast. How does that sound, ma'am?''

''Absolutely perfect, sir.''

They smiled as they looked directly into each other's eyes. Then the smiles faded slowly as senses sharpened.

Christina was nestled against Daniel, her hands splayed on the dark curls covering his hard, bare chest. She was clad only in a T-shirt over bikini panties and was suddenly acutely aware of her skimpy attire and Daniel's half-naked body.

Heat rocketed through Daniel as his brain moved

past his relief that Autumn was on the road to recovery. There in his arms, her breasts clearly defined beneath the thin material of the T-shirt she wore, was Christina Richards, the woman he desired more than any before.

Step back, Shay, he ordered himself. *Drop your arms from around Christina. Now.*

Daniel didn't move.

Christina, think, she mentally yelled. *Don't feel…think. You don't belong in Daniel's embrace. It's too dangerous. Go. Walk away.*

Christina didn't move.

"Ah, hell," Daniel said, then his lips captured Christina's in a searing kiss.

Yes, his mind thundered.

Oh, yes, Christina thought.

Her arms floated upward to encircle Daniel's neck as his hands skimmed down to cradle the womanly slope of her bottom, urging her closer. She complied, her breasts crushing against Daniel's chest with a sweet, tantalizing pain.

She returned his kiss in total abandon, meeting his tongue in the darkness of her mouth, drinking in the taste of him, his aroma and the strength tempered with gentleness of his magnificent body.

It was ecstasy. The embers of desire within them that had been simmering for days burst into heated flames of passion that licked throughout them. Their need was beyond reason, was far beyond dwelling on the consequences of what they were doing.

There was only the moment—and the burning desire.

Daniel broke the kiss and swung Christina up into his arms. He carried her across the living room and into the bedroom, placing her in the center of the bed and following her down to claim her lips once more.

Christina sank her fingers into Daniel's thick hair, urging his mouth harder onto hers. Her breasts were heavy, aching, waiting for Daniel's soothing touch.

Daniel raised his head a fraction of an inch.

"I want you, Christina," he said, his voice gritty.

"And I want you, Daniel," she whispered.

Daniel shifted long enough to shed his jeans as Christina pulled off the T-shirt and panties. The soft glow from the living-room lamp cast a rosy hue over the bed, allowing them to see what they were to receive.

Daniel stretched out next to Christina and splayed one hand on her stomach, propping his weight on his other forearm.

"You're beautiful, Christina Richards," he said.

"So are you, Daniel Shay."

"Christina, when there are nights like this one, there's a morning after. I just couldn't handle it if you regretted—"

"Shh," she interrupted. "There will be no regrets, I promise. We're stealing this night out of time, making it ours, sharing it by mutual consent. Make love to me, Daniel, please. I want you so very much.''

With a groan that rumbled deep in his chest, Daniel gave way to his desire, pushing aside the niggling questions of right and wrong that had inched into his mind.

It was all, everything and more, that they'd fantasized it would be. It was glorious. They kissed, caressed, explored, marveling at the wonder of discoveries made.

Daniel trailed a ribbon of kisses down Christina's slender throat, then on to one of her breasts, drawing the sweet bounty into his mouth.

She closed her eyes, savoring, allowing a purr of feminine pleasure to whisper from her lips. Her hands fluttered over Daniel's moist back and she memorized the feel of the bunching muscles moving beneath her fingertips.

Daniel paid homage to Christina's other breast and she tossed her head restlessly on the pillow as the swirling heat within her built to a fever pitch.

''Daniel,'' she gasped. ''Please.''

He moved over her, looked directly into her smoky blue eyes, then entered her, filling her with all that he was. She welcomed him into her womanly darkness, receiving him with awe and wonder.

He began the tempo, slowly at first, then faster, with Christina matching him beat for beat. The heat within them coiled tighter, hotter, carrying them up and away to a place they could only go to together.

Faster. Hotter. Thundering now, lifting them further toward the summit, flinging them into wondrous oblivion.

"Daniel!"

Christina clung tightly to Daniel's shoulders as he joined her in the place where she had gone. He murmured her name as he found his own release.

He collapsed against her, spent, sated, fulfilled in body and in mind. With his last ounce of strength he rolled off her, tucking her close to his side.

Christina rested one hand on Daniel's chest as tears closed her throat.

So wonderful, she thought hazily. Never, *never* before had she shared lovemaking so exquisitely beautiful. But never before had she become one with Daniel.

No, she would not regret this night. The memory of it was hers to keep for all time.

Christina slept.

Daniel sifted his fingers through Christina's silky hair as he listened to the steady rhythm of her breathing.

Incredible, he thought. Making love with Christina had been... No, he didn't really have words to describe it. Emotions had intertwined with the physical; emotions of protectiveness, possessiveness, of knowing he would lay his life on the line if Christina was in harm's way.

Daniel frowned.

Easy, Shay, he told himself. Those emotions were capable of pulling him into an arena where he had no intention of going. Those emotions were some of the bricks of the foundation of love.

No. He was *not* falling in love with Christina Richards. He was stronger than any spell she might weave over and around him. He was capable of walking away from her and not looking back.

Daniel gave way to the somnolence that claimed him.

Autumn's crying woke Christina and she glanced quickly at the clock on the nightstand.

Six in the morning, she thought. Autumn had been as exhausted as her caregivers.

As she flung back the blankets she looked at the bathroom door, fully expecting it to be closed and answering the question of where Daniel was. The door was open.

After slipping on her panties and T-shirt, Christina hurried into the living room to prepare a bottle for her hungry daughter. A piece of paper was propped against an empty bottle on the table.

"'Need to finish processing visas,'" she read aloud, "'so your group can leave tomorrow. Have a nice day. Daniel.'"

Christina prepared the formula by rote, changed Autumn's diaper, then settled onto the sofa to feed the baby.

Have a nice day? That was what the clerk at the grocery store said when Christina bought a loaf of bread.

Well, what did she expect Daniel to say, or do? Declare his undying love? Tell her she was the woman of his dreams? Ridiculous. Besides, Daniel Shay had made it clear early that he no longer had any dreams. He just accepted life as it unfolded, one day at a time.

One night at a time.

Christina sighed, then set the bottle aside and lifted Autumn to her shoulder, patting the baby gently on the back.

She, Christina Richards, had for the first time in her life taken part in a one-night stand. That was really disgusting.

She narrowed her eyes and stared at the ceiling.

No, in actuality it had been wonderful, beyond description in its intensity and beauty. What she had shared with Daniel was the stuff of which exquisite memories were made.

She'd promised Daniel she'd have no regrets, and she had none. The tricky part would be to act cool and sophisticated when she saw Daniel later that day. He mustn't have a clue as to how emotionally moved she'd been by the night they'd spent together.

She was leaving Guangzhou early tomorrow, and that would be that. She'd never see Daniel again. He mustn't know that every precious moment she'd spent with him was etched indelibly in her mind.

At least she hadn't fallen in love with the man, as she'd feared she might. Yes, he'd had a major impact on her and she would never forget him, but she wasn't in love with him, thank goodness.

"That would be a disaster in its purest form, Autumn," Christina said aloud. "Daniel is a pro at love 'em and leave 'em, at having the ever-famous one-night stand. How do I know? My sweet patootie, it takes a seasoned veteran of such things to write a note the morning after that says 'Have a nice day.'"

Autumn burped.

Daniel sat behind his desk at the consulate and glowered at the mug of coffee cradled in his hands.

Have a nice day? he thought. Lord, he couldn't believe he'd actually written that in the note to Christina. It was so cold, so dismissive, a verbal form of leaving the money on the table.

His only excuse was that he'd been rattled, emotionally off-kilter. He'd stood by the bed, watching Christina sleep, and had had to reach deep within himself for the willpower not to kiss her awake and make love to her again.

His mind had skittered to the image of Christina and Autumn walking out of the hotel tomorrow to go to the airport, where they'd fly up into the heavens and out of his life forever.

In his mental vision a bizarre scenario had formed—him flattening himself against the front doors of the White Swan and refusing to allow Christina to leave him.

In a state of near panic over his jumbled thoughts and emotions, he'd scribbled the note and left the suite in a rush.

Have a nice day? No, he wouldn't. What was he going to say to Christina when he met her later? How should he act? Even more disturbing was the question of why in the hell he didn't know. He was Daniel Shay, playboy extraordinaire, for crying out loud.

But Christina Richards, he thought dismally, was like no woman he'd met before. She didn't play the games of the single scene, didn't know the rules, didn't deserve to find a tacky note the morning after that said "Have a nice day."

"You're a scum, Shay," he muttered, then drained the mug, shuddering at the taste of the bitter coffee.

Get a plan, he told himself, thudding the mug onto his desk. Okay, he'd make certain he didn't encounter Christina between now and when she left tomorrow morning.

No, that was a coward's way out.

He'd see Christina, be pleasant, warm, smile his best diplomatic smile, and wish her every happiness with her new daughter. That would hopefully erase some of the sting of his crummy note. Yes, fine, that was workable.

Then when Christina was gone, taking that heart stealer of a baby with her, he'd begin a determined program to forget the two of them, which was not going to be an easy task to accomplish.

Well, he'd look at the bright side of this tangled mess. At least he hadn't fallen in love with Christina. She was the kind of woman men *did* fall in love with, but he'd count his lucky stars that it hadn't happened to him.

With a decisive nod, Daniel pulled the top file from a stack on the side of the desk and flipped it open, directing his full attention to the papers inside.

Christina tucked one of Autumn's blankets into the suitcase that she'd placed on a chair, then scrutinized the space that was left.

In the carry-on tote bag, she'd pack the supplies she'd need for Autumn during the fifteen hour flight from Hong Kong to Los Angeles, she mused, leaving room in the suitcase for her cosmetic bag. She'd just barely fit everything in.

She glanced at her watch to make certain she had plenty of time to get Autumn ready for the celebration dinner on this the last night in Guangzhou.

Christina had called housekeeping and asked that the crib be returned to her own room. With one last memory-filled look around Daniel's suite, she'd closed the door and walked away.

Libby had contacted everyone in the early afternoon, saying the special dinner was to take place as planned. The babies had bounced back from the flu in fine fiddle, Libby had said. The ailing adults were recovered, but were a tad wobbly.

The evening's festivities would be kept short so everyone could get a good night's sleep before beginning the journey home at 6:00 a.m. the next morning.

Home, Christina thought, lifting Autumn's red dress from the tissue paper. She could hardly wait to enter her cozy house, see Autumn sleeping in the crib in the nursery so lovingly prepared for her. Oh, yes, she was more than ready to go home.

But then again…

Christina sank onto the edge of the bed with a sigh.

Daniel.

Oh, how long would it take for the memories of Daniel Shay to dim, to not be so vivid? The image of him in her mind's eye was so real, it was as though he was next to her at that very moment.

No, Christina thought, getting to her feet. She wasn't going to start that nonsense. She was *not* sitting there like an adolescent idiot daydreaming about Daniel. She'd see him at the dinner, as Libby had mentioned that she'd invited Daniel to attend and he'd said he'd be delighted.

Heavens, Christina thought suddenly, she'd be in a crowded room with the other parents and babies when she saw Daniel. Would anyone be able to sense, see, that she and Daniel had...

"Don't be ridiculous, Christina," she said aloud. It wasn't as though she'd be carrying a neon sign announcing the fact that she and Daniel had made love last night. "A one-night stand," she added with another sigh.

Daniel had not even hinted in his notorious note that he wished her to remain in his suite. So she'd moved back to her own room, and that was that.

"Have a nice day," she said, frowning. "Oh, blak."

"Boo," Autumn said merrily. "Ba. Boo."

"All right, Miss Boo, let's get you all gussied up in your special red dress from Grandma and Grandpa. We're going to a party, Autumn Christina."

The room Libby had reserved for the dinner was beautiful, causing everyone to comment on the decor the moment they arrived.

Two large, round tables were set, including a turntable in the center of each. The tables were flanked by dark wooden chairs in high backs that were carved with intricate detail. The walls boasted narrow pictures painted on delicate rice paper.

Four waitresses in red silk dresses with vibrant, embroidered flowers stood in a straight row by the door, smiling and nodding as the group arrived.

"Isn't this gorgeous?" Kathy said. "I'm so glad I feel better. I would have hated to miss this. I'm not going to eat much, though. My tummy isn't ready for a heavy meal, that's for sure."

"Emily looks darling in her red dress," Christina said, smiling.

"So does Autumn," Kathy said. "Look at all the babies. You'd never know any of them had had the flu. I wonder if the slow adult recuperation has to do with the age of the patients."

Christina laughed. "I wouldn't be surprised."

The mood was festive, the noise level high. They agreed that each person would order a different dish, set it on the turntable and afford the group a vast variety of food to choose from.

Cameras flashed every few seconds as multitudes of pictures were taken of the event that marked their last night in China.

Christina sat with Kathy on her left and Libby on her right. Babies were snuggled on laps. The food arrived in what appeared to be a never-ending parade of the waitresses, the delicious aromas wafting through the air.

"Mmm," Christina said, taking a bite of sweet and sour pork.

"I wonder where Daniel Shay is?" Libby said, spooning fluffy rice onto her plate. "He said he'd be joining us and bringing the babies' visas when he came."

"Christina," Kathy said, "do you know where Daniel might be?"

"Me?" Christina said, raising her eyebrows. "No, I have no idea. I haven't spoken to him all day."

"Really?" Libby said. "That surprises me. It's very obvious that Daniel is quite taken with you, Christina." She laughed. "That's an old-fashioned way to put it, isn't it?"

"He's smitten with Christina," Kathy said, nodding decisively. "There's another ancient way to say it."

A warm flush stained Christina's cheeks. "Don't be silly. Daniel simply stepped in to help me when Autumn became ill, because I was the only one attempting to manage on my own."

"Right," Kathy said, laughing. "Do you have a bridge you want to sell us, Christina? Autumn, tell your mommy that her nose is going to grow."

"Kathy, for heaven's sake," Christina said.

"You're blushing, Christina," Kathy said. "That's so sweet. Blushing is old-fashioned, too."

"Leave poor Christina alone," Kathy's husband

said, chuckling. "It's none of our business if Christina and Daniel are involved with each other."

"But it's so romantic," Kathy said. "I knew something special was happening between them the moment they met."

"Oh, good grief," Christina said, contemplating crawling under her chair. "Could we change the subject, please?"

"Well, darn, okay," Kathy said. "But where is Daniel Shay?"

Good question, Christina thought dryly, and it was the one she'd been mentally asking ever since she'd arrived in that room. She kept sliding glances toward the door, waiting, hoping to see Daniel.

Oh, now, just a second here. Surely Daniel wasn't going to avoid seeing her because of last night. Did the man who'd asked her to promise she'd have no regrets about their lovemaking have regrets of his own?

Was she now destined to leave Guangzhou without a further glimpse of Daniel?

Daniel left the elevator and sprinted down the hallway to his suite. Inside the living room he flicked on the light, then stood statue still, a knot tightening painfully in his gut.

The crib was gone.

Christina had moved back to her own room.

"Damn," he said, then turned and left again, hurrying toward the elevators. He barely made it inside one before the doors swished shut.

He was late, very late, for the celebration dinner Libby had so graciously invited him to attend. It had been a busy day at the consulate and he hadn't had one free second to telephone Christina.

Just as he had finally been leaving his office, an American tourist had arrived, totally distraught over having lost her passport.

"Come on, come on," he muttered, staring up at the blinking lights on the elevator panel.

Despite his tardiness, he'd had to take the time to dash to his room. The only clue he might have as to Christina's frame of mind would be whether she was, or wasn't, still in residence in his suite.

But Christina was gone.

The asinine note he'd written her because of his jangled emotional state had taken its toll. Christina had packed and exited stage left.

It was better this way, he told himself. Another night of sweet, sweet lovemaking with Christina just might be his undoing. As it was, he was on shaky emotional ground in regard to keeping his feelings for Christina in check.

He'd breathe a sigh of relief when Christina and Autumn Richards left Guangzhou.

Liar, he admitted in the next instant. *Ah, Shay, shut up.* He was driving himself out of his feeble mind.

The elevator bumped to a stop and Daniel emerged, looking around for a wall directory that would tell him where the room he was seeking was located. Libby had told him the name of the room, but not where it was.

He muttered an earthy expletive when he scrutinized the directory, discovering he was on the wrong floor. Running back to the bank of elevators, he clenched his jaw in frustration as all the doors remained stubbornly closed.

"All right, everyone," Libby said, flapping one hand in the air, "scoot closer together so I can get all of you in the picture. That's it. A little more…a little more. Perfect. Don't move an inch while I record this on all of your cameras."

The cameras were lined up on the table in front of Libby and she picked up each in turn, capturing the special moment. Just as she focused Christina's camera, Daniel burst into the room.

Daniel, Christina's mind hummed. Daniel was here.

"Got it," Libby said, replacing Christina's camera among the others. "That's all of them. Hello, Daniel, I didn't think you were going to make it. I'm afraid you've missed a delicious dinner."

"It was a killer day at the consulate." Daniel slid a quick glance at Christina, but she was laughing and talking with the others, and most definitely not looking at *him*. "Here are the babies' visas." He handed Libby a large cream-colored envelope. "Signed, sealed and delivered."

"Thank you, dear," Libby said. "You've been such a help to us all, and especially to Christina. I know she appreciated your being there for her while Autumn was ill."

"Well, I..."

"Everyone," Libby said, "Daniel has just brought us the babies' visas. We'll leave early in the morning as scheduled. Remember to be near the front doors in the lobby at 6:00 a.m. so we have plenty of time to catch our flight to Hong Kong. We'll lay over there for three hours, then begin the fifteen-hour flight to Los Angeles."

"Oh, grim," Kathy said. "That is the longest airplane ride ever invented by man. I'm going to bed right now and rest up for the ordeal."

Others in the group nodded, agreeing that an early-to-bed due to the early-to-rise was an excellent idea, considering the long, monotonous flight they were facing. They began to file from the room, greeting and thanking Daniel as they passed him.

Christina picked up her tote-cum-diaper bag and followed the others, not looking at Daniel.

"Thank you again, Daniel," Libby said, then bustled from the room.

Libby, wait! Christina mentally yelled. Oh, darn,

now she was about to move in front of Daniel and there wasn't anyone left in the room for camouflage.

"Christina," Daniel said quietly.

Christina stopped, willing her heart to quit beating in such a wild rhythm, willing the sudden heat that suffused her to dissipate.

"Hello, Daniel," she said, staring at the center of his tie. "Did you see how pretty Autumn is in her special red dress? All the babies were in red. Did you notice that? It symbolizes—"

"Christina," he interrupted, "may I walk you and Autumn to your room? Could I carry that princess in the beautiful red dress?"

"I don't—"

"Please?"

"Yes, all right."

Daniel tucked Autumn into the crook of one arm and they left the room. They were silent as they went to the elevators, rode upstairs, then started down the hallway leading to Christina's room.

The tension between them was a crackling entity, nearly palpable. Scattered thoughts and words slammed in, then out, of their minds, but none were spoken.

At her door, Christina opened it, then reached for Autumn. Daniel slowly and very reluctantly returned the baby to her mother.

"Christina, I..."

"Daniel, don't," she said, finally meeting his

gaze. "There's really nothing to say. I'll always remember you, what we shared, everything. I'll wrap those memories up with all the others from this incredible trip." An achy sensation of threatening tears gripped Christina's throat. "Goodbye, Daniel Shay," she whispered.

Daniel looked at her for a long, heart-stopping moment, then drew one thumb over her lips.

"Goodbye, Christina Richards," he said, his voice sounding gritty with emotion to his own ears. He shifted his gaze to Autumn. "Bye, kiddo. Be a good girl for your mommy. She's the best, remember that."

A sob caught in Christina's throat.

Daniel turned and strode away.

Christina didn't move until Daniel disappeared from her teary view.

Chapter Seven

Christina hurried through the door leading from the garage into the kitchen, dropped her purse and packages onto the table, then snatched up the receiver of the ringing telephone on the wall. Autumn gurgled happily in the crook of Christina's free arm.

"Hello?" Christina said.

"Oh, dear, you're out of breath. I've disturbed you when you were in the middle of something."

"Hi, Mom," Christina said, smiling. "I was dashing in the door. Autumn and I were out and about running errands. There's bad news ahead for my budget. Autumn loves to go shopping."

"Of course she does. She's my granddaughter. All Richards women were born to shop, except you, Christina. You're a changeling."

Christina laughed. "Thanks a lot. Oh, I have a bulletin. They tracked down my pictures that I was having developed, from the trip to China. I was so afraid they were lost forever, but the tracer worked. Even as we speak they're sitting on the kitchen table."

"Wonderful. Maybe some snapshots of Autumn will satisfy your father for a bit. He is such a grumpy bear with that broken leg, Christina. He's continually fuming over the fact that you've been home for two weeks and we are many more weeks away from seeing and holding our granddaughter.''

''I'm eager for you to see her, too. She gets cuter by the day. And growing? Two of the sleepers she wore in China won't zip up over her tummy now.''

''Your father said Autumn will be starting school before we get there.''

''He *is* grumpy, isn't he?'' Christina said. ''I bet he won't climb a tree to rescue a stranded kitten again.''

''No, he certainly won't. The silly kitten has taken up residency on your father's lap. Just what I need around here—a kitten. Well, I wanted to say hello to you two. We think about you both so much. We'll be flying out there as soon as the doctor says it's feasible.''

''Super. I'll mail you some pictures tomorrow. After Autumn is down for the night I'll write on the back of each photo, saying where it was taken. I hope I can remember everything. I have five rolls of film here.''

''We'll be watching for the mail. Goodbye, Christina, and kissies to Autumn.''

''Bye, Mom. Tell Dad to smile.''

Christina replaced the receiver and looked at her daughter.

''That was your grandma,'' Christina said. ''She's going to go nuts over you. And your grandpa? He'll do his best to spoil you rotten. Okay, miss, it's a dry diaper, juice and a nap for you. Off we go.''

When Autumn was finally tucked into her crib for a snooze, Christina returned to the kitchen, unable to resist at least taking a peek at the multitude of pictures. She settled at the table with a refreshing glass of iced tea and pulled the stack of photographs from the envelope.

She smiled and nodded as she began to go through them quickly, lovely memories flooding her mind as she saw familiar faces from the group, as well as the places they'd all visited.

Suddenly her breath caught and her smile disappeared as she stared at one of the pictures.

It had been taken by Libby at the celebration dinner on the last night in Guangzhou. The whole group was there, the babies absolutely adorable in their red dresses.

But it was the expression on her own face in the picture that was causing her heart to race and the color to drain from her cheeks. Libby had snapped the shutter just as Christina had caught sight of Daniel when he hurried into the banquet room.

''Dear heaven,'' Christina whispered, unable to tear her gaze from the photograph.

There, for all the world to see, was a woman looking at a man she was in love with. Her face was glowing, her eyes were sparkling, the soft smile on her lips spoke volumes. It had been captured for eternity in the split-second pressing of a button on a camera.

Christina dropped the picture onto the stack as though it was suddenly singeing her fingers. On trembling legs she rose and went to the window, wrapping her hands around her elbows as she leaned her forehead against the glass.

The image of Daniel Shay had not been far from her mind's eye during the two weeks she'd been home. He followed her through the day and into her sensuous dreams at night.

It would take time, she'd been reassuring herself, for those memories to dim, to no longer haunt her. Yes, time was what she needed to be able to stop missing Daniel, aching for Daniel, reliving every detail of every moment she'd spent with Daniel.

But now? She had been totally convinced that she wanted no part of a serious relationship. Then Daniel had come into her life and... There was nowhere to run, to hide, from the truth she'd been refusing to admit to herself, or even consider.

She had fallen in love twice in China.

She had fallen in love with her precious daughter, Autumn.

And she had fallen in love with Daniel Shay.

"Oh, Christina," she said as tears filled her eyes, "look what you've gone and done. It's all so foolish, so hopeless."

But what if Daniel...

There were pictures of Daniel taken with her and Autumn on the bridge in front of the waterfall at the White Swan. What if she saw on Daniel's face what she'd seen on her own? What if Daniel was in love with her, just as she was with him?

Christina returned to the table, spreading out the photographs with shaking hands. She found three snapshots of them on the bridge and stared at them intently, her heart sinking.

Daniel was smiling his plastic, diplomatic smile in all of the pictures. That wasn't the face of a man in love, it was one of someone satisfying another's whim.

Two tears slid down Christina's cheeks, and she dashed them away angrily.

So, all right, now she knew the truth of her feelings for Daniel and she would have to deal with it, one day, one night at a time.

The only saving grace to the whole disaster was that Daniel would never know that she was in love with him.

He would *never* know.

Daniel sat behind his desk in the small office and shook his head in self-disgust. He started to reread the words on the paper in front of him, realizing he hadn't comprehended one sentence.

Concentrate, Shay, he ordered himself. Even if this *was* just busy work they'd invented for him to do during his stint in Washington, he'd do well to lose himself in it, become completely engrossed in the dry, boring data. If he had his entire brain focused on his work, there would be no part of his mind left over to dwell on Christina.

Nice try, but no cigar, he thought, then smacked the top of the desk with the palm of his hand. He'd just read two lines on the paper again and didn't have the foggiest idea what they said.

"Hell," he said.

"Beating up on government property," a deep voice said, "and swearing in government airspace. I thought I taught you better than that, Daniel."

The first genuine smile since he'd returned to Washington broke across Daniel's face. He got to his feet and came around the desk to extend his hand to the man in the doorway.

"Greg," Daniel said, shaking the man's hand. "Damn, it's good to see you. How's retirement life?"

"Even better than I'd hoped," Greg said, smiling. "I'm becoming quite the golfer, if I do say so myself, and I finally have time to tend to my roses the way I've always wanted to."

"Fantastic," Daniel said. "Come into my cell and sit down, bring me up to date."

"Sure thing. I heard you were due back and I told Lucy I wouldn't rest until I drove in to see how you're doing. Lucy sends her best, by the way."

"And greetings to Lucy. Your wife still makes the best apple pie there is, and I've sampled apple pie in a lot of places."

"I'll tell her you said that." Greg settled onto the chair opposite the desk and Daniel sat down in his own chair. "Lucy will no doubt invite you to dinner and serve apple pie for dessert."

"Sounds like a plan," Daniel said, smiling.

"So, tell me, Daniel, how did it go? Your returning to Washington? I know there are a great many painful memories for you here."

"It was fine," Daniel said. "I was prepared to get punched in the gut by those memories, but it didn't happen. I was very surprised."

"I'm not. It has been many years since your wife was killed. Time does heal bleeding wounds." Greg paused. "Would you like to tell me why you were using your desk for a punching bag?"

Daniel leaned back in the chair and sighed. He stared at his mentor for a long moment, realizing he still liked and respected Greg Manning very, very much.

"Well," Daniel said finally, "for one thing, I was happy working overseas. Washington is not my favorite city. For another, the work they've given me is ridiculous. I'm checking for accuracy what someone else has already checked for accuracy. And then there's the subject of…" Daniel's voice trailed off and he frowned.

"What's her name?"

"Christina." Daniel chuckled and shook his head. "You haven't lost your touch, Greg. I always said you should be a member of the FBI." His smile faded. "Christina Richards and her daughter, Autumn."

"And? What about them?"

"Well, you see, I did a two-week stint in Guang-zhou, China, on the way home, because the consulate personnel was hit hard by the flu. I stayed at the White Swan Hotel."

"Classy place."

"Yes, it is. Anyway, there was a group at the White Swan who..."

Daniel filled Greg in on how he'd met Christina, about being with her when she saw Autumn for the first time, and on and on. He omitted the part about making love with Christina.

"Christina Richards is Auntie Ann?" Greg said. "I'll be darned. I read an Auntie Ann book to my grandchildren the last time they were at the house." He paused. "Color me stupid, Daniel, but I don't see what your problem is."

"I can't get Christina off my mind," he said, fling-ing out his arms. "She's driving me nuts, right over the edge. She's haunting me, Greg. She has cast a spell over me." He dragged a restless hand through his hair. "I'm losing it. Yes, I'm definitely losing it."

"Daniel, I'm still the color of stupid. What is your problem?"

"I don't want to be in love with Christina, be part of a serious relationship," Daniel said, none too quietly.

He glanced quickly at the open doorway and lowered his voice.

"Even worse, Christina has a baby," he went on. "I don't want to raise a kid. Of course, Autumn is a cut above the herd as far as kids go. Cute? She's the epitome of a China doll, that's what she is. Forget that. Now you know what my problem is."

"Yep," Greg said, nodding. "It's as clear as a bell. Daniel, when you left Washington after your wife was killed you were a shattered man, who vowed to never love again.

"As you've discovered upon arriving back here, that pain is gone, long gone. What you didn't do along the way is readjust your stand on living out your days alone. *That* is your problem, my boy." Greg got to his feet. "You're a man in love. A man with hope and dreams. Personally, I think you ought to get off your butt and do something about it."

"But—"

"Good to see you, Daniel." Greg turned and left the room.

"But..." Daniel said to the empty room.

Suddenly he heard the words Christina had spoken what seemed like an eternity ago.

*Maybe you could look a little deeper within your-
self to see if there isn't a dream hiding from your
view, waiting to be discovered.*

Daniel lost track of time as he sat in the quiet
room. He didn't move, and hardly breathed as he
turned his thoughts inward for a journey through his
heart, mind, his very soul.

And slowly, so slowly, came the warmth, the
peace, the comforting realization that he'd traveled
far but had, at long last, reached his destination, had
truly come home.

He got to his feet, drew a deep, cleansing breath,
then left the room.

Christina pulled the lightweight blanket up over
Autumn's tummy, then stood by the crib for a long
moment, watching her daughter sleep.

"Get to work, Auntie Ann," she finally said
aloud, then left the nursery.

As she came down the hallway, her mind shifted
gears to what was waiting for her attention in her
office. The sound of the doorbell ringing caused her
to jerk as she was jolted from her deep concentration.

It was probably a salesman, she thought, crossing
the living room, hoping to find people at home in the
early afternoon. She'd be polite, but send him
quickly on his way.

Christina opened the door, then just stood there
staring at the person standing on her welcome mat.

Daniel? her mind questioned. Daniel Shay was here? No, don't be silly. She'd thought about him so much she was simply imagining that he'd appeared out of nowhere. Right?

"Christina?" Daniel said.

"Oh my God," she said, one hand flying to cover her now racing heart. "You're really here. You're really here? Are you really here?"

Daniel frowned. "I'm here. May I come in?"

"What? Oh, yes, of course."

Get a grip, Christina, she ordered herself as Daniel entered the house and she closed the door behind him. Daniel was probably just passing through town on his way to wherever. She had to stay calm and cool, not give him one clue to the fact that she'd discovered she was in love with him.

Daniel Shay. Oh, he looked scrumptious, although tired. He was in her home, a scene she'd fantasized about more times than she cared to count. She wanted to fling herself into his arms and...

No, no, calm and cool. In control. Sophisticated. She could handle this. She hoped.

"My, my," she said, a tad too loudly, "this is a surprise. What brings you to the wild West, Daniel?"

You! his mind yelled.

Lord, look at her. In white shorts, a red top, sandals on her feet and her dark, curly hair in fetching disarray, she was so beautiful that the mere sight of her made him ache.

"Could we sit down?" he asked.

"Please do," Christina said, sweeping one hand through the air. "Would you care for a glass of sun tea?"

"No, thank you."

Daniel sat on the sofa as Christina took a chair a few feet away. She folded her hands primly in her lap and produced a smile she hoped wasn't as phony looking as it felt.

"That smile is about as real as the diplomatic plastic number I slide into place on command," Daniel said.

Christina jumped to her feet and planted her hands on her hips.

"Well, what do you expect, Daniel Shay?" she said, her blue eyes blazing. "You waltz in here unannounced as though you do it every day of the week. I thought I'd never see you again and—kazoom—here you are. I'm a little shook-up, mister."

Daniel frowned and studied Christina for a long moment.

"Kazoom?" he said finally.

"That does it. That really cooks it. I'm having enough trouble keeping you out of my brain space without your popping in for a chat. I thought I could handle this, Daniel, but I can't. Now, on top of everything else, I'll envision you sitting there on my sofa every time I look at that cushion."

''Why would you do that?'' Daniel said quietly, staring at her intently. ''Are you in love with me?''

''Yes, I am, darn you, and it's very upsetting because...'' Christina stopped speaking and her eyes widened in horror as she realized what she had said. ''Erase that,'' she added in a small voice.

''No way,'' Daniel said, grinning. ''You said it. I heard it. It's officially recorded.''

''Whatever,'' Christina said wearily, sinking back onto her chair.

Daniel's smile faded and he leaned forward, propping his elbows on his knees and lacing his fingers together loosely.

''Christina,'' he said, looking directly at her, ''I left Guangzhou about a week after you did and reported in to work in Washington. My body was there. My mind, my heart were here with you and Autumn. I put in for vacation time and flew out here.''

''I see,'' Christina said.

But she really didn't, she thought. Exactly what was it that Daniel was leading up to?

''You once told me,'' Daniel said, ''that I might have a dream hiding within me, waiting for me to find it. Someone else recently said a very similar thing.

''So I looked deep within myself, wanting to know if it was true. And, Christina? It *is* true. I *do* have dreams, and they all center on you and your daughter.''

"What…what do you mean?" she said, having to remind herself to breathe.

"Christina Richards, I love you. The past is gone, forgotten. I want a future with you. I'm asking you to marry me. I'm asking you to be my wife and to allow me to be Autumn's father." Daniel got to his feet. "Will you marry me, Christina? Please?"

Christina was up and moving before she realized she'd left the chair. She flung herself into Daniel's embrace as tears glistened in her eyes.

"Yes, I'll marry you," she said, smiling through her tears. "I love you so much, Daniel. My past is behind me, too. We'll have a wonderful future together."

Daniel lowered his head and kissed Christina to seal their commitment to forever.

"Daniel," Christina said breathlessly when he finally ended the kiss, "what about your job, your desire to live overseas?"

"I'm finished with running from memories that don't even exist anymore. In the Immigration and Naturalization Office in Phoenix there's an opening that's mine if I want it. I definitely want it."

"Oh, I'm so happy. I've missed you, I…" Christina sniffled. "Don't get me started."

Daniel chuckled. "Okay. Could I take a peek at Autumn? At my…my daughter?"

"Yes. After all, Daniel, you were in the *delivery*

room at the orphanage when the babies arrived. You definitely qualify to be Autumn's daddy.''

They went down the hall to the nursery to stand next to the crib, Daniel's arm snugly around Christina's shoulders.

"Hi, kiddo," Daniel said quietly to a sleeping Autumn. "We're going to be a family, the three of us, and we got it all figured out just in time. It's perfect."

"In time for what?" Christina said, looking up at him.

Daniel shifted his gaze to Christina, love radiating from his dark eyes and matching the love in her eyes of summer-sky blue.

"To celebrate Mother's Day this Sunday," he said.

"You're right," Christina said, smiling. "It's absolutely perfect."

* * * * *

READER SERVICE™

The best romantic fiction direct to your door

Our guarantee to you...

The Reader Service involves you in no obligation
to purchase, and is truly a service to you!

There are many extra benefits including a free
monthly Newsletter with author interviews,
book previews and much more.

Your books are sent direct to your door
on 14 days no obligation home approval.

We offer huge discounts on selected books
exclusively for subscribers.

Plus, we have a dedicated Customer Care team
on hand to answer all your queries on
(UK) 020 8288 2888
(Ireland) 01 278 2062.

Escape into

Just a few pages
into any Silhouette®
novel and you'll find
yourself escaping
into a world of
desire and intrigue,
sensation and
passion.

Silhouette

Diana **Palmer**

Beloved

Rebecca **YORK**

Nowhere Man

The **Marriage Bargain**

Jennifer Mikels

A Husband Waiting To Happen

MARIE FERRARELLA

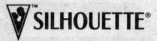

▼ SILHOUETTE®

GEN/SIL/RS

SILHOUETTE™ DESIRE®

*Provocative,
sensual love stories for the
woman of today*

Capture the intensity of falling in
love in these fast-paced, intense
love stories with strong, rugged
heroes who are just *irresistible!*

Six new titles available every
month from the

READER SERVICE™
on subscription

GEN/22/RS

SILHOUETTE
SPECIAL EDITION®

Satisfying, substantial and compelling romances packed with emotion.

Experience the drama of living and loving in the depth and vivid detail that only Special Edition™ can provide.
The sensuality can be sizzling or subtle but these are always very special contemporary romances.

Six new titles available every month from the
READER SERVICE™
on subscription

GEN/23/RS

Danger, deception and desire

SILHOUETTE
INTRIGUE™

Enjoy these dynamic mysteries with a thrilling combination of breathtaking romance and heart-stopping suspense. Unexpected plot twists and page-turning writing will keep you on the edge of your seat.

Four new titles every month available from the
READER SERVICE™
on subscription

GEN/46/IRS

A thrilling mix of passion, adventure and drama

™
**SILHOUETTE
SENSATION**®

If it's excitement and adventure you seek in your romances, then join these dynamic men and women who are unafraid to live life to the fullest in these complex and dramatic stories.

Let us carry you away on the tides of passion!

Four new titles are available every month from the

READER SERVICE™
on subscription

GEN/18/RS